The Stolen Heart

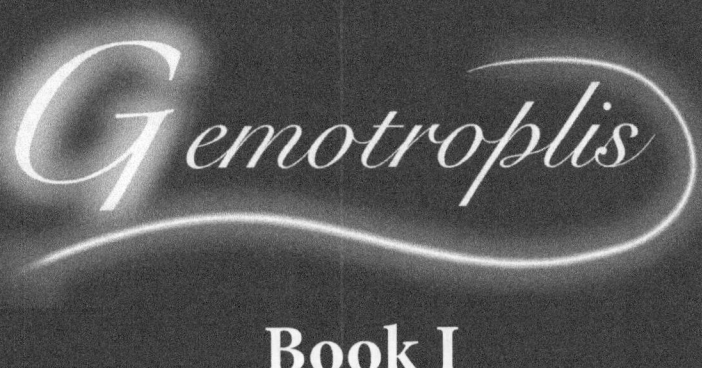

Gemotroplis

Book I

Jack Haligo

Paperback edition, ISBN 978-0-6458634-3-7

Map by Jack Haligo
Illustrations by Kylah Davis
Cover Illustration by Jeffery E. Doherty

Printed by InHouse Publishing Pty Ltd, Australia

Dedicated to my mum,
whose love & support are
the foundation
of my writing journey.

For greater insights into
Gemotroplis' lore, the special
plants, potions, and gemotros
subscribe to

www.gemotroplis.com

About the Author

Jack Haligo is a teenager living on the Gold Coast in Queensland, an Australian author who began writing the "Gemotroplis" pentalogy at only twelve years old. Through his writings, Jack aims to reshape perceptions of autism, advocating for recognising the unique talents and perspectives that autistic individuals bring to society.

He wrote Gemotroplis – The Stolen Heart to reflect his vision of a fantasy world: a magical place where he can escape the harsh realities of school, bullying, and his struggles with what he describes as a 'normal life'. Autism has allowed him to see the world differently, and this perspective, along with his life lessons, has influenced his storytelling. Authoring this first book has provided Jack with the resilience and self-reflection needed to cope with his early years and to learn that being different is okay.

Jack fell in love with writing at a young age and has made it a significant part of his life. He particularly hopes his fantasy will help autistic readers shape and reflect on their thoughts and actions, guiding them to learn right from wrong and navigate the complexities of human behaviour, matters that Jack himself struggles with.

Contents

GEMOTROPLIS THIRD ERA

N

50 MILES

The Forbidden Ocean

The Emerald Channel

The Grandor Bay

Azareni

Crimson Bay

Emerald Forest

Grandor

Sapsascuia

Sapphire Valley

Perilous

White plains

Dendank

Irindot

Neil

The Sapphire Ocean

The Neilan Sea

Arelor

Prologue

Late in the third era, Gemotroplis was considered a place of relative peace among the four nations. It was once a mystical land of trade, diversity, and culture, torn by war a few decades prior. Now, each nation sat in discomfort, not knowing whom to trust. The nations grew apart, trapped in medieval times, relying less on foreign trade and allies as they became more individual.

The nations were named after the individual jewels they worshipped. There was the wealthy Topaz Nation, the wise Sapphire Nation, the mighty Emerald Nation, and the spiteful Ruby Nation. The Ruby Nation was not trusted, as it had attempted to invade the other nations. An invasion led by the power-hungry and evil Ruby Emperor Cranium. It was dubbed the Ruby War, fittingly after the nation responsible for starting it.

The invasion ultimately failed; it resulted in thousands of deaths and a hatred that stained the reputation of Ruby Nation. The emperor died during the short war, but not in the way you would think. The emperor's spirit endured due to the very life force that every nation relies on, the raw, unequal phenomenon known as magic. It was a powerful and strange force. For once a person reached the age of maturity, they were granted magic, allowing them to modify physics in their favour with an arsenal of spells, curses and charms.

But, of course, the magic is not permanent. A person can only use magic until they grow old and frail. Each nation's population possess a unique type of magic. Emerald magic focuses on healing and nature spells; the Sapphire Nation focuses on construction and taming spells. The Topaz Nation is focused on summoning and defence spells, and the Ruby Nation is focused on attack and destruction.

In the past, there was also dark magic, spells so terrible that nations agreed to erase them. Dark magic became forgotten, and books and teachings were destroyed. Now, only a few souls held these guarded secrets. Fortunately, Ruby Nation had lost its dark magic during the second era, well before the Ruby War. However, tales say other nations still exist, isolated and far away, where magic is still the most powerful. These nations are focused on illusion, deception, and other strange spells.

There is one spot in the centre of Gemotroplis which each nation fears. It is called Ravena. A field of basalt and magma surrounds a gigantic volcano whose eruption occurs once every thousand years, indicating the end of each era. This place is almost always infested with horrible, foul, man-eating creatures called gemotros. Ravena still holds scars from the Ruby War, littered with skeletal remains dressed in rusting steel armour, some even still impaled with arrows and swords protruding from their decaying bodies.

Every nation has unique creatures, some more dangerous than others, but the most terrible are in Ravena. Magic as a strange force still had limitations; some Topaz gemotros couldn't be killed with Topaz spells, the same with other gemotros who couldn't be killed with their own nation's magic. This forced each nation to defend itself from the strongest gemotros with primitive weapons, such as swords, bows and spears.

The Topaz, Emerald, and Sapphire nations tried to maintain peace, ensuring the Ruby Nation never started another war. They decided the best way was to starve the nation by giving it giant, unpayable fines. This led to the vast population growing poor and desperate, resulting in an explosion of crime and thievery.

Currency was also a significant part of each nation's development. The currency used was the corresponding gemstone for each nation. For example, rubies, the shiny, blood-coloured gemstones, were used as payment within the Ruby Nation. This meant that each nation's currency was unequal. Rubies are considered next to worthless compared to rarer and more valuable emeralds. One emerald would be the equivalent of about twenty fat rubies. Different gemstones had different values within each nation, and rubies were at the bottom of the chart, adding to the reason Ruby Nation was starving.

Shortly after the downfall of the failed Ruby War, they crowned a new Ruby emperor named Emperor Maroon, son of the deceased Emperor Cranium. Maroon was left with all the responsibility of the Ruby Nation, which had collapsed into poverty thanks to his father. The only logical thing, the only solution the inexperienced Ruby emperor could think of, was to mine more rubies within the nation to pay off these fines the other nations were demanding. This is where it all started, with two young miners deep below Ruby Nation. Two regular boys, friends from the beginning, were waiting for the day they discovered something that would change their lives and Gemotroplis forever.

Chapter 1

The Discovery

"Rusty, found anything yet?" Lustre paused his mining to ask.

Rusty glanced over at him.

"No," he sighed. "Just some stone, more stone, and granite."

Lustre breathed deeply before returning to chipping away at the wall with his pickaxe. The two boys had found nothing all day, and they had been labouring inside that tunnel for hours, with Lustre wanting to give up on several occasions. The only reason he was still going was Rusty. He was reassuring him that they would find something soon.

"If we find nothing in the next few minutes, I'm sneaking out." Lustre groaned.

Rusty stopped, a sudden flash of concern on his face. "But you know the guards won't let any miner leave for the day until they have found at least one ruby." Rusty reminded him.

Lustre ignored Rusty. He kept mining, his motivation dying fast. Lustre hoped a ruby would reveal itself with every swing of his pickaxe. Lustre was the oldest and tallest of the two. He was seventeen rots old, meaning he had experienced the same number of rotations of the Gemotroplis sun. The only thing that could be said about Lustre was that he was very gutsy, energetic, and willing to do anything Rusty didn't want to. He had pure black hair, pale skin, and red freckles sprinkled across his stubby nose.

On the other hand, there was Rusty. He was scrawny and two rots younger than Lustre. He was timid and unwilling to take any risks of any kind. Whether exploring, fighting, or sneaking out of the mine without a ruby. He was seen mainly as a small, weak boy. He was short and bony, with filthy red hair that could not be brushed or styled. It was permanently messy, usually the first thing anybody noticed about Rusty. Around Rusty's neck was a long fibre string with a dangling ruby pendant. It was the first ruby they had ever found. Instead of spending the ruby, Rusty fashioned it into a necklace as a motivation booster. On a few occasions, he had wanted to exchange it for food, shelter or even his daily ruby to leave the mine. But he always hesitated and stopped himself from doing so.

The two of them were homeless. They spent most of their time confined inside the mine, working to earn as much as possible. It was their means of survival in the harsh Ruby Nation and was all they knew. They had both been orphaned at a very young age, and any thought of life before they worked in the mines was a blur.

Minutes passed, but minutes quickly turn into hours when doing something repetitive. At that point, they both lost all concept of time. The one thing they knew was that their efforts had not produced a single ruby. They had only uncovered some ordinary stuff that littered the shaft, like granite and elder maroon.

Lustre squinted at the wall he had been working away at. For a hot second, his eyes widened, and he held tired hands high above his head in celebration. "I found a ruby!" cheered Lustre.

"Really?" Rusty gasped.

Rusty immediately dropped his pickaxe and rushed over to Lustre. "Let me see!"

Lustre pointed at the wall, and Rusty's heart sank. He saw a red lump of rock protruding from the wall. It was obvious what Lustre was cheering about. Rusty slowly turned back to face Lustre.

"That isn't a ruby," Rusty muttered. "It's just elder maroon."

Almost every day, Lustre managed to uncover one of these ruby impostors. They were as familiar and worthless as a lump of glass. Yet, they were virtually identical to rubies and convincing enough to excite Lustre.

Lustre stared at the wall as if it had insulted him, teasing them and taunting them with these fakes. Elder maroon had earned itself a nickname by many miners. It was a fool's ruby. Lustre's patience sank faster than a ship's anchor. He was done!

"Fool's ruby again! Yesterday, I tried to leave with one of those, but the guards took one look at it and made me walk the stairs back down here," complained Lustre. The guards were trained to distinguish between a genuine ruby and an elder maroon. He bent down, picked up his pickaxe from the floor, and smashed the fool's ruby into shards.

"Hey! Calm down, we will find something eventually," reassured Rusty.

Lustre was relieved of some anger, but it did not restore his motivation to keep mining. "No. We won't. This tunnel is empty! It's got nothing to offer," he yelled. Lustre then apologised. "I am sorry for yelling, Rusty!"

"It's fine, Lustre." Rusty smiled. Rusty opened his arms and hugged Lustre tightly.

Even though a hug wasn't enough to restore his motivation, it was comforting nonetheless. Lustre softly replied, "Thanks."

Lustre leaned his pickaxe against the wall and led himself out of the tunnel, squeezing himself through the narrow gap at the beginning. It was the only exit and entrance, barely large enough for Lustre or Rusty to pass through.

Rusty sighed. "I guess the hug wasn't enough."

"Are you coming?"

He heard Lustre's voice echo from outside the tunnel. Rusty had no choice; he had to follow Lustre, feeling like he was tied to him with an invisible chain. He held all responsibility when Lustre did something stupid. Lustre was the kind of boy who would do something dangerous without thinking. In contrast, Rusty was the kind of person who would always consider the consequences before trying to talk Lustre out of it.

Before Rusty followed Lustre out of the tunnel, he heard something. He looked back down the tunnel for the strange noise and heard it again.

Rusty felt curious. The noise wasn't like what he usually heard in the mines. It didn't sound like the soft clattering of their crimson oil lantern, which was the only thing his mining experience knew. It sounded like rubbing a finger around the rim of a wine glass. A very gentle and peaceful ringing. Almost like the lingering tail of a church bell chime. He pressed his ear against the tunnel wall, trying to pinpoint where the sound emanated.

After thoroughly investigating each wall, he eventually found the point where the sound was the loudest. He could even feel the sound vibrating behind the stone and dirt. He was very confused. Picking up his pickaxe from the ground and seizing it with two hands, Rusty pulled back his arms and slung it forward into the wall. The wall crumbled, flooding the tunnel with thick, grey chalk dust. The deafening crack echoed. Rusty coughed violently after inhaling a mouthful of dust. He glanced up, his vision obscured.

After a few seconds, when the dust had settled to the tunnel floor, Rusty was in shock. Before him was the most beautiful, flaring light buried deep in the tunnel wall. The light pierced through the darkness, illuminating the entire tunnel with multiple colours. Rusty was instantly mesmerised. It was like he was staring into the eyes of the goddess Peroa.

Never taking his eyes off the source of the light, he slowly stepped closer, reaching his hand out. He extended his fingers, and he touched it. He felt the light. It was smooth and round, like polished marble. Then he realised, "Oh, Peroa! Mother of life."

Rusty excitedly announced, "It's a jewel." Lustre came running. He squeezed himself back down into the tunnel.

"Rusty, what is it? Are you alright?" Lustre cried out.

There was a moment of silence. Lustre stared at the light glowing from the inner wall. He pinched himself. "Rusty… Am I dead? I'm seeing a bright light."

Both weren't hallucinating. They stared at the brightest and most beautiful jewel they had ever seen. Lustre stepped closer to investigate.

"How do we get it out of the wall?" Lustre asked over his shoulder.

"I guess we just pull it out," Rusty replied in an unsure voice.

Lustre reached out and wrapped one hand around the lump of glowing stone. He put his other hand around his wrist for extra leverage. He yanked on it with full force. It didn't move. He tried again. And again. After many unsuccessful attempts to free the jewel, Lustre figured that the only way was to hammer it out. "Pass me my chisel and peg," Lustre called out.

Rusty scoured around for the large brown sack holding all of their tools. Once he found it, he reached inside and handed

Lustre a hammer and a long steel peg. Lustre positioned the peg next to the jewel and began pounding the end with the hammer. Rusty watched nervously as Lustre chipped away at the surrounding stone.

"Be careful!" Rusty reminded.

"I'm always careful," Lustre replied confidently.

Rusty moaned, "Debatable."

Lustre stopped and grabbed hold of the jewel once again. It was much looser in the stone, so Lustre wriggled it around, tugging at it aggressively, almost like he was trying to rip out a loose tooth. Finally, it popped out, revealing its actual size. This was when Lustre realised how big it was. They had only been seeing the tip of the iceberg. It was almost bigger than Lustre's hand.

Never had Rusty felt more relieved.

"Got it!" celebrated Lustre.

"Wow!" It was the only thing that Rusty could say. It resembled a giant glowing opal, with rays of colourful light beaming inside. Rusty asked, "Do you think that will be enough to convince the guards?"

"Wait." Lustre paused. "What if we don't tell anybody about this and take it to the emperor? He will pay anything for this jewel. Then we will be rich and won't have to work tirelessly in the mine anymore," Lustre suggested confidently, admiring his strenuous efforts. Lustre seemed very confident. Rusty, on the other hand, seemed very doubtful.

"So, you're saying we sneak out, travel a hundred miles. To sell this… thing to the emperor?" Rusty clarified.

"Yeah!" cheered Lustre, excitement bursting from his face.

"I don't know, Lustre."

Lustre didn't wait for Rusty to approve. He thought it was a brilliant idea. "Let's just get to the train," replied Lustre, scrambling out of the tunnel.

The tunnel they had just emerged from was a claustrophobic nightmare, a confining space where the walls seemed to close in around them. A stark contrast awaited them. As Lustre pushed through, he stepped into a vast underground expanse, a colossal cavern stretching out for nearly a mile. Once a thriving mining hub, this cavern had been hollowed out decades ago. Its walls, carved from jagged stone, glistened with moisture seeping through from deep below the surface. Rows upon rows of entrances to other tunnels scarred the rough-hewn walls, carved out by the generations of folk who had toiled here.

Despite the absence of natural light, the cavern was bathed in a surprisingly bright illumination. Sunlight had never found its way into this subterranean abyss, but miners had ingeniously compensated for the darkness. Overhead, many brass lanterns dangled from the ceiling, suspended by sturdy steel brackets, casting light across the expanse.

Lustre stared blankly back at the entrance to their tunnel. Through his inward-looking eyes, he saw a timber sign firmly bolted to the wall that bore the inscription '341' designating their specific tunnel. Rusty wriggled through the entrance, emerging on the other side with a dust-covered visage. With a shake of his head, Rusty straightened up and brushed the dirt from his clothes, ready to disembark from their day's work in this vast underground world.

"I despise that bloody entrance. I wish they'd make it bigger," groaned Rusty. "And if I eat in there, I won't be able to get out. I can barely fit through that hole as it is."

"Well, you're lucky we can't afford to eat most of the time. Being skinny probably helps." Lustre chuckled. Rusty didn't find his hunger funny. "Okay, now put the jewel in your pocket," ordered Lustre.

"Okay," replied Rusty.

"Now, we just must make our way through the crowd. Without anybody noticing the jewel." Lustre whispered, but even when whispering, a nosey miner heard them.

"Jewel? Did you find something, Lustre?" the miner said, stepping out before them.

"Oh! Amber, it's you," stuttered Lustre.

Rusty quickly hid behind Lustre. Amber was a braggy miner who coincidentally looked very similar to Lustre. He was identical in height, skin and hair colour. Rusty would sometimes refer to them as twins. It bothered Lustre, as he didn't want to be associated with Amber in any way. It also bothered Amber that every time he saw him, it was like he was staring into an annoying mirror.

"You said you found a jewel. That would be a first," snickered Amber. Rusty shoved the jewel into his pocket but quickly realised the coloured light could be seen through the fabric. He tried to hide it with his hand, but it didn't work.

"Hey, I say. What's Rusty got in his pocket?" asked Amber, raising an eyebrow.

"None of your business," spat Lustre. "Did you find anything today?" asked Lustre, trying to change the subject. Lustre didn't care if Amber found anything; Amber took it as an opportunity to brag.

Amber said proudly, "Oh yeah! I found twenty-three massive rubies! Oh, I also found a fossil in the stone! I'm pretty sure it's fossilised grombler vertebrae."

The grombler is one of many gemotros native to the region of Bandeira. It is a gemotro that has evolved over hundreds of years. Gromblers tend to be fond of exploring caves and rocky terrain. It is not uncommon to unearth grombler fossils underground.

"Interesting," remarked Lustre sarcastically.

Amber didn't find it sarcastic, instead taking it as a compliment. "Thank you," he boasted.

Even though Lustre didn't care about Amber, he still felt mildly jealous.

Rusty was the first to say, "Well, I think we'd better get going."

Lustre agreed. "Yes, we probably should be on our way."

Amber grinned. "Well, it was nice talking to you. I'm heading to the surface, but I am not taking that old rust bucket train like you lazy lads. I have my method." He smirked. However, Amber also provided some solid advice. "Hope you boys have a ruby. The guards are unusually strict today," pointed out Amber, dropping his grin.

"We're right!" replied Rusty. Lustre nudged Rusty.

Strangely, to their relief, Amber dismissed Rusty. "Okay then. I'll leave you two to it."

"Okay, bye!" Lustre farewelled sarcastically.

Amber couldn't help noticing the light seeping through Rusty's back pocket as they walked past him. Although he said anything, he sure found it suspicious.

The crowd was dense, with miners crawling in and out of their tunnels. Lustre and Rusty pushed through the crowd, keeping a low profile. At the very end of the cavern was the platform. It had an arched stone roof with two dark tunnels on either side. It was the railway station used for hauling rock and stone out of the mine. It wasn't meant to transport miners, and travelling by train to the surface was prohibited. Usually, all miners had only one way of getting in and out of the cavern: the gigantic, agonising stairs stretching upward five hundred feet. Lustre and Rusty hated these stairs; they were exhausting and slow. The worst thing was the climb after a long, tiresome day of mining.

Fortunately, the train's conductor took pity on them and let them catch a ride instead. They stood on the stone platform at the edge of the rails, waiting in the eerie silence.

The only noises were the faint sound of distant miners and the clock ticking on the platform wall. Rusty counted each second as the sizeable golden clock ticked away, each tick sounding in his head. Anxiety was growing within him. The clock was well known to the boys. Miner lads would tell the true story of the most beautiful and intelligent girl in the realm, an inventive girl who could service the mine's locomotive. They said she built the beautiful clock to look after the miners so they would not work too long and hard. Haley embodied Peroa's looks; she was in all the miner lads' dreams. The clock was also named Haley.

"Lustre, do you think we missed the train?" Rusty was clearly worried.

Lustre looked around. "Of course not; it arrives here every two hours. It will get here at exactly…" Lustre then paused as he peered up at the clock for a moment.

He confidently replied, "4.00."

Rusty also peered up at Haley, but it didn't make him feel better. "It's 3:58!" said Rusty, panic growing inside him. Rusty would always panic relentlessly over the most minor things; it was a part of his personality.

"Yes, it will arrive in about two minutes," Lustre assured. Rusty took a cautious step forward and glanced down into the tunnel, hoping to see the approaching headlights of the train, but it was empty and much too dark to see anything inside.

"I don't know, Lustre. We might have missed it," remarked Rusty.

Lustre shook his head.

Suddenly, they were startled by a loud chiming noise interrupting the silence. The noise echoed down the tunnel, ricocheting off the jagged stone walls. Lustre glanced back at the clock before realising it had struck four.

"Lustre! It's four o'clock! It's not here!" screamed Rusty.

Lustre rolled his eyes. "Don't you think there could be a chance the train is late, Rusty?"

Then, to their relief, they heard the train. The steel wheels squealed loudly as the train used its brakes to slow its approach.

"Rusty, what did I tell you? Only one minute late."

They both watched the train roll down the tunnel, with plumes of smoke spewing out from behind it. Slowly, the train ground to a halt. The train was tiny, with no roof or doors. It was built decades ago to transport mining rubble back to the surface. It was considered much faster and safer than carrying loads back up the manual way, even though Rusty thought that was arguable.

It was a compact steel locomotive powered by steam from burning crimson oil. It only had enough space for one conductor in the front, but the train's locomotive towed five large minecarts, most full to the brim with rocks and stone. Since it was so old, it had been prone to a few breakdowns in its long history, which is the main thing that inspired Rusty's fear of the train. Plus, it wasn't the cleanest. Years of being down in the mine had riddled it with dents and scratches, and the outer steel was covered in flaking rust.

The scrawny conductor stepped out onto the platform, straightening his weathered conductor's hat. He cleared his gravelly throat. "Sorry for the delay, boys. The tracks a bit further up almost broke apart today."

"Well, I think they will be fine for one more trip, Conductor," Lustre confidently replied.

The conductor replied, "Okay, in you get! Don't tell anybody about this arrangement; the guards might get angry at me."

Lustre and Rusty climbed into one of the empty minecarts in the back. Even though each cart could fit five people; miners weren't usually permitted. Lustre and Rusty got into the minecart adjacent to one overflowing with stone. Rusty convinced Lustre to sit at the back, preparing for his motion sickness. He had ridden this train before; his stomach knew it was like a twisted rollercoaster.

The conductor sat back down in the front. On the dashboard, below the musty windscreen, were three large gauges and various buttons and switches. The conductor tapped one of the gauges with his finger, squinting at it.

"Almost empty. Should last one more trip." He then whispered to himself, "Oh, I almost forgot." At that moment, he got up and strolled onto the platform. He reached up to Haley on the wall and took her down. He opened the face of the clock and turned the hands to midnight until a slight click was heard. Suddenly, the face sprang open like a trapdoor, and two fat rubies fell from the hidden compartment. "Right where I left them." He grinned. After he retrieved them, he reset Haley to the correct time.

Then he returned to the locomotive and secured them in a small lockbox beneath the seat. The conductor grabbed the handbrake before calling, "Okay, are you boys ready?"

To which Lustre shouted, "Yes!" Rusty whined, "Not really."

The train jerked forward as the handbrake was released.

It crept forward, slowly at first. The conductor blew the

train's horn twice as it entered a rail tunnel. Rusty prepared himself.

The train rattled violently as it hurtled along the tracks, starting its climb. It wasn't a smooth ride, to say the least, but it didn't bother Lustre. Rusty was huddling in the corner of the minecart, covering his eyes. "Just tell me when it's over," Rusty grumbled. Lustre rolled his eyes.

They were now enveloped in darkness, with the only illumination coming from the locomotive's headlights. These headlights were not fire-lit but contained glass reservoirs filled with a luminescent powder called crimson bloom dust. This pollen, sourced from the crimson bloom flower or blood orchid, glows a vivid blue in the dark. Lustre was first captivated by the headlights when he saw them. Additionally, crimson bloom pollen is used in lanterns, lasting longer and shining brighter than standard oil lanterns.

Rusty was terrified of the train, but preferred it over climbing the stairs any day. The train was shaky and would occasionally hit the walls as it moved. The worst part of the ride was crossing a long, flimsy bridge built over the deep cavern. It was the most dangerous part of the mines. He feared that the bridge would collapse under the weight of the train, and they would plummet to the bottom of the cavern, which seemed reasonable, as the bridge would creak and crack. But now, since the conductor had said the rails were dodgy, he was especially worried.

Lustre and Rusty were thrown to one side of their minecart as the train swerved around a bend. "Ouch," Lustre squealed.

"Sorry about that," the Conductor called out.

Lustre propped himself back. He noticed Rusty's heavy breathing. He placed a hand on Rusty's shoulder to calm him down. "It will be fine, I promise." Lustre smiled.

Rusty peered up, revealing his scrunched-up face. Lustre noticed his nose was runny and tears were trailing down his cheeks.

"Have you been crying?" Lustre asked.

Rusty quickly wiped his face with his sleeve before responding with his quivering voice, "No. I'm fine."

"Do you need a hug?" Lustre offered out his arms.

Rusty stared at Lustre for a few seconds. "I'm fine, but thanks," he replied again. "I don't understand. How are you never scared?" Rusty wondered.

Lustre paused for a second. "Well, I guess you grow out of being scared," he said firmly.

"Are you scared of anything? Like being alone? Or drowning? Or gemotros? Or the dark? Or just dying in general?" Rusty asked.

It took a second, but Lustre responded with an answer that shocked Rusty. "Well...No!" He had no noticeable doubt in his voice.

Rusty inhaled. "I wish I were like you..." He yearned.

Right then, the train hurled around a tight bend, and Lustre was flung into the side of the minecart.

"Ouch...that's gonna bruise." Lustre flinched.

Once again, they both heard the conductor yelling a slightly amused apology from the front of the train: "Sorry, boys, it's a bit of a bumpy ride!" At that point, the lockbox fell open without the conductor noticing, and the fat rubies spilled out onto the locomotive floor just by the conductor's feet.

"Maybe he should slow down a bit..." Rusty suggested.

"I'm going to stand up to see how fast we are moving," Lustre bravely stated.

The train was now moving faster than ever before. Lustre peeked over the edge of the minecart, exposing himself to the drag from the train's speed, which was not the wisest thing to do. At first, he almost lost his balance, but he grasped the rim of the minecart to regain stability. The rim felt cold against his fingers. He leaned over the edge, glancing below the minecart.

"Be careful!" Rusty cautioned.

He glimpsed the rails below, sporadically flashing with sparks at the point of contact with the wheels. The depths below were a blur; it was far too dark for his eyes. He didn't get to see too much before he was sprayed with grit and dust kicked up from the wheels. He pulled his head back in. "This train is moving fast!" Lustre was now starting to get nervous.

Rusty's face flashed with concern. He tried to stand up to communicate with the conductor over the carts, but it wasn't easy as his voice was fighting the wind, the rattling noise and the engine sound.

"Can we slow down a bit?" Rusty called out.

The conductor turned his head. "No, buddy! We must move fast so the bridge doesn't break on us."

This was not the answer Rusty was looking for. Suddenly, there was light. The loud train noise dispersed as they were above a chasm. They had exited a dark tunnel and were now careening across the bridge, which was much brighter than the tunnel. Torches lined each side of the bridge, which was not much wider than the train itself. The dozens of timber support pillars and scaffolding were the only things preventing the bridge from collapsing.

Rusty stared down over the edge of the minecart at the endless pit below him, holding his breath every time he heard the bridge creak or crack. Lustre kept his eyes glued to the tunnel opening on the other side. He watched as they moved closer and closer. They were about halfway across the bridge.

Suddenly, they both jerked forward as the train slowed down, eventually stopping in the middle of the bridge.

They were both confused. They stood up in their minecart and glanced across at the conductor.

"What happened? Why did we stop?" Lustre called out. The conductor didn't reply. Lustre watched him step out of the train onto the railing. "Hey! What happened? Why aren't we moving?" repeated Lustre a little louder this time.

This time, the conductor responded, "We can't go any further."

"Why not?" yelled Lustre, cautiously climbing out of the minecart.

"Look!" The conductor pointed at the rails a few yards before the train. "Those rails are bowing downwards; if we put more weight on them, they won't hold us. All of us will plummet down into the chasm, along with the train." He then made his way to the front of the train and sank in defeat, leaning against the locomotive's hood.

Rusty refused to get out of the minecart. Lustre was shocked at how easily this guy gave up. Even though there was a pretty solid reason, Lustre felt like this guy was lying to him. "I know we can get across," Lustre said confidently.

"It's suicide," remarked the conductor. The conductor held his head in his hands. "The emperor doesn't care about us. They don't even fund the mines. They use them as profit farms. They expect us to work in these unsafe and rotten conditions." The man sighed.

Lustre turned away from the conductor with an insulted expression on his face.

"Lustre, maybe we should just wait until help arrives," suggested Rusty.

"There is no help coming," Lustre voiced the facts. "There is only one train."

Lustre climbed into the conductor's chair and gazed at all the levers and switches before him. He had no clue how to operate any. But what stood out to him was the apparent handbrake and two gemstones under his feet. He secretly stuffed them in his pocket. He leaned over the windshield and shouted. "You might wanna move."

The conductor slowly rose, glancing at Lustre before frowning. "You're bluffing. You can't operate the train." With scepticism in his eyes, he manoeuvred around the front of the train towards Lustre. "Get out!" the conductor ordered. "We will just have to wait until somebody comes down and helps us."

"When will that be?" asked Lustre. The conductor gave a quick glimpse at his wrist; he pushed back his tattered sleeve.

"Well, it will be when they realise the train is missing. I do a lap of the mine every two hours. So, about then," assumed the conductor.

This didn't make either Lustre or Rusty feel any better. Lustre was so impatient, and Rusty was still filled with gut-wrenching fear. The only other option in Lustre's mind was to take matters into his own hands. He didn't want to wait for the conductor's approval because he already knew what he would say. Lustre grasped the ignition key and twisted it. The engine gasped loudly before it began to rumble. The conductor's scepticism was immediately replaced with fear.

"Hold on, Rusty!" called out Lustre.

He reached down beneath him and released the handbrake. The train lurched forward, and the conductor tried to grab hold of a minecart, but his fingers slipped.

The conductor stumbled as he attempted to catch up, inevitably tripping on the rails. He was left on the ground as the train bustled away, spraying him with grit and crimson oil fumes from the stack. The conductor's final word was a distant cry of "Thief!"

Lustre grinned at the sight of the conductor in his rearview. He held the handbrake firmly in case hesitation would stop him before he made any decisions permanent. But the train stayed on course, speeding towards what could be its final stop. Suddenly, Lustre heard the loudest crack yet, proving that the conductor wasn't making anything up. Lustre now knew the bridge was indeed about to collapse.

He could almost consider himself across the bridge; the train was only a few yards from the exit tunnel. Then, the darkness consumed their surroundings, and the light vanished. They were now in the tunnel. Lustre heard Rusty cheer behind him.

"We made it!" Rusty broadcast his voice as it echoed through the tunnel.

Lustre felt proud of himself; although it was risky, he had pulled through. The real reason he survived wasn't confidence; strangely, he wasn't lucky either. That bridge should have fallen; it had been holding the train's weight for some reason. It's almost as if someone or something had been supporting the bridge for him.

After a few more minutes of travel, they emerged at the surface. Lustre applied the handbrake, bringing the train to a halt. The boys then stepped out onto the platform. A sprawling, spacious tent greeted them on the surface. Its vast expanse was built from brown sheets of grombler skin stitched together into a canopy. These sheets were draped over poles, shielding the exposed tracks from the rain and wind. Grombler skin, which resembles rubber, provides a firm and waterproof covering. Yet, it did have one downside. Grombler's skin emitted a nauseating stench that permeated the air.

Thanks to Lustre, the train rested securely on the tracks, preventing any further problems, such as rolling back into the mine. The train wasn't meant to give miners a free ride; its only purpose was to haul the rubble out of the mine to be dumped at the surface. The mine was built with cost-efficiency in mind, aiming to maximise profits. Rusty was especially eager to get off the train. "Finally, I am off that death trap!" He cheered, pinching his nose.

"I told you we would be fine." Lustre reminded. They then hastily exited the station tent.

A few ruby mines were scattered throughout the Ruby Nation, but the largest rubies were found in the region known as Bandeira. The local peasant folk also named places, such as forests and villages, using the word Banderian. Lustre and Rusty worked in this mine in a cleared section of the Banderian Forest. The mine didn't look very impressive on the surface; it only resembled a cluster of tents. The tents were fashioned from the readily available grombler skin and used to house the miners. Gromblers were a troublesome gemotro species that infested the Banderian forest and provided an abundant source of leather.

Unfortunately, life on the surface was no better than within the mine. A crowd of miners, exhausted from climbing the stairs, milled about near the tents, creating a cramped atmosphere. Each miner was obligated to visit the collection tent to deposit their slaved haul of rubies, after which they were granted freedom to eat and rest until the next shift. At the end of every octave, they were paid a token wage and some leave. However, the boys were usually too tired to venture.

A long, agonising queue of miners had formed at the collection tent. Most were turned away and sent back into the depths of the mine; only a tiny fraction were permitted to finish work. Witnessing a miner at the front of the line get rejected offered Lustre solace, which affirmed that bad luck inside the tunnel didn't just happen to him.

"Come on! That's elder maroon! There's a difference!" They overheard the inspection guard at the front of the line boom.

"But it's ruby. I swear!" pleaded an unfortunate miner.

"Go back down the stairs. Come back only when you've found a genuine ruby. Don't return until you do!" threatened the guard.

"Oh please, I don't want to go back down. It took me almost half an hour to climb those bloody stairs!" begged the miner.

"Don't care! Be gone."

"How are we going to get past? They're being unusually strict today," Rusty whispered, noting that Amber was right.

They both paused, having not yet formulated a plan. After a moment of contemplation, a solution emerged.

"Umm," Rusty hesitated, scratching his head. "That minecart back at the train. I'll hold our place in line, and you search for something amongst the rubble. Just make sure you do it quietly."

Lustre nodded and retraced his steps into the station tent. There, he was met with a sombre sight: a minecart full of rock and just elder maroon. With care, he retrieved the two rubies from his pocket. This was the first time he had admired fat rubies for octaves. Bad luck in the mines had left him craving to hold these beautiful gemstones. He felt a bit guilty about stealing, especially from his friend, the conductor, but the voice deep in his head kept assuring him it was fine. Then, out of nowhere, he heard another voice behind him.

"Stealing, are you? You rotten little reatrit." A reatrit is similar to a rat, but much worse.

"Peroa!" Lustre was startled. He spun around, his back pressed against the minecart. He was shocked, for standing before him was Amber with a devious grin stained upon his face. "Amber!" said Lustre, dropping the rubies in a panic. There was a brief moment of silence. "How did you get here so fast?" Lustre questioned.

"I bought some incredible teleportation potions from the Banderian Village two octaves ago. I can afford them," taunted Amber. Potions were a costly item. Guards could buy them from a couple of markets across Ruby Nation. Usually, the higher-quality potions were more expensive, and some could sell for hundreds of rubies. They were also illegal for regular folk. That's why it was very uncommon to see miners with such things.

He took a step forward towards Lustre.

"What do you think that guard is going to say? About a boy stealing other people's work?"

Lustre stood firm and replied, "What do you think that guard's gonna say about your potion?" Unexpectedly, somebody else entered the station tent. Amber quickly spun around. Lustre breathed a massive sigh of relief when he heard Rusty's voice.

"What's taking you so long, Lustre? I had to sacrifice our spot in the queue to come here."

Amber turned.

"Amber?" stuttered Rusty. "Why don't you ever just leave us alone?"

Amber sighed. "You guys are up to no good. I can tell." Amber mumbled, "Little reatrit bastard," and quickly left the tent.

"What was all that about?" asked Rusty.

"Amber is going to snitch," proclaimed Lustre. "Let's just grab these two rubies I found in the rubble, one for each of us, and get back in the queue." With that, they were in the queue again at the back. Rusty was now extra paranoid about being snitched on. However, he assumed it was about the train ride. He also couldn't see Amber anywhere in the queue or around them.

Fortunately, that was the last time Rusty ever saw Amber. He wouldn't be a problem anymore.

Once at the front of the queue, they both tried to seem honest and convincing to the inspection guard, to the point where the miner behind them scoffed, "Just a tip. Sucking up would increase your chances."

Lustre hated being judged and replied, "How do you know that? Suck up."

At that point, the miner behind them fell silent. Rusty would never do something like that; he rarely reacted to an argument or insult and was never the ignition for one. Lustre had been through rigid inspections on occasion; the last one had happened octaves ago. He knew what to expect, but he was still unexpectedly nervous.

Unlike most people, the inspector guard stood firmly, towering over Lustre by a few inches. He glanced over the edge of his clipboard, showing only his wrinkly forehead. He spoke in a dull tone. "Name?"

Lustre cleared his throat. "Umm… Lustre and Rusty."

The man brought the clipboard back, covering his face. "I can't find a… 'Lustda' and 'Rust tea' on my list." The inspector grumbled.

Probably as a result of Lustre's heavy Ruby accent. The accent had more minor pauses between each word, which could sometimes hinder conversations.

Lustre had to clarify to the inspector that they were again separate names.

"Okay, rubies, please. Both of you," said the inspector, holding his free hand out to the boys. "We have only mined tiny rubies today, very few big ones. So, if you have a big ruby, I'll let you both off."

Lustre placed the fat rubies in the man's hand. The inspector brought them up to his face, glancing deeply at them.

His expression remained dull and emotionless throughout the whole process.

The silence between them made the boys feel nervous. Tension and anticipation swelled inside them. Then, the inspector confirmed, "All right, those are rubies. You may go on through." Relief fluttered inside them.

"Phew." Rusty exhaled.

As the boys walked past, the inspector guard gave them a suspicious look, potentially noticing the strange glow from Rusty's back pocket. Either way, the boys had made it through the collection tent. Of which they exited almost immediately out of the opposite end. They partially knew the surrounding forests, but not enough to be confident of where they were going. Rusty had a map of the area. It was in his tool sack, the sizeable brown sack containing all of his and Lustre's mining equipment. However, due to the boys' forgetfulness and excitement, they had left all the mining equipment back inside the tunnel. This quickly became apparent after they lost sight of the mine tents, having already ventured far into the Banderian Forest.

Chapter 2

The Encounter

They roamed through the forest, occasionally having to duck and weave around overhanging branches and nettles that grew from the vines dangling above. Many considered the Banderian Forest safer than the Crimson Forest up north in the Ruby Nation. The Banderian Forest was denser, like a jungle of exposed roots of various plants and vegetation. The Crimson Forest had much softer and level ground, with the crimson trees growing equal distances from one another.

The Banderian Forest also had some nasty gemotros that inhabited it. The most common is the grombler. It wasn't hard to kill, but it was dangerous to the inexperienced, like two innocent, vulnerable boys who were about to discover that they were lost, just like a snowflake in a blizzard.

"Okay, Rusty. I need that map," Lustre requested, then added, "You said it was in your pocket before we left."

"Oh, yeah, of course. Just hang on..." Rusty replied, reaching his hand into his pocket.

Rusty's skin turned pale; his mind felt tangled. He froze for a second, enough time for Lustre to realise.

"Rusty... did you forget the map?" Lustre paused, trying to calm the panic inside him. Rusty hesitated; he didn't know what would be better, telling the truth or lying. But he ended up nodding. After gasping, Lustre quickly tried to slow down his breathing. He muttered between breaths, "It's fine as long as we stay en route. We should be able to make it back to the camp."

Minutes passed, and not knowing if they were going in the right direction, Rusty stopped for Lustre to guide him. "Lustre, are you sure we are not just blindly walking? I can't see the camp anywhere!"

"Of course, the camp is this direction. When we return, we can retrieve the map and find the palace." After Lustre lied, they both kept walking, feeling a little unnerved.

"You told me this place is swarming with gromblers!" Rusty remembered bedtime stories that Lustre would tell him at the mine camp.

"If we just stay quiet, no gemotros will hear us." After Lustre said that, Rusty realised how loud he was being. His breathing, his heart pounding in his chest, and even the simple sound of leaves crunching under his feet felt like they could be heard for miles.

"Lustre, what if a gemotro jumps out and eats us?" said Rusty.

"It's fine, Rusty. Just make sure you don't lose that jewel," reinforced Lustre.

Rusty glanced down at the jewel in his pocket, ensuring it was still there. The rustling sound of leaves interrupted Lustre. Not anything they hadn't heard before, but this time, just a little out of the ordinary.

"Stop stepping on leaves," Lustre whispered.

"But... I didn't make that noise," said Rusty.

They both stopped.

"What did then?" Lustre asked.

Both waited to hear the sound again, listening for anything through the ambience; they heard nothing. Rusty's hearing something and not knowing made him feel uneasy, a common side effect of his paranoia. Lustre stopped at the foot of a fat Bandeira bush weed. Lustre noticed a prominent puddle in the soil. He bent down to investigate. An untrained eye would probably overlook the puddle, but the odour was conclusive. "What is it, Lustre?" Rusty asked.

He lowered his face toward the puddle, sniffing it. Lustre recognised the stench almost instantly. He stumbled backwards, gagging violently. "That's a grombler footprint," Lustre confirmed.

"Well…What do we do? How old is it?"

The stench of a grombler lingered. The fact that this one still reeked heavily meant it had to be pretty fresh. Lustre turned to face Rusty.

"Ne…New?" It was evident that Rusty found the whole situation very troubling.

"Come on, let's not worry about it. It's probably a few days old," reassured Lustre.

This didn't make Rusty feel any better. Unconsciously, Rusty kept very close to Lustre as they walked.

"Lustre, I still don't get it." Rusty again brought it up. "How are you scared of nothing?"

Instead of responding, Lustre stopped. All his attention channelled in one direction, he stood perfectly still, gesturing to Rusty to stop as well. Lustre stared off into the distance, this time focused and silent.

"Lustre, why do you always ignore me?" whinged Rusty.

"Shhh!" Lustre snapped.

A gust of wind rushed past them. It was cold and bitter, like a blizzard of sharp glass. It stung their faces and the tips of their fingers, but that wasn't what concerned Lustre. What made him shiver was the pungent smell. The wind carried a horrible, rotten stench. It was an early warning sign.

Lustre ordered, "Rusty, don't move!" Rusty obeyed. Suddenly, a gigantic, monstrous figure stepped into view. It was only a few yards away. Rusty held his breath.

The humanoid figure stood ten feet high, towering over them both. Lustre couldn't look away, didn't blink, flinch, or even dare to breathe. It was a terrifying sight!

It had blood-red, damp skin, similar in texture to a human. Its back was arched, as was its neck; it was the only gemotro with such a distinctive posture. It was a grombler. The creature turned, revealing its gruesome face to the boys. Its unhinged jaw of yellow-stained teeth and long demonic horns protruding from the front of its face were enough to scare off anybody. Its arms were irregularly long, dragging its knuckles along the forest floor as it walked towards them. It stared into Lustre's eyes. Its throat bulged as it breathed.

There was a moment of silence, each waiting for the other to move first. In the end, the first to move was Rusty. He couldn't take it and snapped into panic mode. Rusty stumbled backwards, hyperventilating. Lustre sprang into action. He aimed his hands at the grombler before him, tensing his fingers.

"Gamber Goth-Gorian!" Lustre yelled the magic words. His veins filled with adrenaline. The tips of his fingers sparked, spewing out strings of luminescent red dust. The dust then took the shape of a ball in Lustre's hands. "Stand back, Rusty!" Lustre warned.

The ball caught fire. Lustre thrust his hands forward, hurling the fireball toward the grombler. It zipped through the air, striking the grombler between the eyes. The ball shattered upon impact as if it were made of glass. A plume of fire engulfed the grombler's face. With a shriek of pain, the grombler stumbled backwards, quickly regaining its balance. The spell was to startle and knock it over, but the creature was only aggravated further.

Ruby spells can't kill or seriously harm Ruby gemotros, and a grombler was a Ruby gemotro. The best they could do was stun them or resort to primitive weapons. Lustre was still an amateur caster, so he wasn't the best at spells. The known Ruby stun spell 'Re-tentro-mjana' was still too advanced for him! "Rusty, run! My magic is useless against it!" cried Lustre. The grombler wrapped its claws around Lustre's waist, lifting him to the level of its face. Rusty wanted to run, but hesitation overcame him. He had to do something. Lustre begged Rusty to escape, reassuring him he could handle it. Rusty didn't believe him.

"Just go... Rusty!" ordered Lustre. The grombler widened its mouth, exposing its teeth. The gemotro lifted Lustre above its mouth and lowered him towards its jaws. Lustre kicked and flailed his legs, but he couldn't slip free of the gemotro's grip, and even if he did, he would still fall straight into the grombler's mouth.

Rusty wasn't old enough to cast magic. He scoured through his pockets for something, anything that could be helpful. But the only thing he found was the jewel. Rusty thought that its bright glow could be enough to distract the grombler. He waved it above his head, trying to get its attention, without any effect. Rusty was out of ideas. He clutched the gemstone tightly in his hands and pulled his arm back. Just before he threw it, he paused and brought it back up in front of his face. He felt something. It felt like peace. It felt like hope. At that moment, Rusty had no control over his actions. The jewel was in control, and it was unexplainable.

Then he closed his eyes. Aimed the jewel up at the grombler.

FLASH

Blue light blinded him. His vision was clouded, and everything was muffled in his ears. His head was spinning.

The next thing Rusty knew was that he was lying down, staring at the treetops, with Lustre kneeling before him.

"Come on, buddy, wake up," he heard Lustre say. Rusty slowly sat up with some assistance from Lustre.

"What just happened?" was the only thing Rusty could utter.

Lustre seemed to be just as clueless. The main thing Rusty noticed was that the grombler, who had been attacking Lustre a moment before, was lying motionless on the ground.

"Wait. You're alive!" exclaimed Rusty.

Lustre nodded. "Yeah, I thought I was about to die. Then there was this big flash of blue light, the grombler collapsed." Lustre turned around and approached the dead gemotro, glancing at its face for a few seconds before concluding. "It's a male, thirty to forty rots; I still don't understand how it died, though."

Rusty slowly regained balance on his legs. He rose off the ground, still a little dizzy. "Lustre...I think I cast a spell."

Lustre spun around. "Don't be silly. You're not old enough to cast magic. Besides, even if you're an early caster, how could you kill it? It's a Ruby gemotro!"

They kept walking. After considering the situation, Lustre thought that Rusty was just an early caster. He is much younger than average, but there's some variation. Still, that didn't explain how the grombler died. Lustre then noticed a tiny speck of sunlight through a bush in front of him. Not wanting to get too excited, he moved closer to have a better look.

"It could just be!" Lustre pulled the branch up, revealing the glaring sun. They had found a way out. "Rusty, the forest ends here!" Lustre called out. Rusty came running, fluttering with relief.

Seeing Bandeira's vast, treeless fields, Lustre pushed his face through the bush. A massive wheat field was before them, stretching far into the distance. A blanket of gold lay across the horizon. The sky was no longer obscured with leaves, and the ground was no longer littered with exposed roots and shrubbery. Lustre loosened his boots and took them off. The soil felt soft between his toes, and he inhaled a huge breath of fresh air.

"Wow, it's morning already." Lustre was surprised. Rusty followed behind, pulling the branch above his head and stepping out into the field. His first reactions were both positive and negative. The main thing that echoed in his mind was the lack of navigation. They had no clue where they were. The positive was that they were no longer at the threat of gromblers.

Rusty gazed around for clues, some obvious marker that could be helpful. Maybe a distant village or town. Every direction looked similar to the one before it. It was just a slightly slanted field of wheat. The field was so vast with no sign of any distant objects. There was just wheat and sky separated by the gleam of the sun upon the horizon. There was not much to go on.

"Maybe there is a village nearby. Then somebody could tell us where the mine is," said Rusty.

"Wait, why do we need to return to the mine now? We have already found a way out of the forest. Why don't we head straight for the palace?" suggested Lustre.

"Well, we need directions either way," remarked Rusty. "Maybe we could go find the Banderian Village. It shouldn't be far."

Lustre smiled and said, "The last one to find a village is a rotten egg!"

Rusty was already annoyed. But being playful at a bad time could often soften it into a good time, which could be shaped into a nice memory. And for some reason, he felt he was running out of good memories. His whole past was a stain on his current life.

"Hey, you can't have a head start!" laughed Rusty. They both began chasing each other through the wheat fields, playing a game of hide and seek. Being able to run without trees in every direction felt so much better. After a few minutes, they forgot they were trying to find the village. They hadn't gone far, but Rusty ensured they didn't lose sight of the forest's edge. The wheat was up to their waists. Soon, Rusty grew impatient; he proved he was the more responsible of the two and reminded Lustre. "Hey, Lustre, we need to find that village," Rusty called out.

Lustre didn't respond. Rusty spun round, glancing across the field. Nothing. Rusty got a little concerned. "Lustre, this isn't funny!" Rusty yelled out. Lustre always played tricks when they were younger, without Rusty's agreement. Lustre was the boy who took simple games very seriously, and once he started, he was committed.

When Rusty was ten, Lustre hid from him for two hours before he found him. Knowing that Lustre could repeat this, he called, "I will leave without you!"

Rusty would never actually do something like that. But he hoped it would be enough to convince Lustre to show himself. Lustre probably knew Rusty was bluffing because it didn't work. Lustre was nowhere to be seen. A few seconds later, just before Rusty started to panic…

"BOO!"

Rusty squealed and lost his balance. Fortunately, the wheat beneath him softened his fall. Rusty gazed up to see Lustre laughing hysterically. "That's not funny. That's really immature." Rusty was crying and embarrassed. Lustre continued laughing without a speck of guilt. After Rusty got back to his feet, he asserted himself. "You almost made me drop the jewel; it could be fragile."

Lustre stopped to catch his breath and to apologise, obviously with insincerity. Right at that moment, something caught Lustre's attention. It was a noise, something unnatural. Lustre overheard a loud creaking through the wind and the gentle rustling of the wheat. Lustre could only compare it to the squealing of a loose floorboard. The sound was quite distant, but audible.

"What is that...creaking?" Rusty was the first to ask.

"I don't know, but I will find out."

After following the sound for a few minutes, they lost sight of the Banderian Forest, which was concerning to Rusty. Surrounding them still was the vast expanse of golden wheat. In every direction, the field seemed to go on for miles. However, they did see something new. A long dirt road cut the field in two. The road stretched miles into the distance, snaking over the hills, weaving its path through the land. It was so long, yet only a few yards wide.

"That is one long road. Maybe we should follow it?" Lustre suggested.

"Hang on...What's that? The creaking sound is getting louder," Rusty interjected, pointing out into the distance. About a mile away, a solitary figure emerged, slowly moving along the winding road. Lustre and Rusty squinted to get a better look, and it became apparent that this figure was leading a caravan. The creaking was the noise of the wagon wheels carried by the wind across the fields. This caravan was the only thing in sight on the long, empty road. Its presence felt like a mirage, a sudden speck of civilisation.

The caravan was striking, with its arched, white canopy standing in stark contrast against the backdrop of golden wheat fields. The noisy caravan proceeded along the road, but what caught Lustre's curiosity were the two strange creatures towing it—two massive centipedes, a sight neither of the boys had ever witnessed.

Eager anticipation held the boys in place by the roadside. Then the boys cautiously approached it. The centipede- like creatures scuttled, their multiple legs startling Rusty. He stumbled backward, taken aback by their peculiar appearance.

"I have never seen those gemotros before." Rusty was scared.

Lustre mustered the courage to call out to the coachman seated lazily at the front of the caravan. Initially undisturbed by the boys' presence, the man was visibly disrupted when he heard Lustre's voice. He resembled a typical merchant, clad in worn, tattered attire, and his long silver beard cascaded down his chest. His narrowed eyes rested atop a wrinkled nose.

Turning his head abruptly, his beard swaying with the motion, the man uttered an abrupt shriek of annoyance. "Aye! What... What?" he grumbled, clearly awakened from his sleep.

Lustre asked politely, "Sir? We were just wondering where you're headed."

"Where am I going?" the proud man repeated, his tone irritable. "I am heading to the Banderian Village to sell all these crates of ruby wine and see my son, but you're not getting a ride!"

"Please, can we?" Rusty implored, desperation in his voice.

"Can you two boys scram? You're frightening my pelatas!" he groaned with a crack of his coacher's whip. The caravan sped up a bit faster, a little more than running pace. Leaving the two boys behind.

"Hey, maybe we should follow him," Rusty suggested.

Lustre sighed and pointed down the road. "No, it's probably a long walk."

Then Lustre smiled cunningly and said, "I know!"

Rusty knew that smile all too well. It was an obvious hint, telling him he was about to do something incredibly smart or dumb. Most of the time, it would end up being the latter.

"What if we climbed onto the back of his caravan, staying low and quiet? Then he will take us there!" Lustre suggested.

It seemed like a good idea. But Rusty was already counting the risks that the idea would come with. "But what if he sees us?" said Rusty nervously.

"Then we will just jump off," Lustre reassured. With no other options, Rusty accepted. They raced to the caravan before it got too far down the road. They matched its pace, moving quietly behind it. Lustre went first, clutching the back of the caravan. Once he got a sturdy grip, he lifted himself into the caravan. He stayed low, out of sight.

Then it was Rusty's turn. This time, the process wasn't as swift. Rusty was much weaker and struggled to lift his weight, especially while maintaining pace with the caravan. By himself, he couldn't make it.

"Lustre, grab me, please!" begged Rusty.

Lustre rolled his eyes and replied, "Come on, just pull yourself up."

Rusty made a second effort to pull himself up. He made it halfway up but ultimately just fell back down. He didn't have the strength. "Please, Lustre, just pull me up," Rusty again asked. After watching Rusty fail for a second time, Lustre was satisfied. He offered his hand out over the edge. Rusty gripped it, using it to pull his weight forward. Then he jumped. Lustre hauled Rusty over the edge, dragging him into the caravan.

"Yes, thank you." Rusty sighed.

Minutes passed, and Lustre leaned against one of the ruby wine crates as he sat. At the front of the wagon, he saw a fine blade mounted on an ornamental rack; an inscription on the blade read, 'Dazzldern forged by IronShard'. Bottles rattled loudly inside as the caravan went over a bump, drowning out all noise. Rusty sat on the edge, his feet dangling over, watching the sun start its afternoon arch. He held the jewel in his lap, admiring it. He glanced at it, watching the coloured lights swell within it.

Lustre broke the silence. "I still don't understand how you killed that grombler?" Rusty then stuffed the jewel back into his pocket.

"I just don't know. I am not an early caster," responded Rusty.

Lustre then scratched his chin. "Strange."

Suddenly, all the sunlight around them vanished. The caravan halted in the shadow of a gigantic gateway enclosed by surrounding stone walls. The two boys rushed to the front, peering over the coacher's head.

"Wow! That's one tall wall," Rusty commented.

Lustre shoved his hand over Rusty's mouth, pulling him back out of sight. Fortunately, the man didn't hear them.

Lustre reminded, "We can't let that coachman know we are here. Keep quiet." Now that the caravan had stopped, the sound of the wheels and wind didn't mask out their voices. They heard the coachman crying loudly and gravelly at the guardhouse.

"Hello! Who goes there?" returned another voice from the top of the gate.

"Phil IronShard! I am here as a merchant. We have a stall selling fine weapons and ruby wine across Bandeira!"

"Oh, Phil, I know your son, Henry. Come on in!"

The portcullis had a very archaic design, built more for beauty than practicality. They overheard the sound of rattling chains and squealing steel. The gate rose inch by inch until it stopped at a height large enough to fit the caravan through. They heard another crack of the coacher's whip. The caravan began moving. The sight just beyond those gates was nothing short of magical.

Chapter 3

The Banderian Village

Every second octave or twenty-four days, in the Banderian Village was a market day. It was the only day when crowds would flood the streets, and tradespeople and merchants would travel miles to exchange goods with the village. The main street was purposely built very wide to accommodate all the carriages and people passing through. Off this street, many narrow alleyways branched.

Lustre gazed at the abundance of barrels, crates, and benches along the roadside. No market stall was like the other, each varying in size and colour. Some even had their own smaller crowds of people surrounding them. Every direction was bustling with activity. Tantalising smells wafted from the marketplace. The rich and warm scent reminded him of spicy stews, soup, and sugar. The smell made him think of his favourite place, Tether's Tavern in the Crimson Village.

The crowd divided itself so the caravan could pass through the street without the pelatas trampling somebody. Lustre thought this was a good opportunity to leave the caravan. "Come on, let's get off. Hopefully, somebody can give us directions here."

Looking very worried, Rusty said, "Um, okay, as long as it's safe. Wait, before we get off…" He reached up to his neck and untied his necklace. "Here, please take my necklace. You can trade it for a map or directions." Rusty placed it into Lustre's hand. Even though Rusty did want to keep it, he thought now was the most necessary time to trade it.

"Thanks," replied Lustre, tightening the necklace around his neck. "Okay, let's go."

Then they jumped. Soon, they scrambled amongst the crowd, being pushed and shoved in every direction. Lustre was quite tall for his age, so he could see over most people around him, but Rusty felt as if he was submerged beneath a wave pool. There was no organisation whatsoever; everybody wanted to move in different directions. Briefly, the two boys were split from each other. But Lustre managed to spot Rusty amongst the crowd and guide him to the roadside.

"Well, that was horrible." Rusty breathed deeply.

"Yes, let's stay together so we don't get lost," Lustre advised.

Only seconds after saying that, Lustre abandoned Rusty to go and see all the market stalls lining the roadside. He raced over to the first one that caught his attention, a stall with an ornamental red cup as its banner. It was quite a simple stall compared to most others he had seen. A simple wooden bench decorated with a red-patterned tablecloth. This market stall wasn't as lively as the others; it had no crowd surrounding it whatsoever. This further prompted Lustre to go over to it. From the lack of customers, the man behind the stall was fast asleep, leaning his head on his table. Lustre cleared his throat.

"Hello sir," Lustre greeted politely.

At that point, Lustre noticed the man's loud snoring and decided to do the first thing that came to mind. "Sir!" he repeated loudly. The man jerked his head up, glaring at Lustre.

"Wha-Wh-What…Who? Oh," mumbled the seller.

"Hi," Lustre smiled.

"Sorry… I don't get many customers." The man introduced himself, straightening his glasses. Guards normally policed this stall, patting down and frisking customers, which was terrible for business. "Would you like to buy something?"

"Okay, what is there to buy?" replied Lustre.

"Oh! Well, there are lots of things. I am an old shoemaker by trade, but I work here now and am licensed to sell potions and ingredients; most stock goes to the Ruby Army. I have the rare golden devtark orchids, which I sell for only forty small rubies per pound or just five fat rubies. I have crimson berries, crimson leaf, Bandeira bush weed, fluro flutters, aztel ferns and plenty of potions. I even have spellbooks! You name it, I have it!" The seller listed.

"Wow," gasped a curious Lustre. "Spellbooks!"

"Yes, I have the whole collection of Ruby spell books."

Lustre's face lit up. "The whole collection. I only have the beginner-level spell book and the second," said Lustre, realising those were all back at the mine camp.

"Well, let me get you the third." The seller then whistled.

He turned away from his stall and toward a tall bookshelf behind him. Skimming across each row with his finger, reading the spines, one stood out. "Here it is," he murmured. He carefully slid the book from the bookshelf and placed it on the table. Lustre glanced at the cover. The cover wasn't new. The cover and spine were made from leather that had begun to fray along the edges. Curly writing, written in silver to contrast against the brown, decorated the front. The centrepiece of the cover was a ruby embedded within the leather, and it caught Lustre's attention.

"Is that ruby real?" Lustre asked.

"Of course," replied the seller. "The book contains many spells, such as defence, disarm, and stun."

"May I?" Lustre asked.

"Sure, go ahead."

Lustre carefully picked the book up. After thoroughly admiring the cover, he opened it, revealing the inner cream-coloured pages. Even though the outside seemed quite worn, the inner pages were unharmed. Lustre skimmed through the pages, thinking to himself, "This is incredible."

"If you want to buy, it's four small rubies or one fat ruby. But otherwise, I am willing to trade."

Then Lustre's heart sank. He had forgotten entirely. "Oh…" Lustre sighed. "I don't have any rubies." Lustre placed the spell book back on the table.

"Wait, you have nothing? So, you woke me up for nothing?" grumbled the seller.

Lustre gave off a nervous and slightly humiliated grin. The man shook his head with disappointment.

"Well, I have this necklace," Lustre said, lifting his chin and exposing his neck to the man.

The man stared at it for a few moments. "A single ruby pendant is worthless," he concluded.

Lustre lowered his head back down. Then a thought dawned on Lustre.

"My mate over there might have something we could trade. We found it in the mines." This one statement restored the man's interest once again.

"What is it?" said the seller curiously.

Just as Lustre was about to answer, he felt a cold breeze drift past him. Lustre heard a faint voice within that breeze, unlike anything he had heard. The voice was shrill and very subtle. Lustre only recognised three words. Those three words would spark a new sense of uneasiness within him. "Don't tell him!" whispered a strange voice.

At first, Lustre was puzzled. It was so clear, yet so impossible. He assumed it was just the wind.

"Did you hear that?" asked Lustre.

"No."

At that point, the seller thought Lustre was just another beggar, scavenging through the markets, like reatrits, searching for food. Starving beggars were a common aspect of almost every village within Ruby Nation. The seller realised this and decided to take pity on Lustre. "It's okay. You don't have to pretend to be somebody else. I know what it feels like to have nothing." The seller smiled. He reached below his table, eventually producing three glass vials and a potion bottle reserved only for official guards. He placed them both down on the table and leaned inwards. The seller spoke, suppressing his voice.

"Okay, my friend, because you can't afford any of my stock, you may have one thing for free." Lustre leaned in.

"Here, in my left hand, is a potion called Muzzle Mud. It is scarce and pricey. But I will give you this fifteen-ounce bottle of it for free," he stated.

"Muzzle Mud?" Lustre repeated.

"Yes. It is a potion that can heal almost any wound or poison in one sip." The man smiled as Lustre stared at the spherical glass bottle. It contained some blue sludge, sealed off with a small cork at the top. It was intriguing, but Lustre was sceptical. The seller continued, "In my right hand are three shots of Gone Gazz."

"Goon jazz," Lustre replied, doubting whether he pronounced the words correctly. Lustre always struggled with names, especially ones that were difficult to pronounce.

Which is the main reason he never calls Rusty by his real name. So, once again, he was trapped in an awkward silence of waiting for somebody to correct him.

"It's pronounced Gone Gazz. Not goon jazz. I am pretty sure that's a weird band or... something."

Lustre acknowledged, "Yeah, yeah, okay."

In the seller's right hand were three small glass vials, each containing some yellow water. "Gone Gazz is a teleportation serum. You drink the whole vial in one go. You must picture and announce where you want to be teleported, then whoosh. You're there!"

Again, Lustre was intrigued, but sceptical.

"Which one do you want?"quickly muttered the man, hoping any guards were not watching."

"Wait, I can have one of these potions for free?" Lustre clarified. The man nodded.

Lustre was surprised by this man's generosity. However, it also significantly increased his scepticism; it seemed too good to be true to have a potion. With a few seconds of consideration, Lustre took the three vials of Gone Gazz. Teleportation seemed like the most useful.

"Good choice." The man smiled.

Lustre slipped them into his pocket. After thanking the man, Lustre turned away, expecting to see Rusty waiting for him. However, Rusty had managed to get lost amongst the crowd once again!

"Seriously, why can't he stay put?" Lustre cursed.

Rusty wasn't curious in any way. After losing sight of Lustre, he went on a journey. He ignored most market stalls, which were exceptionally crowded. He believed the majority of what merchants had to sell was pure junk, fakery. Most things that appeared to have value were worthless. This especially applied to jewellery, art, and antiques. Desperate villagers would overprice everything.

Rusty stayed on the roadside to avoid getting lost amongst the crowd. Even though finding Lustre was his main priority, he also wanted to find somebody who could give them directions. Everything was so loud.

"Exotic herbs and spices! Fresh from Emerald Nation!" he heard one merchant say.

"Swords! Get the finest swords here from Henry IronShard, the blacksmith!" he heard another cry.

But then, over the thumping instruments and prattling crowd, he heard some merchant say, "Maps! Get your maps here! Everything cartography!"

Rusty rushed to the market stall with a tall man behind the bench. "Hey! Could I please have directions to the palace?" asked Rusty.

The man smiled graciously. "Oh, of course. Just hold on while I get a map." Rusty waited patiently. Everything was going perfectly; he could find Lustre and get going once he had directions. But something gained his attention: a scream across the crowd from the other side of the street.

It was the most blood-curdling scream he had ever heard. Convinced that something was wrong, he left the market stand to investigate. With a struggle, he pushed through the crowd until he reached the other side. Standing before him was a distressed woman. She was no different from the other villagers. She wore a long, tattered dress with a white apron tied around her waist. Rusty noticed she was hugging a stick of bread.

Something didn't seem right. A guard approached the woman. Rusty quickly realised that the guard had ill intentions.

"Get away!" the woman shrieked.

Rusty raised an eyebrow. Before the woman could get away, the guard grabbed her by the wrist. The guard overpowered her, twisting her arm behind her back.

"Just hand it over!" He heard the guard groan.

The woman made a strong effort to hold on to the bread, even as the guard tried to rip it from her grasp. The guard grew impatient quickly. Without thinking, Rusty bravely stepped in. Not usually a thing he would do. He didn't consider how easily things could go wrong. Before things escalated further, Rusty yelled at the guard, "Hey! Let go of her now!"

The guard stopped, turning his head with visible confusion on his face. "Leave her alone, you reatrit," Rusty again yelled. The guard lowered his eyes to see the stumpiest and most timid child he had ever seen. Confusion turned into laughter. "Scram, kid, or else," chuckled the guard.

Rusty wasn't about to obey this guard. Sure, Rusty was timid; he had many fears and was weak. However, his one trait that Lustre soon found out was that he was also stubborn. He stood his ground, unfazed by the guard's threats. "No! I am going to say this one more time… leave her!" yelled Rusty.

The guard briefly let go of the woman, giving her time to scuttle away to the street side. Then, losing interest in the bread, the guard stepped toward Rusty, a gleaming smile on his face. "Or what?" he smirked.

Rusty felt shy. His bravery was short-lived. He said nothing.

"Exactly," chuckled the guard before walking off. Instantly, Rusty ran over to help the woman, who was now huddled and crying.

"Are you okay?" Rusty enquired, with empathy on his face.

"I am fine, son. Thanks for that. But don't stand up to those guards in the future. They will always have an excuse to arrest you." The woman gathered herself before retreating into the crowd.

Rusty thought, "Well, at least she still has her bread." It was appalling to think that all these innocent people had to live in such conditions. Fighting over what the emperor would consider worthless things, like bread. The guards weren't treated any better. They still lacked food and shelter, so they pillaged the markets, stealing food and gems from the already-starving citizens. Since guards were provided with armour and weaponry, they abused their power to steal from the citizens. This added to why the Ruby Nation was so corrupt compared to the others.

Suddenly, Rusty felt a strange sensation in his back pocket; he reached inside it and pulled out the jewel. Unlike before, the jewel shone brightly like a flaring torch, even in direct daylight. "I don't understand. Why is it glowing now?" Rusty wondered, staring at it. Unfortunately, the jewel was dazzling and caught somebody else's attention.

"That's a pretty rock you got there." Rusty heard a deep voice from behind. He spun around, startled by the horrifying grin of the guard from earlier.

"You know, I am sure that's worth a lot," added the guard.

Rusty was speechless, too shocked to react. The guard then seized Rusty by the hand and attempted to snatch the jewel, but Rusty refused to let it go.

Rusty screamed at the crest of his lungs, "Let go!" The guard clenched his teeth, his anger swelling his face. Rusty kept hold. The guard probably thought this scrawny kid wouldn't put up such a fight. Usually, kids would feel terrified in such a situation. But no, Rusty was different. To regain superiority in the fight, the guard briefly let go of Rusty's hand to draw a knife from his belt. He held the knife above his head, aiming the blade down at Rusty.

Rusty was traumatised. Was this guard really about to stab him? Over a rock? Could one man feel that desperate? He could see the fire in his eyes. Rusty's heart pounded. The guard's expression was one of pure heartlessness without a drop of guilt, thinking that violence was the only option. The guard thrust his hand down, plunging the knife toward Rusty's face. The jewel in Rusty's hand swelled, increasing in luminosity.

Time stopped. Rusty's pupils flashed bright yellow.

"Hella-scaren-peta-shingo," Rusty whispered unknown words to himself. A loud crack pierced the air like a coacher's whip. Lustre, now amongst the crowd searching for Rusty, was exhausted. Then he heard it, followed by the frantic screams of villagers.

"Terrorism!" Lustre heard a passing villager scream.

Lustre was puzzled. The crowd quickly became a stampede, and everybody rushed toward the village gate. Merchants abandoned their stalls and joined the crowd. Lustre was almost trampled by the sudden hurry to leave the village. He could only wonder what they could be running from. Then he saw it. In the distance, a thick tower of smoke swirled upward into the sky, a fire whirlwind. Only minutes later, the entire crowd was leaving, hurrying out the gates. The market was deserted.

Lustre arrived at the cause of the smoke. It was not what he expected: a fire twister moving rapidly. The firestorm emitted immense heat upon his face. He coughed violently, his lungs filled with that horrible smoke, as he gasped, "What could have started such a fire?"

Fire licked the sky, blackening the surrounding road. Henry IronShard's blacksmith shop had collapsed under the fire's pursuit. It consumed everything flammable, twisting and weaving through the square, leaving only charred remains. A few of the remaining villagers who didn't evacuate with the crowd came running. They chased and dumped buckets of water upon the fire, doing little to prevent it from worsening.

Lustre considered helping them, but something else crossed his mind.

He heard somebody scream. It wasn't a villager this time. Lustre recognised this scream immediately.

"Lustre, help!" It was Rusty. Lustre snapped back into reality. Just a bit further up the road were two guards, easily recognisable by their bright silver armour. Amongst them, Lustre spotted a small boy getting dragged away. "Rusty!" screeched Lustre.

Lustre raced towards them. His hands trembled, and his heart felt like it would never stop pounding. He felt the effects of adrenaline rush through his body; although tired, this rush gave him the energy to keep going. Lustre never thought he could run so fast; his best friend needed him.

"Hey, let him go!" Lustre managed to speak between breaths. Rusty was wrestled along, his arms restrained behind his back.

"Lustre! Please tell them I'm not a T-" Rusty screamed. Before he could finish, one of the guards bound a strip of cloth around Rusty's mouth, muffling his voice.

"Who are you, boy?" One of the guards scowled.

"I am not telling you my name! All you need to know is that's my mate. And you have to let him go," responded Lustre.

"Your mate? This young boy here is a terrorist! He is from the Topaz Nation, here to cause destruction!" snapped the other.

Lustre was baffled. "No, he's not! He's Ruby by birth!" argued Lustre.

"Well, explain that summoned firestorm." Both guards pointed down the road at the quenched fire. "No Ruby spell can do that! But I know a Topaz spell that can do as such! So, he is a Topaz!" they claimed.

Rusty couldn't have done it; he couldn't be Topaz. Yet, all the evidence suggested otherwise. Lustre was lost for words.

"That couldn't have been him! It was probably an accident!" Lustre struggled to answer.

Suddenly, two other guards rushed in carrying a wooden stretcher. "Out of the way, guard down!" they cried as they hurried past. Lying motionless on the stretcher was a guard, not like the others; his armour was deformed, with a large dent right in the centre of his chest. His underclothes were tattered from the force of his chest armour collapsing in on his stomach. Lustre glimpsed the guard's face as they hustled by. His skin was pale and smothered like coal dust. It was so seriously burnt that it was almost unrecognisable as a human face.

"Rusty…Would never…He can't be… It's not true."

Lustre refused to believe that Rusty was responsible. It couldn't be possible.

"This little reatrit… He killed our brethren… He's dead now because of him!" bellowed the guard holding Rusty's arms.

Rusty stared into Lustre's bloodshot eyes. Lustre was full of anger.

"Now scram! We're taking this reatrit to the Bandeira Jail." They scowled, dragging Rusty further up the street. Lustre stood there, anger brewing within him. He fought to hold in his anger, but the sight of Rusty being handled like a prisoner by those guards meant he couldn't hold himself back. He stormed back up toward them.

"Oh, seriously! Didn't we tell you to get lost?" one remarked.

"I am only going to say this one more time. Let him go. Now!" uttered Lustre through clenched teeth. Even though they appeared unthreatened, the two guards still took a few seconds to consider.

"Bear, I know this boy injured a guard…"

"Killed!" the other guard interjected.

"Well… we don't know for sure, but can't we just let this boy go? He is just a kid."

"No, Ryan, he's a Topaz kid! We can't just let him go; he could cause even more destruction," argued Bear.

"Well, fine."

The guards ultimately agreed to disagree. "We are not letting him go, kid! We are taking him to jail, and that's final!" Bear exclaimed, "Now scram, you little…"

Lustre was done. He lurched forward and swung his fist toward Bear's nose. Dazzled, Bear stumbled backwards. At that moment, both guards briefly released Rusty's hands, stunned by what had just happened. Bear collapsed to the ground, losing consciousness only seconds after being punched.

Lustre saw his opportunity and took it. Whilst the other guard was distracted, Lustre grabbed Rusty's hand before bolting in the opposite direction. With his hands now free, Rusty tore the cloth off his face. His first words were, "Peroa, mother of life! That was wild! How did you do that?"

"We have to get to the exit fast!" yelled Lustre.

"I know the gateway isn't far! It's just down the street from where we arrived on that merchant's caravan!" Rusty reminded his friend.

Lustre glanced across the street; the gatehouse wasn't far from where they stood. Better yet, the gate was wide open, most likely due to the stampede of villagers all trying to exit at once.

"All right, do you still have the jewel?" Lustre asked.

Rusty quickly reached behind him, feeling his back pocket. "Yes," he confirmed.

"Good, make sure you don't lose it."

They both raced down the road. Lustre could almost consider themselves through the gate before disaster struck.

Since there was no crowd to hide in, the guard who stood high up in the village watchtower could easily spot them approaching the open gateway.

Upon seeing them, he quickly signalled for the gate to be shut. The portcullis was released and slammed down right before them. They turned their backs against the gate. Dozens of village guards swarmed toward them, closing off every direction outwards from the gate. They huddled behind their shields, pointing their spears inwards. "Hands above your head!" They roared.

Lustre was out of ideas. He had to obey.

"What's your plan now?" Rusty trembled. Lustre couldn't respond.

The ground began to vibrate beneath their feet. It was unnoticeable at first, but the sensation grew rapidly. Then, the ground burst into flames in front of the boys unnaturally. The ground was made from stone bricks glued in place with cement. It wasn't flammable. The guards were undeterred by the sudden fire, almost like they were expecting it.

The fire roared upwards, sending ribbons of flame into the air. Then, as quickly as the fire grew, it collapsed, dissipating into the ground. The scalding heat cast upon the boys was enough to rid their faces of all moisture, even in the few seconds the fire was present. Standing in the fire's place was a man dressed in a golden silk robe draped over his shoulders. His expression was dull, with a slight hint of anger. There was something about his appearance that didn't feel altogether, something that made him look uncanny.

"Here, Autumn, it's these two," a senior guard pointed at them.

Rusty felt a spear prod him in the side, forcing him forward toward the man. Rusty sneakily transferred the jewel from his pocket into Lustre's as he moved forward.

"Wait...Rusty, what are you doing?" Lustre whispered.

"It will be fine, Lustre..." Rusty responded, unusually calm. Lustre stared into Rusty's eyes. "Why are you doing this? I will find another way to escape this...I am sure," spoke Lustre. But then, Rusty said something that made Lustre's heart sink.

"I am not scared anymore...Lustre. I am just like you now. That's all I have ever wanted. When I saved that woman back there from the guard. I wasn't scared! When, usually, I would normally be terrified."

"Wait...Rusty..." stuttered Lustre.

Rusty turned to face the strange man, willingly stepping forward. Instead of fearing the outcome, he just accepted it. The strange man raised his arm, curling his fingers into a fist. The man scrunched his eyebrows and clenched his teeth.

"Loomapa-lingera!" spoke the man.

A blinding, brilliant flash erupted, abruptly shrouding the surroundings in silence. Lustre instinctively shielded his eyes from the searing light, and time seemed to stand still in the following heart-pounding seconds. With trepidation, Lustre cautiously lowered his hands, and his vision gradually became focused, revealing a bewildering sight.

A cloud of yellow mist enveloped Lustre's field of view. As the dust gently descended to the ground, it revealed Rusty, who stood there with his skin now drained of colour, transformed into a pallid, ashen grey. He remained eerily motionless, his posture frozen in place, but it wasn't just his stance that had stilled. Even his hair no longer danced in the breeze, and the ripples and creases in his shirt were frozen. It was an inexplicable sight beyond the reach of words, leaving Lustre speechless and swelling with disbelief.

"What... What! What did you do to him?" Lustre's voice erupted in a torrent of fear and anger. Driven by concern and desperation, Lustre moved toward Rusty, only to be pulled back by the guards.

"He's been turned to stone, son. We are taking him to the palace where he will cause no more trouble. The emperor loves his trophies."

Lustre felt his heart skip a beat. "Turned…To…To…Stone?" Lustre felt something tighten around his wrists.

"Quickly, Autumn, turn this one to stone as well." Lustre then heard the senior guard protest.

The strange man took a step forward toward Lustre. "Sorry, bud," he said insincerely.

Lustre attempted to free his hands just once more, but to no avail, as the guard's grip was tight. The man held his arm up high, his wrinkly hand inches from Lustre's forehead. Then it happened. It was inexplicable. It could have been luck. But Lustre's hands were now free, just for a crucial second. The guard that had been binding Lustre's wrists let go, the reason being unknown.

Since Lustre's back was hidden, nobody had noticed at the time, not even the man standing directly before Lustre. The man began to utter his spell.

"Looma-"

Lustre was first. "Gamber Goth-Gorian!" screamed Lustre, aiming his hand at the man. Veins bulged in Lustre's wrist. His arm tensed. The guards were blinded as red light rippled outwards from Lustre's hand. The light birthed a small ball of fire. He thrust his arm forward, sending the ball of light whizzing towards the man and shedding a trail of sparks behind it. The point of impact was right in the man's stomach; it didn't just knock over the man as initially expected. Usually, the fireball would strike the victim, barrelling the person over and then dispersing into the air. But on this occasion, the fireball launched the man with it.

The man was thrown backwards into the air. His body twisted and turned until landing on his back, hurling him so far backwards that he cleared every guard and protruding spear behind him. With a few seconds, Lustre was spared, and he reached into his pocket and pulled out one of the three glass vials of Gone Gazz. He popped the cork off with his thumb, uttering. "Please work." He tilted his head back and gulped it down. The guards advanced to surround Lustre. With his back pressed against the gate, Lustre shouted, "Take me to the Crimson Forest!" In the panic, it was the first place that came to his mind.

The Crimson Forest was another vast forest north of Bandeira, much different from the Banderian Forest. Even though it was considered twice as dangerous as the Banderian Forest, it was the only thing his mind could produce in the two seconds he was given. The forest was so massive that it took up half of Ruby Nation. It was a place of refuge for most outlaws, as guards had difficulty finding people. It was like spotting a shard of glass in a pool of water.

Crunch

Lustre was tackled to the ground. Guards had rushed towards him. Logically, he should have expected this; free potions were too good to be true. Lustre's face was rubbed in the dirt, his wrists firmly tied behind his back twice.

"You're goin' to jail now, buddy." A guard spat.

Chapter 4

The Crimson Forest

The next thing Lustre knew, he was floating. His arms and legs felt weightless, as if gravity wasn't there. His hands were still tied behind his back. His chest was throbbing in pain as darkness consumed his surroundings. He was just as confused as he was panicked. It only took a few seconds for him to realise he was very deep underwater. He turned his head upwards. Thirty feet above him was the sun, shimmering in the disturbed water. Peroa's rays pierced through the first few feet of water, dancing and sparkling above him. Lustre began to panic. Instinctively, he inhaled to replenish his lungs, mistakenly filling them with water, which further added to the pain. Lustre coughed again, only to swallow even more water.

Completely out of breath, he tried desperately to swim back up, but without his hands, he couldn't. Seconds passed, and Lustre felt his back hit the sandy floor. That was the point where he started to feel lightheaded. He knew he didn't have enough time to reach the surface before he drowned. Lustre cried in pain. Luckily, seeing his tears would be impossible. At least there was one upside; he hated people seeing him cry. All seemed hopeless. His vision slowly darkened; it was failing in the black water around him. But somehow, it wasn't dark enough to see the flare of light directly in front of him. It wasn't the sun. It was much too bright and far too near. What was it? It glowed white with an ominous blue tint.

Lustre squinted his eyes, adjusting them to the brightness. When he realised what it was, he almost gasped. It was the jewel. Whilst he was struggling, it must have drifted out of his pocket. It didn't make sense. It was a rock; it shouldn't float, let alone go upwards. When his eyes saw the blurred white object in the water in front of him, he knew it could only be the jewel. Its peaceful glow illuminated the surrounding water.

Then Lustre's hands were separated. Something severed the rope around his wrists. He slowly moved upwards off the sand, feeling a pushing sensation against his back, but he couldn't see behind him; his eyes wouldn't look away from the glow. Lustre reached out his arm to touch it, extending his fingers. He was so close. He darted upwards as soon as he felt the jewel touch his fingertips. Like a torpedo, he cut through the water faster than he could comprehend. The water's colour got lighter as he ascended. His face breached the surface in only a few seconds, and he was breathing air. He coughed violently, exhaling mouthfuls of water.

Oxygen had never tasted so sweet. So fresh. He tried to process his surroundings. The first thing that became apparent was that he was in the centre of a vast lake bordered by trees. Lustre swam to the shore with the last of his energy. Even though Lustre wasn't the most knowledgeable about gemotros, he knew enough to know that being in a deep freshwater lake anywhere in Ruby Nation was a bad idea. Lakes in these areas could be home to mosa-gac-laga, giant scaly lizards with snapping jaws. Emerald Nation was also home to these dangerous creatures, who were named herpeta-mosa.

He crawled out of the water, the waves sweeping in and out, pounding his body. His clothes were heavy and drenched, and his throat was sore after swallowing so much disgusting lake water. To regain his strength, he lay on his back, his body nourished by the warmth of the sand. Then he glanced at the rope around his wrists.

"It doesn't make any sense," Lustre uttered. The rope had been cut somehow. It's almost like a knife had done it, for the cut was so clean. But there was nothing inside that lake that could cause such a thing. Lustre propped himself up, leaning against a tree. He looked across the lake. There was so much red. The entire surrounding scene was red. The sky, the trees and the lakes' reflection. "I guess that potion worked; I am in the Crimson Forest," Lustre mused.

Crimson trees were like pine trees, with sturdy trunks and a rough, crumbly coat of bark. The only difference was that the leaves were bright red. The water looked like blood, stained over time by the oil and tannin of forest leaves, settling to the bottom. The light enhanced it, but it had a good purpose, which deterred people who wanted to swim. People nicknamed these large forest lakes blood baths. The name was a stark reminder of what dwelt below the depths. The mosa-gac-laga would drag victims down in bloody, vicious attacks, sometimes large forest creatures as well, those that just wanted a drink at the lake's edge.

Looking at the jewel in disbelief, Lustre raised it before his face. "How?" he asked himself. "This jewel... It saved me." He was still profoundly unaware of what power he held in his possession.

* * *

Meanwhile, to the far north of the Ruby Nation. A fire began to grow just outside of Royal Ruby Town. It started as a stray spark on the ground and grew rapidly into a blazing red fire pillar.

Once it reached a height of ten feet, it shrank back down, leaving nothing but smoke and two guards carrying a statue of Rusty.

"I hate travelling by Fazz Fire. I would much rather have the weird aftertaste of Gone Gazz than feel like I am being cremated," complained one of the guards.

"Suck it up, let's just get this kid inside, and then we can go find that other one."

"Okay, then. I saw him drink Gone Gazz before we jumped him, and I think I heard him say *Crimson Forest*."

"Okay then, that's where we'll look."

The gravel road leading through the town to the market square became a concrete path as it reached the palace stairs. The market was centred on the grandest structure ever built in the Ruby Nation, the towering statue of Emperor Maroon.

"Don't tell the Emperor! We must wait until we have captured him. Imagine if he knew we let him slip through our fingers," said Bear worriedly.

On the stairs was a long red carpet that everyone except the emperor was forbidden to walk on. The two guards made their way up the cobblestone stairs, avoiding the red carpet to the palace doors, but both started to get nervous. The guards passed through the massive wooden doors with two brass knockers. Many crimson banners could be seen with large centred black wavires. They hung from everywhere, the intimidating symbols of power. The palace was the foundation of Ruby Nation. Inside, the palace was a maze of rooms, corridors, and hallways. The main hallway was situated directly after the entrance. Priceless artwork and decorative furniture lined the walls. The arched roof had ornamental chandeliers hanging down the corridor, but none were lit. The only light was the sunlight from the entrance door behind them. The guards, trying to act confidently, made their way down the corridor, looking for the dungeon while carrying Rusty.

* * *

Back in the Crimson Forest, Lustre gazed uncertainly at the jewel. "It has to be cursed…" he assumed, placing the jewel back in his pocket. It seemed to be the only thing Lustre trusted. He then massaged his neck, trying to numb the pain and also swallowed continuously. Muck and sludge that had made its way into his throat. The ruby pendant hanging beneath his coloured shirt was tangled, so he pulled it out into the sunlight.

"Rusty, I must save him," he vowed. "I need to find my way to the palace… alone."

He stood up, trekking into the trees away from the lake. Being unaccompanied for the first time in rots almost certainly impacted Lustre's morale, and he knew it.

Compared to the gruesome Banderian, this forest was much calmer, with less tension and fear. There was much less ground vegetation and overgrown shrubs, almost none. The ground was plain soil sprinkled with decaying crimson leaves. This made navigation a lot easier, as the trees didn't block out the sunlight entirely, and the ground was even, making it much more apparent if one was walking in circles.

However, similar to the Banderian Forest, the Crimson Forest was riddled with foul, horrible gemotros, all adapted to devouring human flesh somewhere within their diet. Lustre only knew about the amphibious mosa-gac-laga. That water lizard was avoidable; most other gemotros weren't.

Lustre walked in the silence of the forest. He only made it a few yards from the lake before a thought hit him. "Hold on. I still have two vials of goon… gazz left," realised Lustre. "It worked before. I could drink another and teleport right to the palace!" Lustre pulled out another shot of Gone Gazz, which surprisingly hadn't been lost in the swim. He saw his reflection in the glass.

It seemed like a great idea. But then Lustre did something he had never done. He considered the consequences. "Wait, the guards would expect that and arrest me," Lustre thought, scratching his head. He placed the vial of Gone Gazz back in his pocket. Those guards back in the village now knew his face and were actively hunting him, which was a problem for Lustre. Regardless, for Gone Gazz to work reliably, one must see a clear picture of the destination in their mind, and Lustre could not envisage the Ruby Palace.

"Well, I guess I am just gonna have to think hard." He sighed.

Lustre began to hear something. It was so faint that he would have missed it without Lustre's extraordinary hearing abilities. It sounded like a dull screeching, like the squawk of a crow mixed with the howl of a wolf. Gradually, the sound increased in volume, and eventually, Lustre could point out where it was coming from. He glanced above him. Apart from the sun's flare, he made out three squiggly figures orientated in the sky. They were very high up, only visible by their silhouettes as they moved across the sun. He had no clue what these things could be. Questions flooded his mind, igniting his curiosity.

"What are those things?" He asked himself.

The figures moved in a wavelike motion, coiling their bodies to fly forward through the air, almost like a sidewinder snake would move across the sand. They circled in the sky, inconsistent in direction. Lustre watched, his eyes following the figures as they glided around. They mesmerised him. After a few minutes, Lustre still couldn't figure out what they were and grew bored.

"Whatever, I shouldn't get distracted. I need to stay on track," he reminded himself, bringing his eyes back down. He continued his walk, battling his hesitation to drink a Gone Gazz. It seemed like the clear answer, but he only had two left, and being resourceful was the only option. After an hour, he lost sight of the lake, and all the forest looked the same.

He stopped briefly to take in his surroundings. Out of nowhere, a crackle of thunder shattered the silence. Lustre shivered, awakening from his calm state. His eyes darted back up to the sky. One of the three figures had burst into smoke and had begun barrelling toward the ground. The figure lifelessly twisted and turned as it plummeted downwards. Lustre's eyes followed the figure until it disappeared behind the trees before him.

There was a loud but distant thud. Surely, whatever creature did that was likely dead!

"Peroa, mother of life!" gasped Lustre. Even though this seemed like a good opportunity to satisfy his curiosity, it wasn't a priority. Travelling miles through the forest to find the corpse of gemotro, which he had never seen before, could make him even more lost and vulnerable. Even with every form of logic against him, Lustre couldn't resist. He had to see what it was.

Changing course, he travelled towards where the gemotro had crashed. It didn't matter in his mind; every direction looked the same. Ten minutes into the search, Lustre was startled by a crack of thunder for the second time. He gazed up at a clear blue sky, not a cloud.

"Strange?"

Lustre spotted something. It was not what he was looking for, but it made him stop in his tracks. A stray flower standing in the dirt. It was roughly ten inches tall, just visible above the soil and away from other small shrubs. The flower had beautiful red petals, fanned out like a sunflower. However, when Lustre got close, the petals closed almost shyly. He recognised the flower, though he couldn't recall ever seeing one. "I know these flowers are called blood orchids," thought Lustre.

He admired the flower for a few minutes, wishing he could pick it up, but it was so beautiful that he didn't want to disturb it. The flower lost its beautiful reputation after Lustre sniffed it. He leaned down, took in one whiff and almost threw up. It was horrible, even worse than grombler stench. It smelt like shit mixed with the sap from crimson trees. Lustre got back up and continued his search. He didn't take long to find something else that caught his interest. Before long, another foul stench began to pollute the air. It was very different, almost like burning flesh. Rising above the trees, only about ten yards before him, was a tower of smoke.

Curious, he stepped closer, pulling back the shrubs that obscured where the smoke was rising from. What he saw sent a cold shiver rushing up his spine. He was terrified. Instinctively, he froze in place. Before him, lying on the ground, was a gigantic serpent. Its scaly body glistened in the sunlight. The serpent was green with contrasting yellow patterns across its scales. It lay motionless. Although it was obviously dead, Lustre was still scared of the imposing creature.

Once he built enough courage, he stepped forward, keeping a safe distance from the gemotro. He glanced at the long, protruding fangs from its upper jaw. Inky blood trickled freely down the front of its face, directly below its giant beaming eye. The eye lens was clouded, but its pupil was still visible. It stared at Lustre's ominously increasing fear.

Every nerve in his body was begging him to back away. But Lustre still had one question he needed an answer to. "So, how did you die if you're a flying gemotro? You were flying perfectly, and you just caught fire and fell." Lustre looked into its massive, unsettling eye.

He began circling the gemotro, trying to pinpoint where the smoke was coming from. When he reached the tail, it quickly became apparent. The smoke was rising from beneath one patch of scales. These scales weren't like the rest. They were blackened and charred as if they had been smeared with coal dust. Blood gushed like a river out of the wound with some pressure. Lustre gasped. Its heart had to be still beating.

It was alive, only unconscious. Even though Lustre realised this, he felt more pity than fear. The gemotro would be dead from blood loss soon, anyway. Eating a bony, homeless teenager before he died probably wasn't one of his priorities. "How did this happen?" Lustre questioned.

He was startled again as another clap of thunder whipped through the sky. He squealed before letting out an embarrassed and slightly peeved grunt. "Oh my gosh, what keeps doing that?" Lustre groaned. "It's getting annoying."

Lustre wanted to put the gemotro out of its misery, but he had no weapons or painless spells to do such a thing. So, he decided to leave the giant serpent to bleed out. He felt terrible, yet there was no other option except for cremating it with a fire, which definitely wouldn't be painless.

More than anything else, he wanted to know what was causing the random claps of thunder. They were very loud, so they must have been close. During the walk, Lustre kept his eyes on the sky, searching for any more of those giant flying serpent creatures. He found himself standing at the edge of a circular grassed clearing. It was a small temporary break in the forest with trees encircling it.

The clearing was much brighter, with bleaching sunlight beaming down on him. Without trees for shade, it was unusually hot. However, what caught Lustre's eye were two men dressed in glimmering plate armour standing in the centre. "Hey!" Lustre called out, approaching them boldly.

"Umm... Hi, buddy," one said, diverting his attention from the sky. The two men appeared familiar to Lustre. Although he hadn't processed their names, their faces rang a bell somewhere in Lustre's mind.

"What are you guys doing here in the Crimson Forest?" Lustre asked.

The other stepped forward, "Could ask the same of you, bud?"

Lustre stuttered before quickly assembling a somewhat believable excuse.

"Um, I was... Exploring, then I got lost. I'm Lustre," he said rather unconvincingly. Somehow, they bought it.

"Well, I am Recruit Bear," he greeted with a deep and unwelcoming voice.

"And I am Recruit Ryan. We are both guards. We only graduated from the Ruby Army Preparatory a few octaves ago." Ryan instantly seemed more likable.

"That's cool," Lustre replied. He had always been curious about the Ruby military. The different ranks of authority, the weapons, and even the army training camp located in Banderia had sparked his interest. But before asking any questions about the military, he needed another answer. "Okay, so do you two know anything about all these random claps of thunder?"

"Oh yes, that's us," Bear stated.

Lustre's face dropped. "You? Why? It keeps startling me. I hate loud noises," Lustre exclaimed.

Ryan subtly glanced upwards at the sky before pointing in the same direction. Lustre glanced up.

"You see, there are these horrid gemotros called sacro slithers."

"What are Sack-crow...Slappers?" struggled Lustre.

"No, sacro slithers," corrected Ryan.

"They're vicious gigantic serpents that can fly. They're some of the most dangerous gemotros there are! We teleported here to… find somebody. We looked for a bit until we both got bored. Then, we spotted a flock migrating over the Crimson Forest a few minutes ago and decided to hunt them."

"Why are you hunting them?" asked Lustre.

"For their scales, mate!" exclaimed Bear.

"Sacro slither scales are worth quite a bit. They are tougher than steel. The IronShard blacksmiths use them to craft armour and shields for us guards."

"Casting bolts of lightning is the best spell we have against flying gemotros, but it lacks accuracy. I am pretty sure we have only hit one," added Bear.

"Wait…You can kill them?" Lustre gasped.

Bear replied, "Yes, they're not Ruby gemotros. They have migrated from Emerald Nation."

It was nagging him; Lustre had to have seen these guards somewhere before.

"I SEE THEM!" Bear shouted, interrupting Lustre.

They both returned their attention to the sky. Sure enough, there was a flock of three sacro slithers. They travelled in a triangular formation that snaked across the sky. Lustre squinted his eyes to focus his vision on the gemotros. However, he couldn't, as they were moving so quickly that it was all just a green blur. The sacro slithers propelled their bodies forward using their tail, beating the tail side to side aggressively like a furious fish. This unique way of flying meant these gemotros could fly up to one hundred and thirty miles per hour.

"Stand back, please, kid!" Ryan ordered.

Ryan and Bear aimed their hands at the sky, clawing their fingers.

"Wezdorth Dazzagar!" They called out in unison.

A pillar of light discharged from their hands, crackling upward. Lustre was briefly deafened as a loud, shrill ringing clouded his ears. He stumbled backwards, his eyes and mind dazzled. The flock scattered as soon as the lightning bolt struck the sky, becoming three individuals zipping around. This severely increased the accuracy and luck needed to hit them.

They streaked across the sky so quickly, only visible because of the stark contrast between their dark green bodies and the clear blue sky. Both lightning bolts missed. Bear groaned.

"Can you give a warning next time?" Lustre grumbled, massaging his ears. After the gemotros had disappeared from the sky, Ryan glanced back down, feeling defeated.

"Sorry mate, I know it's loud and annoying, but no other spell can kill these gemotros." Ryan hated the death of any creature.

Then, Lustre noticed something. "Hey, look!" He yelled, pointing up at the sky.

Ryan and Bear looked up at the sky, their eyes widening. One sacro slither had broken away from the flock and changed its course.

"That's strange! Sacro slithers fly together. I wonder what it's doing?" Bear questioned. The sacro slither had begun flying in the opposite direction to the rest of the flock. Its beaming eyes scanned the ground beneath it before barrelling downwards.

"Oh, Mother Peroa. It's aggravated!" Bear exclaimed, his voice filled with concern. "It's coming right for us!"

Ryan and Bear immediately raised clawed hands, preparing to cast another lightning spell. Lustre didn't know what to do. Should he run? Should he watch everything unfold before him? He had no clue. They watched nervously as the gemotro rapidly descended, its green-scaled body gleaming in the sunlight.

The creature was much closer now, and Lustre could see the sharp fangs protruding from its mouth as it hissed threateningly.

"Wezdorth Dazzagar!" Ryan and Bear chanted again, releasing lightning bolts toward the diving gemotro. However, despite their best efforts, the gemotro dodged every attempt. Bear drew his sword without wasting time, preparing for the absolute worst.

"Look out!" Lustre shouted, instinctively leaping to the side as the gemotro whizzed past them, its size causing a gust of wind to buffet their bodies. Bear quickly regained his composure and attempted to strike the gemotro again, but he managed to miss again. The creature soared back into the sky, circling above them, crazed, a renewed sense of aggression blazing in its eyes.

"We need to come up with a new plan," Ryan said, his voice tense with determination. "Lustre, stay close to us, and be prepared to take cover." Lustre nodded, his eyes fixed on the gemotro as it continued to hover above them, its eyes locked on them, its prey. The situation had escalated, and it was clear that dealing with the sacro slithers without any effective ranged weapons or spells was difficult.

"Here it comes!" Bear shrieked. The sacro slither began its second swoop down toward them. This time, it intended to snatch a person off the ground.

Bear's eyes widened in terror as he watched the sacro slither's jaw unhinge, designed to swallow a man whole. It soared towards them with incredible speed. Lustre's heart pounded in his chest, his breath catching in his throat. The atmosphere around them turned tense, as if the air held its breath in anticipation.

Lustre paused. His expression went blank. He pondered his thoughts, feeling strangely calm despite the situation. He lowered his eyes. He noticed a strange glow in his pocket.

Thin, white rays escaped through the fabric. Lustre reached down, pulling the jewel out. It shone brightly in the palm of his hand, brighter than the midday sun.

Lustre held it high above his head. "What if… What if…" He uttered to himself.

Ryan and Bear were unsettled. They both knew the sacro slither was moments away from devouring them, but they had no clue what Lustre was doing.

"Buddy…What are you doing? RUN!" Bear yelled.

Gradually, the wind began to pick up. In several aggressive gusts, the wind blew dead leaves and loose material across the grassy ground. It kept growing stronger. Lustre stood perfectly still, immersed in the jewel's glow, his only focus unbreakable by the cries of Ryan and Bear demanding him to stop.

The surrounding crimson trees swayed gently at first, but soon the wind was strong enough to shed the leaves from the branches. Now, the wind was spearing. Clouds began forming in the sky, blocking the sun and plunging the Crimson Forest into the cold. The clouds swirled in the sky, creating a ring. Lustre's veins bulged from his skin, his hand tensed, and his pupils rushed to the roof of his eyes. His head slowly tilted backwards, consciousness fading from his body. The clouds then funnelled down from the sky as they sped up. They spiralled towards Lustre's hand, dispersing their dark shadows across the ground.

The strong wind peaked, causing trees to crack at the base, slowly eroding their roots. Ryan started to lose his balance. He called out once more. "What is happening?" But Lustre couldn't hear him. The clouds erupted into a tornado. The sacro slither couldn't reach them before it was sucked up into the clouds.

Bear was already on his stomach; he lost his balance when the wind picked up. But Ryan was still standing. Before, he ended up like Bear, outmatched by the wind. Ryan leapt toward Lustre, grabbing for the jewel.

The jewel flew out of Lustre's grasp, ending up on the ground a few feet away. This caused the tornado to dissipate and the wind to soften. With the sun back in the sky and not a cloud to obscure it, thousands of leaves and small shrubs fluttered down from above them like rain. Lustre snapped back into reality.

"What in Gemotroplis just happened?" Bear was the first to announce.

"I second that!" Ryan added.

Lustre was left wordless because he wasn't quite sure either.

"That was not a Ruby spell. You must be foreign!" Ryan remarked. Lustre immediately hit back. "No. No. I'm not! It wasn't me...It was...This... Je-"

"Hold on," interrupted Bear

"Weren't you the kid who punched me in the nose back at the Banderian Village? I did not recognise you earlier because I was concerned with sacro slithers."

That's when it struck Lustre. He had seen these guards in the village.

"Yeah, you were the kid with a Topaz terrorist. You both must be from Topaz Nation!" Ryan was now convinced, placing a hand on the hilt of his sword. All guards wore a leather belt around their waists, which held their swords. Only the hilt was visible; the blade was concealed inside the sheath for safety purposes and protection from the weather.

Lustre stepped back nervously. "No, I swear. I was born in Ruby Nation!" Lustre yelled back.

"Well, how did you just summon a tornado? That's not a Ruby spell." They argued.

Lustre bent down, picking the jewel up off the ground. He offered it to Ryan. "It was this."

Ryan snatched the jewel from Lustre's hands and gazed at it briefly. His eyes widened. "Buddy...Listen very carefully..." Ryan cautioned.

"I have seen books in the Royal Ruby Town library and have heard tales about powerful artifacts from era: 1st, tales from over a thousand rots ago. There was said to be a jewel that emitted a radiant-coloured light. It was said to be the heart of a god. The wielder of the heart held great power; I can't remember exactly what it was, though I think it was destroyed," explained Ryan. He grabbed Lustre's hand and drew it close to him. He placed the jewel into Lustre's palm, curling his fingers around it tightly. Ryan leaned his head forward, his mouth beside Lustre's ear. He whispered in utter seriousness. "Go north towards the White Plains, where you will find a cottage. There is a man there of great wisdom. They call him the Crimson Chalice."

Lustre nodded.

"What did you tell him?" Bear asked nosily.

Ryan replied, "Nothing. Anyway, we better get going. Those sacro slithers could be anywhere by now."

Both recruits stepped back from Lustre.

"Right, Bear, where's that jar of Fazz Fire?" Ryan asked. After rummaging through his pockets, Bear glowered unconvincingly.

"Uh! I must have lost it." Bear sighed.

Ryan shook his head, sighing dramatically. He pointed his finger at Bear's pocket, seeing the apparent jar-shaped lump in his pants. "What's that then?"

In one last effort, Bear lied again to save his embarrassment. "Umm... That's not the jar. That's...Umm," Bear tried desperately to construct an excuse.

Ryan narrowed his eyes, squinting into Bear's. His eyebrow rose high into his forehead. "What is it then?" Ryan asked cautiously.

Bear gave up. "Fine. I didn't lose it. I hate teleporting with it! Please, can't we go by Gone Gazz?" Bear confessed, reaching into his pocket and taking out the jar shamefully.

Ryan was disappointed and mildly relieved. "Oh…Okay. If it bothers you so much, we will use Gone Gazz," agreed Ryan. Both men produced a vial of Gone Gazz from their pockets. They positioned themselves side by side, shoulders touching. Ryan gave Lustre one last advising glance, along with an assuring nod.

Both men announced, "Banderian Village," and they vanished. Lustre was left standing there, nervous and confused. He had no clue why the two guards who had previously tried to capture him had just helped him. That seemed very out of the ordinary. Perhaps they realised that he was not really a criminal.

"Travel on foot to the White Plains in a dangerous forest!" Lustre considered his options. He could take the easy route to the palace with Gone Gazz, but he knew that he would be arrested on the spot. He knew any other Ruby guards wouldn't take it as well as Ryan, and he could not picture the palace.

But it would be at least an octave before he reached the White Plains. It would be a risky journey, likely encountering many obstacles. However, he still wanted to know more about the jewel he possessed. So, he took Ryan's advice and began his journey.

"Rusty can wait… I am sure this journey will be worth it. And if I get stuck or have second thoughts, I can always use Gone Gazz." Lustre reassured himself. He walked wearily back into the forest.

Even though Lustre was not a professional navigator, he knew enough to pinpoint the north direction from the clearing using the sun's position. It was an ancient saying. '*The sun rises in the east, dies in the west.*'

However, it was noon, so the sun was perched directly above him. Lustre had to wait a few minutes to see which way the sun was setting before he could find north. He set off once again, occasionally glancing up at the sky through the obscuring canopy of leaves. He wouldn't let any more sacro slithers go over his head without his knowing. The afternoon sun was starting to sink; Lustre was unaware of how long he had been walking; only dappled sunlight was visible through the leaves.

Lustre was immersed in the sound of rustling leaves and gentle wind. Colaies filled the ambient silence with their chorus. They were songbirds, usually hidden amongst the trees, but they were heard. The colaies shrieked incredibly high yet beautiful notes, which no human could ever reach. Their song was so beautiful that it was the only thing in Lustre's mind.

"What beautiful gemotros," Lustre thought, humming along with their song. Only twenty minutes later, something broke the repetitiveness. Lustre stumbled upon an old chest sitting alone at the foot of a tree.

As Lustre approached the old chest, he couldn't help but notice the carpet of mould that blanketed its surface. The wood was warped and faded; the once intricate designs were barely visible under the grime. It looked as if it had been neglected in the crimson forest for centuries, abandoned and left to rot at the foot of the tree.

As he got closer, the smell of must and decaying wood overwhelmed him, making him wonder what could be inside. There is always something captivating about a mystery. At the front was a small padlock, which had also aged into a crusty brown colour. "I wonder who left this thing here?" He considered, "Maybe I could pry it open." Lustre kneeled in front of the chest and grabbed the padlock. He was surprised by how easily it snapped off. As he lifted the lid, the hinges squealed, revealing the damp and foreboding interior.

Lustre gazed at all the contents. Inside the chest was a collection of strange objects: two glass bottles, a long dagger, and a tarnished paper scroll. "Wow…" Lustre gasped.

Truthfully, Lustre was expecting a dead reatrit. First, Lustre reached inside for one of the bottles. The glass was clouded in grime, almost opaque. Lustre rubbed the bottle clean with his sleeve. Inside the bottle was some blue gloop. "Oh, it's a potion," Lustre said. It didn't look very appetising, and he left it untouched. Lustre was hoping for water because all that walking had made him thirsty.

The other potion was identically dirty and looked identically strange. The only difference was that this one had yellow water inside and a label on the neck. It was in words that Lustre couldn't understand. Or even pronounce - to be honest, he could not pronounce anything. It read 'Wav-va-wire stella lo-compo.'

"Maybe it's in a foreign language," he assumed. Unknown to Lustre, it meant wavire juice. Curiously, Lustre pulled off the cork. Immediately, a horrid stench filled the air. "Gross! What is inside that bottle?" Lustre gagged, swiftly pushing the cork back on. "Why have I smelt so many horrible things today?"

Lustre returned both potions to the chest and reached for the dagger. Carefully, he drew it from the leather sheath. Lustre was astonished by the dagger's condition. Unlike the potions, the dagger looked unharmed. The blade, although slightly blunt, showed no rust or fracture. After closely examining the blade, Lustre noticed some words inscribed on the handle.

"Jackie Fletcher"

"Maybe this dagger belongs to that person," Lustre said, sliding it back into the sheath. Lastly, Lustre unravelled the scroll. "Oh! It's a map of the Ruby Nation! This is helpful."

This discovery lifted Lustre's spirits. The charcoal-drawn map gave Lustre a clearer idea of where he was going. He decided to take the dagger and the map, as they both seemed the most helpful. He fastened the sheath around his waist with the attached belt and held the map before his face.

"Okay, so the map shows a known route to the White Plains through the forest," Lustre realised. "A dirt road once used for trade. I should be close." Lustre continued his journey, and the map gave him more confidence than before. It didn't take much longer for Lustre to find something else new. Only a few minutes later, as the sky began to dim, Lustre spotted a sign nailed to a tree. The sign also seemed made from wood, but had grown rotten like the chest. Green vines and ivy clung to the sign, their tendrils snaking around the edges and dangling over the top. Lustre stepped forward, getting a better look at the words carved into it.

Warning!

Blood, urine, and fire will attract

Wavires.

Lustre read it to himself and paused for a moment. "Blood, urine, and fire may attract… Wavires?"

Lustre thought nothing of it and kept walking. The wind carried the sound of whimpering. He stopped walking and listened carefully; it sounded like somebody in fear. Then Lustre saw him. A man with a scared expression on his face was trying to hide behind a tree. Lustre boldly approached. The man's back was pressed firmly against the tree. Sweat rolled down his forehead, and he took in rapid, wailing breaths.

"Hello?" Lustre said, his voice steady despite the situation.

The scared man hesitated for a moment before shaking his head slowly. The man didn't look at Lustre. He stared off into the distant forest, his bright green eyes narrowing as the wind gushed past his face. Lustre was beyond disturbed.

"What are you hiding from?" Lustre asked. This time, though annoyingly, the man did respond without answering the question. "Shh!" He snapped, bringing his finger up to his lips.

Lustre stuttered. "Wh-Why? Who are you? What's happening?" Lustre persisted.

The man ignored Lustre once again. Without much to go off, Lustre also stared into the distance for clues about what the man could have been hiding from. But he only saw the vast, tree-lined horizon, accompanied by the glare of the twilight sun. When Lustre looked back at the man, he noticed something he hadn't seen before. The man's left leg was drenched in blood, and there was even a puddle forming beneath his foot. But what stood out to him the most was the arrow. It looked to be a hunting arrow, impaling his left ankle with the iron tip protruding from the other side.

"What happened…" Lustre gasped. Between breaths, the man replied.

"They're here. I've gotta go."

"What? Who's here?" Lustre still questioned, beginning to get nervous himself.

Lustre stared off into the distance again, still unable to see anything. Either the man was paranoid, or he could see something in the forest that Lustre couldn't. Suddenly, as soon as Lustre's back was turned, he heard a loud shattering noise, like glass. Lustre spun around to see that the man had vanished from the tree, and a small fire was burning tall and bright in his place. The fire shrank back to the ground, and its heat dissipated in the wind. Yet it still took a few stamps to be completely extinguished.

"Where did this fire come from?" Lustre gasped. After checking that the shattering noise wasn't one of his potions, Lustre gazed around, more dazzled than ever. Everything was missing an explanation. Where did he go? What was that noise? How did a random fire appear from nowhere? So many questions bombarded Lustre's mind. It was probably the strangest thing Lustre had witnessed today.

"Where did he go?" Lustre asked.

After a few minutes, Lustre decided to move on from the strange occurrence, but his mind would not let it go. After trying to recount his steps, Lustre still wanted to know what the man could have been seeing. He positioned himself against the tree, just as the man did. In this position, Lustre saw something he could have sworn he hadn't seen earlier.

Faintly in the distance, there was a speck of glimmering light. It felt like he was looking at a window, angled just the right way to shine light into your face. It couldn't be a lantern; it was far too bright. It had to be sunlight. Even though the sun was dimming, there was still sunlight. That had to be it. The dusk sunlight had to be ricocheting off something reflective.

"It must just be the sun's reflection off a puddle," assumed Lustre. Even though it was a reasonable answer, Lustre was still not convinced. The ground was far too dry; it couldn't be a puddle. Lustre narrowed his eyes, trying to focus on the distance. He found himself listing things in his head that could cast such a reflection. "Umm. Is it a ruby, a mirror? Maybe it's a broken piece of glass? Wait, could it be metal? Metal is reflective." Lustre had so many thoughts. "Okay, what's made of metal... A sword... umm... A bucket?" Lustre scratched his head. Then, the answer came to him. "Wait... It's armour!"

Lustre froze.

Chapter 5

Frostbite

"It has to be other guards from Bandeira out looking for me," Lustre uttered, panic swelling. It was a group of three guards, all moving in Lustre's direction with a sense of urgency. It was as if they were looking for something… Or somebody. Lustre didn't know if they had spotted him yet, so he took his opportunity to back away. But, as soon as he moved, he heard.

"There's that little Emerald reatrit!"

Lustre didn't think. He just bolted. He spun around sharply and ran in the opposite direction. The sound of shuffling bushes and hurried footsteps grew behind him. He glanced over his shoulder before realising he was indeed being chased; his worst fear was being realised with three guards hunting him. Even though they were all quite distant, Lustre was still terrified.

Lustre's breath quickened, and his heart thundered within his chest as he sprinted through the dark forest. Thankfully, his agility and the absence of heavy armour gave him an edge, allowing him to outpace the pursuing guards. Relief washed over him momentarily, but it was a fleeting emotion.

Lustre overlooked the tree root exposed along his path. His foot got caught, and he tumbled, landing awkwardly on his ankle. As he could not continue running, his only option was to hide. The thought of using the Gone Gazz potion didn't even cross his mind in the heat of the moment, and using his dagger just seemed stupid.

Crawling over to the nearest tree, he propped himself against it, desperate to still his strained breathing. Tension hung heavy in the air, and an eerie silence descended upon the scene as all three guards caught up and began to scour the surroundings, knowing full well that Lustre was lurking nearby.

"Come on out, we won't hurt you..." one of the guards chuckled.

"Yeah! We just want to talk," another added.

A sharp sound pierced the silence, similar to that of a blade being unsheathed. Lustre's spine raced with a shiver. He assumed the guards had drawn their swords, but this noise wasn't their doing. It had the same effect on the guards, making them tense as they tightened their grip on their hilts, warily scanning their surroundings.

Out of nowhere, a figure in a ragged brown cloak lurched from the underbrush. Though this face remained hidden beneath the hood, the guards did catch a glint of a sword in his hands. They lunged forward, their cloaks billowing behind them like a flag in the wind. In one swift motion, the cloaked figure swung his sword, the edge swiping across one guard's neck.

A strangled wheeze escaped from one of the guards as he clutched his throat. "Oh... Peroa," he screeched before collapsing to the ground, his life slipping away. Panic and fear combined always result in rash and hasty decisions. One of them stepped forward, taking action, while the other hesitated. The mysterious figure's sword clashed with one of the guard's blades in a deafening clang, the two weapons locked in a static bind. Exchanging threatening glares, their swords crossed in a deadly dance of wills.

At that very moment, the final guard intervened, swinging his sword toward the figure's exposed head. A quick maneuver allowed the figure to drop to one knee and parry the attack. This parry smoothly led into their next move, bringing the fight to a decisive end. The figure brought his blade to the left, slicing both guards' vulnerable legs.

Blood sprayed, and the guards crumpled to the ground, their lives extinguished in a gruesome tableau. The figure held his pose for a few breathless seconds, breathing heavily. Lustre, concealed behind the tree, could only listen to the violent clash; he dared not risk a peek. The pungent scent of blood hung in the air. It was Lustre's signal to move. With the strange figure distracted, Lustre seized the opportunity to crawl away, moving as silently as possible until he reached a safer distance. He gingerly sat up, rolling his trousers to inspect his injured ankle.

"Ahh..." Lustre winced, drawing in a sharp breath through clenched teeth. "I've sprained it good," he groaned. His ordeal was far from over. Lustre slowly rose to his feet, trying to keep his weight off his left ankle. He gave one last glance back. "That was crazy...I have to get far away from here." He limped off, occasionally grabbing trees for stability. Once completely out of sight, he pulled out his map again. He carefully unravelled it and stretched it out before his eyes.

"Ok... Alright... I think I know where I am going." Darkness had settled in under the moonlight, and he dragged his finger across the map.

Lustre quickly grew watchful of the logs and bushes he passed. He felt that every sound he made could be heard for miles. He had lost his bravery and gained more self- awareness. Lustre's courage and boldness are massive traits in his personality. Losing them would be like a fire losing its heat. The fire inside Lustre was already beginning to die. He was now even getting startled by the occasional snap of a twig under his feet.

After a few minutes in the darkness, Lustre noticed his footsteps sounded different. They were a lot slushier rather than fluffy soil. He gazed down to see what was happening. The sound was of him walking through a mud puddle.

"Gross!" Lustre remarked.

At first, Lustre was annoyed. The mud oozed through holes in his boots, and it was the most uncomfortable feeling he had ever had. Lustre kept walking, hoping he would return to dry ground. But the forest floor grew progressively deeper and slushier, and Lustre's boots were encased in mud. Before Lustre turned around, he realised something. "Wait, if there's mud, that means there's...Water!" He was energised.

He heard, then hobbled to one of the many streams branching off the giant, powerful river that cut through the Crimson Forest. He cupped his hands and scooped the water into his mouth. The water was icy cold, but Lustre couldn't let that stop him. He felt his body grow stronger with each handful as the water nourished his mind. Even though the water was unfiltered and potentially filled with parasites, it had the most refreshing taste he had ever had.

Unlike the rest of the forest, the stream's edges were crowded with lush green foliage. Their leaves rustled gently in the breeze. The roots of the nearby crimson trees clung to the banks, their gnarled fingers gorging on the water. The stream must have been there for a while. It had eroded the surrounding soil, carving a trench where water could flow freely.

He pushed himself back off the ground, wiping his sleeve across his mouth. He had finally satisfied his thirst. "Ok..." Lustre sighed. "Now, all I have to do is find which way is north again..." He thought. All that running and panic mangled his sense of direction. However, there was no sun. The sky was lit only by moonlight, on which Lustre didn't know how to pathfind. Lustre considered just waiting until morning, but he was impatient. He pulled out his map again for clues.

He again skimmed across the map; it was very difficult to read the scroll. But he recognised the huge wavy line cutting through the giant cluster of trees, which he assumed represented the Crimson Forest. The river was named 'The Great Ruby River'. The river that meandered through the forest.

He knew the water flowed downstream from Bandeira towards the northern Ruby Nation. The Banderian Village heavily relies on the river, using the downstream current to hydrate their farmland and power their watermills. Lustre knelt at the yard-wide stream of water. This stream rushed, cascading over rocks.

Then a thought hit him. Lustre rolled the map back up and slowly stuck his hand into the stream. He felt the current's resistance on his hand, pushing it to the right. "Okay… That must mean…" He glanced down the length of the river on the map. "That must be north, upstream."

Convinced that he was correct, Lustre continued his journey, marching alongside the stream. According to the map, the south was downstream, so he only had to refer to the water's current to find the poles. Lustre's logic was flawed; streams can only flow downhill. He had no one to discuss the matter with. Once Lustre had made a decision, no one could shift his thoughts. Even if he had a travelling mate like Rusty, an argument was the most likely outcome. However, in his mind, he was right; this gave him the confidence to continue walking. Soon, after what felt like ages, Lustre sank to the ground, overwhelmed with fatigue.

"I have to stop. I will continue in daylight." With that, he gathered some rest. As it was starting to get cold, Lustre awoke.

"Maybe I could build a fire," he thought. Even though a fire sounded like a good idea, Lustre didn't want to venture far out into the dark to find wood. He couldn't risk losing the stream.

There were plenty of large branches near him that could be cut up into logs, but he had no axe. He still needed some kindling, like dry leaves and twigs, for a flame anyway. His hands explored the damp ground around him. He ventured only until the rushing stream grew faint.

"Why does this feel so familiar?" Lustre asked himself. He felt a strange connection with the situation of collecting firewood in the Crimson Forest.

"Why do I feel like I have done this before..." After a brief search, Lustre retrieved three fat, small logs from the surrounding forest. He stacked them beside the stream in a tepee formation ideal for a campfire. Usually, you would start with kindling and gradually add larger sticks to the fire. But Lustre had no kindling.

Even though he was certain this fire would not light, he gave it a go anyway. He crouched down, aiming his shivering hands at the log pile.

"Paxta-holla," he whispered. Paxta-holla was a common Ruby spell. The spell offered a substitute for flint and steel. Paxta-holla would normally summon a small but critical spark in the caster's palm. It was a quick flash and sounded almost like an electric spark with a trailing zip. The small spark ignited kindling, which would eventually evolve into a fire.

A brief spark flared in Lustre's hands. But then, as quickly as it came, it vanished. It did nothing to the logs, as they were still damp from being alongside the stream. Lustre was out of ideas. "What do I do..." Lustre moaned. He sat down, leaning his overworked back against the nearest tree. He placed his hands on his forehead and stared at the ground.

"Come on…Think… Think!" He ordered himself. Then, it hit him… Quite literally. A sharp bead of what he thought was rain landed on his forehead. The raindrop slid down his nose, irritating his skin. Lustre swiftly brought his hand up and wiped it off. Unexpectedly, it didn't feel like rain on his fingertips. It was far too glutinous, with a consistency similar to glue. Confused, he brought his hand down to his nose and sniffed it.

It smelt nothing of rain. It was a very strong, bitter scent. Almost like blood! Lustre stood up, scratching his head. "What in Gemotroplis was that?"

He examined the tree above where he had been sitting. The lack of light meant Lustre constantly missed things hidden in the dark. "How did I not see that before…"

An arrow was above Lustre's head, protruding from the upper tree. It hung six feet from the ground, its tip firmly wrenched within the bark. But what Lustre did notice was the glue-like sap trickling from the wound. When Lustre reached up to get a closer look, he found the sap around the arrow tip had crystallised, turning into a red, glass-like material. It could even be mistaken for ruby. Lustre tried to yank the arrow free, but it was too deep into the tree. "I heard something before about crystallised sap from crimson trees…" Lustre thought to himself. He could remember something about how these sap crystals could burn. Crimson tree sap on its own is not flammable, but when crystallised, it becomes something like a reservoir holding extremely flammable oil. Lustre carefully sliced off a shard of crystallised sap using his dagger and brought it down to the log pile. He placed it beneath the tepee and stepped back.

The spark leapt from his hands into the logs, and they flashed to life. The shard of sap burned an ominous red colour.

It emitted a great heat that warped the air above. Lustre held his hands to the fire, and the warmth revived his skin. He had never felt more relieved. The campfire sent sparks drifting into the sky, and Lustre watched them dance in the wind until they vanished. He huddled beside the fire for as long as he could until he grew drowsy.

"Maybe I could just close my eyes…For a bit." Lustre yawned. He tried to make himself comfortable on the sodden ground but felt pain in his ankle. On his back, he stared at the canopy of leaves and the night sky. Speckled starlight surrounded one giant moon with its comforting silver glow. It was truly beautiful. It was then that Lustre truly realised he was alone! His closest mate seemed hundreds of miles away, a statue.

Nobody relied on him. Nobody was around him. Nobody was watching him. He was a stray orphan lying peacefully in the forest, although wet and in pain. He dozed a little. What felt like only seconds later, Lustre was disturbed by the sound of a sizzling, like water being dripped onto melted fat in a very hot pan. His eyes slowly opened, glaring at his surroundings.

Then, everything happened at once. The next thing Lustre knew was that he was wrestled up from the ground, and his hands were forced behind his back. He felt somebody's hand dig into his back, and he was shoved against the tree. He was dazzled; one second, he was nearly asleep, and the next second, he was being attacked.

Lustre's face was then forcefully pressed into the tree bark. Its rough texture was most uncomfortable against his cheek. Then another sharp thrust delivered more pressure into Lustre's back. The force restricted his breathing severely, with his chest now also hammered against the tree. Whoever or whatever was doing this had abnormal strength.

It felt like the weight of a thousand gromblers, all asserting their force into Lustre's back. Lustre couldn't let himself suffocate. Instinctively, he acted. Lustre turned his neck slightly, but it was enough to see who was doing this. A man he had recognised before stood there, his expression aggravated. He was the same man who had killed the guards.

With his feet being the only thing not being forced into the tree, Lustre manoeuvred his right foot back, stomping down hard on the man's foot. He let out a grunt of pain before releasing Lustre to clutch his foot. At that moment, Lustre leapt away from the tree.

He replenished his lungs in one tight gasp. After finding that Lustre had broken free, the man stopped, staring at Lustre with anger brewing in his eyes. Lustre had the urge to run, but his strained ankle said otherwise. The man loaded a hunting crossbow that had been slung over his shoulder. He aimed it at Lustre. His finger slowly squeezed the trigger. Lustre froze. He was too stunned to move, which made him an easy shot.

The sound of the arrow whizzing through the air must have snapped him back into reality, as he jumped away moments before it hit him. A shot that was not intended to kill, only to maim. A second later, it would have pinned Lustre to the forest floor. The arrow glided, missing Lustre's legs by only inches, before striking the tree behind him.

Lustre didn't think; he let his instincts decide his actions without properly considering them. His next move was one he would later regret. He drew the dagger from his sheath and charged towards the man. Without time to reload, the man dropped his crossbow and reached for his sword. However, he didn't draw it in time before the dagger entered his chest. Lustre then lost his balance after attempting to withdraw the dagger.

The man shrieked in pain and staggered backwards. It was when the man shrieked, "Oh, Peroa. I have been stabbed!"

Lustre realised what he had just done. He was wordless. Lustre stood there for a few seconds, his mouth hanging open in disbelief. He approached the man for a second time. He gripped the dagger again and made a second effort to withdraw it from the man's chest. Despite the man's pleas otherwise, Lustre pulled it out.

"No! Don't take it out! I'll bleed to de-" the man screamed.

As soon as the dagger was free, Lustre bolted off, the adrenaline forcing him to run despite the pain in his ankle. He ran until he reached a safe distance. Unbeknownst to Lustre, he had dropped one of his potions during his haste. And he'd also lost the map, which was critical for his journey. Fortunately, he still had the jewel. Traumatised by his actions, Lustre dropped to his knees.

"I just stabbed somebody..." Lustre truly realised. He stared at his red fingers, discoloured from the blood-smeared dagger. His hands shivered in his lap. Slowly, his forehead also fell forward into his lap, on top of his hands. Fat tears began to form in his eyes. Usually, he would try to hold them in, but this time, he just let them fall, as nobody was around to see them. They ran freely down his face, dripping one by one into his lap.

"I just stabbed somebody..." He kept repeating to himself. "I can't keep going; I just want Rusty... I want my simple life back."

Lustre reached into his pocket; he felt wetness, a broken glass vial. After cutting his finger, he found only one vial of Gone Gazz left, and he did not hesitate. He pulled the cork off and held it up to his lips. It was the appropriate time, alone in the most dangerous forest in the Ruby Nation at night. His situation wasn't good.

Lustre was very tempted, to say the least. "I just need to drink it," Lustre told himself. His mind wavered. "Just drink it!"

Lustre ordered himself. Suppose he could teleport straight to the Crimson Village and get a cold pint of crimson cider at Tether's tavern? All this could go away. Lustre had no idea why he was so hesitant. But after a few seconds, he realised why. "I… I don't need it."

He pushed the cork back into place. "I can't stop now. I have to find this bloody cottage," said Lustre. His heart fluttered with resilience.

That was the critical point when he realised that he didn't need to be strong for Rusty, so he didn't need to hide his fear. He didn't need to pretend. He didn't need to wipe his tears. He could be himself. Deep down, he knew he was scared of many things, but the one thing he feared the most was being alone!

Lustre pushed himself up from the ground. A cold breeze gushed past his face; the tears felt like ice on his skin. "I can do this," he reassured himself.

This moment of confidence was shattered quickly. A horrid hissing noise murmured from the bush to his side. He quickly wiped his sleeve across his face. "Who's there!" He called out, his voice still quavering. He was answered by another hiss from the darkness. It was a very distinct hissing noise. It was only faint, but so high-pitched that it stood out among other noises. It also had an eerie undertone. It differed from the sound of a snake. The noise disturbed Lustre, and it certainly wasn't a person.

He gripped his dagger tightly. If Lustre had been familiar with the sound, he would already be running. Hunters and outlaws living in the Crimson Forest knew this sound all too well. It was an early sign to start running.

Yet, Lustre stood still. Lustre pointed his dagger out into the forest with a confidence that he didn't have. Something came into view. A dot of red light beamed in its black surroundings. It was pretty distant, but it couldn't be missed.

It lingered for a while, twinkling like a red star. Lustre watched it disconcertingly. Then, another red dot adjacent to the first one came into view. It almost looked like a pair of eyes.

Lustre couldn't stand the tension in the air; every instinct in his body wanted him to flee. He couldn't stand the silence any longer, either. So, in a move he would regret, he spun around and darted in the opposite direction. As soon as he moved, he heard something dashing behind him. Lustre wanted to think it was a person, but the sound of its footsteps alone suggested otherwise. It was a rhythmic clapping, like a ferinthor galloping, except if the ferinthor galloped with twice the legs.

After that, he bolted, however, ready to look back to see what was chasing him. He peeked over his shoulder.

His eyes widened with fear as they were met with the chilling sight of a gigantic spider advancing behind him. It had two bulging red eyes that stared right through him. Its entire body was covered in needle-like hairs, which were the same colour as the ground, making its hair like camouflage.

This was why wavires were so hard to spot in the Crimson Forest, let alone in the dark. Suddenly, Lustre felt a sudden burning sensation on his knee. The pain was so sudden that he tripped over. Most likely because he wasn't paying any attention to where he was running, his leg had brushed against a bush of Banderian nettle. The nettle's name was misleading; it grew everywhere in Ruby Nation. It was a terrible weed with serrated leaves, which some locals also called the plant Bandeira bush weed.

The nettle caused a huge cut along Lustre's knee, which happened to be the same leg he'd sprained earlier. He couldn't run anymore; his nerves were triggered, and the pain had taken over.

Using his very limited knowledge of gemotro survival, Lustre took a gamble and veered off to the left. He knew what he had on him wasn't enough to survive this time, so he had to use the environment to his advantage. Lustre leapt forward, tumbling into a steep ditch. He hoped that putting himself out of direct eye level would be enough. He made himself as low to the ground as possible.

Lustre pressed down firmly on his cut, trying to slow the bleeding. There was a spike of pain. Lustre clenched his teeth, holding in the urge to bellow out. Slowly, the blood trickling down his leg eased. His mind wanted to take the pressure off, but he couldn't. He had to stop the blood. Then Lustre heard a guttural sniff near him. This sound alone made Lustre shiver in fear. He knew that the wavire could smell the blood.

He was conflicted, and both options for survival were flawed. If he moved, he would die. If he didn't move, he would die. And he couldn't defend himself with magic, as it was a Ruby gemotro. Yet, he had to pick one. He began to hear the unsettling sound of very close footsteps, accompanied by a horrible hiss.

Lustre had to decide now. He didn't have time to plan; he just had to act. He pushed himself up from the ground. But he didn't run; he stood there on one leg, staring directly into its two beaming eyes. As soon as Lustre exposed himself, the wavire turned and scurried towards him. Lustre watched it with no thought of running. Calmly, he reached into his pocket and pulled out the jewel. It was glowing brighter than usual. He briefly diverted his attention to stare at the jewel. He was mesmerised again by it. The soft, white glow was so tranquil and calming. He turned back to face the wavire.

Seconds before the wavire trampled over him, Lustre raised the jewel and pointed it at the wavire. Then, something happened that he couldn't explain. He lost all control of his mouth and began to utter words he couldn't understand.

"Archna-stela pelsitch-avia-bonwax-aroasiza." This was especially unusual as he could not pronounce difficult words, let alone unfamiliar ones.

After he had spoken, the light of Peroa shot out from the jewel. It shone with utter purity, illuminating the entire forest for a second. The ray of light struck the wavire right in its most vulnerable and sensitive area, the eyes. It immediately ground to a halt and let out a shriek of pain. It stopped only inches from Lustre before it began to cower backward. Then it collapsed, rolling onto its back, curling its eight legs inwards.

Right after that, the jewel's glow died down, and Lustre snapped back into reality. Fear swelled within him as his skin tingled from the aftershock of what had just happened. Whilst still baffled, the thought of running finally popped into his mind. He took his chance and hopped away.

After catching his breath, Lustre sat down. He gazed at the jewel for a few seconds. "How did I just do that? I just killed a wavire with magic...But that's impossible...Wavires can't be killed with Ruby magic...This all makes no sense." Lustre was confused.

Lustre rubbed the back of his neck. "Did...I cast a foreign spell?" Lustre asked himself. This couldn't be the answer; a person can only cast spells from the nation in which they were born. But it seemed like the only explanation. How did Rusty cast a Topaz spell in the Banderian Village? And how did he kill a grombler? How did Lustre create a tornado? And how did he just kill a wavire?

All these questions seemed unexplainable, but the jewel in Lustre's hands knotted all these questions together, and Lustre managed to assemble an answer in his mind. An answer that just clicked, like a puzzle piece, nestling perfectly into place.

"Does this jewel grant magic? Does it gift the wielder every form of magic, no matter their nation of origin?" Lustre asked himself.

That had to be it. That had to be the answer. It may explain all the unexplainable. However, Lustre needed to be sure. He needed to know what the jewel was. It had to be more than just a cursed rock if it could grant magic.

"I can't worry about it now. I must keep going. I need to learn more." With pure will, Lustre hobbled on. He used a tree branch as a makeshift crutch. Sunlight began to seep through the canopy. This was good for two reasons: one, he was no longer uneasy about his surroundings, and two, he could use the old pathfinding skill to pinpoint north once again.

Two hours passed, and the weather shifted faster than predicted. Every tree, rock, and bush was blanketed in snow. The air felt like a mist of shattered glass. Lustre was forced to breathe only through his mouth as his nose was stuffed with ice. Even though it was midday, little was visible.

The top of the Ruby Nation was a lot colder than Banderia.

His lips were chapped, and his face was pale.

"So... c-c-cold," said Lustre through his chattering teeth.

His whole body was numb. He wanted to turn back or stop for a few minutes, but his mind kept forcing him to position the crutch and coordinate his other foot in front.

He felt hyperthermia slowly stealing away his consciousness. He shook his head violently, trying to make his mind snap out of it. But it didn't help. Lustre tucked his free hand under his armpit for even the slightest protection against the wind, feeling the top of the crutch as he lost all balance.

THUMP

Lustre found himself face-first on the ground. The ice burned his face. He tried to get up, but he was entirely out of energy. His muscles were far too weak. Lustre lay there until his body finally gave in.

The next thing Lustre knew, he was no longer in the snow. Instead of the howling wind, Lustre could hear something much more comforting—the faint crackling and popping of a fire. Lustre was relieved by the warmth on his skin. Sitting up, he realised the wind was no longer biting his skin. He slowly opened his eyes and squinted at his new surroundings. He sat on a timber floor in the middle of a dark room. To his left, he saw a small fireplace with stone bricks towering up to the ceiling. He warmed his hands by the fire. Its light screened across the floor, partly illuminating the furniture around the room. An old table was the first thing Lustre spotted. Cobwebs dangled like nets between each leg.

Sitting upon the table was a candle and a tea set. Before Lustre saw anything else, there was a loud creak. Suddenly, the entire room was filled with silver moonlight. A door on the opposite end of the room opened. Standing in the doorway was the looming silhouette of a man. Lustre squeezed his eyes shut and pretended to be asleep. The man trudged into the room, grunting loudly with each step. Then he slammed the door shut behind him.

The man was wearing a coat made from treated grombler leather and gloves, all of which were covered in snow. The man unbuttoned his coat and lazily tossed it into the corner, out of sight. Then, everything fell silent. When Lustre reopened his eyes, he was greeted by the sight of the man staring right back at him. He gasped.

"Don't kill me!" Lustre screamed, shielding his face with his hands. The man sighed deeply before replying in a calm tone. "If I'd wanted you dead, I would have left you in the snow."

The man offered his hand to Lustre. "Come on, get up. I haven't cleaned that floor in ages."

Lustre refused to take the man's hand, instead pushing himself up. Lustre noticed a window beside the door, a good opportunity to find out where he was. He limped over towards the window and pulled back the ragged curtains. Unfortunately, what he saw still didn't answer much.

The window was coated in frost, and Lustre could hardly see through it. He could tell of the battering winds. Even inside, he could still feel the wind edging his skin. Everything was covered in snow; the only thing visible was the vast expanse of trees, but even those were just a dark backdrop in the blizzard. Everything visible was obscured or lost in a white void. Lustre felt so isolated. "So…Where am I?" Lustre asked.

A calm voice replied, "Son, you are in White Plains Cottage."

Chapter 6

Hazel Tea

"So, my name is Winston. I know this may all seem a bit strange, but before I explain anything, let's fix your leg," the stranger said in a concerned voice. His chestnut brown hair was peppered with grey. He looked over fifty rots, although he was only forty-six. The effects of age were beginning to overrun him. Winston also had a prickly grey beard sprouting from his chin.

Lustre turned around. "My leg? What do you mean?" asked Lustre, who had forgotten about his leg. It came as a surprise to him when he peered downwards. "Woah. That's a lot of blood," uttered Lustre. It was strange; he didn't feel any pain. The snow must have numbed his skin.

Winston quickly slid a chair out from beneath the table, saying, "Have a seat. I will brew up some disinfectant for your leg before things get really bad!"

Lustre limped back to the centre of the room and sat at the chair.

"Lift your leg," Winston instructed Lustre. Winston lifted Lustre's leg and propped it up on a second chair with a pillow to make it more comfortable. Lustre didn't yet trust Winston, but he seemed sincere because he was trying to help.

After reviewing the cut knee, Winston said, "Okay, I won't be a minute." As he walked away, Lustre asked, "So, what is this place?"

"Oh, this is my cottage. I live here in White Plains. It's not much, but there is a fireplace. That's all you need as a brewer…"

"So, you're a potion maker," interrupted Lustre.

"No…I'm a potion brewer. I have been crafting potions for many rots; I value my privacy and research." Lustre's eyes widened at being corrected. After a few seconds, Winston returned to the table, carrying a bronze kettle. He placed it before Lustre and turned his attention to the dying fireplace.

"I better re-light that," he uttered to himself. He rubbed his gnarled fingers. The logs were strewn around the floor, and he couldn't bring himself to fetch them. Instead, he shuffled across the room to the hearth. Kneeling down, he picked up the nearest log and cradled it in his arms. He struggled to lift it onto the grate. Lustre felt like he should help, but he could only watch.

Once the log had been plonked into the fireplace, Winston arranged all the remaining kindling around it. He took a deep, contented breath and held his hands toward it.

"Paxta-holla," he spoke. There was a flicker of light. The spark leapt into the fireplace and slowly grew into a flame. Winston swiftly hooked the kettle over the fireplace to heat.

The flame lingered for a few seconds before dying out. Winston let out an irritated groan. "It's wet. Where's the crimson…Oh! Here it is," Winston exclaimed. Beside the fireplace was an old water canteen labelled 'Crimson oil'. Winston grasped the canteen and splashed just a bit over the kindling. Winston tried again.

This time, the kindling roared to life instantly. Satisfied, he turned his attention back to Lustre. With the addition of crimson oil, it didn't take long for the fire to gnaw right through the kindling, so Winston tossed on another handful to keep it burning long enough to boil a dangling bronze kettle.

As Winston waited for the kettle to boil, Lustre broke the silence with a question. "So… How did I get here again? I could have sworn I was laying in the snow a few minutes ago."

"Ha! Minutes for you. Almost a day for me!"

Lustre was confused. "What do you mean?"

"I was heading back to White Plains after delivering potions to Bandeira market. I teleport there when I am weary to check in on a drowsy business friend. However, I forgot to take a second vial, so I was left to travel the bloody forest road. Anyway, I did drop in on my best friend Derek and his family in Crimson Village. Blizzards make these forest paths bloody dangerous; lucky I found you!"

The Crimson Village was south, days away in good weather; one needed to use the ferry to cross the Great Ruby River. It was also at least a couple of days more to Bandeira from Crimson Village.

"Go on." Lustre leaned in.

"Okay, I spotted you lying in the snow on my way back. At first, I thought you were dead, but when I turned you over, I noticed you were still breathing. So, I used a sled to carry you back home with me, and here we are!" Winston concluded.

"Right." Lustre paused. It seemed like the truth, but Lustre couldn't stop himself from doubting it. It just didn't add up. Nobody had been that nice to him before. Also, why would somebody go out of their way to save a scrawny orphan? Right before Lustre brought up another question, the kettle's whistling interrupted him.

"Oh, the disinfectant is ready," announced Winston. He got up from the table and grabbed the kettle from the fireplace.

Steam arose out of the nozzle, filling the room with a ghastly but familiar smell. Placing the bronze kettle on the table, he reassured Lustre. "Just keep still, okay?" Lustre's fingers drummed nervously on the table. Winston poured the contents over an old brown rag, a common substitute for a bandage. The smell of the liquid alone was enough to make Lustre question its legitimacy.

"Are you sure this will help my cut?"

"Oh, I am quite confident." Winston smiled.

"You know, my disinfectant always works. It is a secret recipe. No other potion brewer in the whole Ruby Nation knows how to make disinfectant," explained Winston proudly. Winston guarded his secrets well; he was a master brewer and businessman. This particular secret ingredient was Wav-va-wire stella lo-compo or wavire juice. He only shared his knowledge with family.

After bathing the rag in disinfectant, Winston brought it over and pressed it down firmly on Lustre's skin. There was a sudden, intensive stinging. Lustre tensed his muscles. Winston could tell that Lustre was in discomfort.

"Just hold still," Winston repeated calmly. Lustre quickly held his breath and squeezed his eyes shut. Every time Lustre accidentally hammered his finger back in the mines, that's what he would do to stop himself screaming like a child. Of course, he didn't want to do that in front of Rusty. Somehow, the urge to breathe overpowered the urge to flinch or scream out. Winston knotted the rag around Lustre's knee tightly, finishing off with a knot.

"You're welcome." Winston smiled.

"Umm...thanks."

Winston sighed contentedly before falling into his chair. He sat opposite Lustre in front of the old tea set. "Oh, I almost forgot about the tea," Winston exclaimed. He carefully lifted the teapot and poured himself a cup. A much more pleasing smell filled the room: sweet lemon mixed with mint leaves. Winston lifted the cup to his nose, deeply admiring the scent. Wisps of steam rose from the teacup, warming his face. He brought his lips to the edge of the cup and took a sip. "So sweet, yet so bitter," he remarked. Then Winston generously filled the second teacup to the brim and offered it to Lustre. "Want some hazel tea?"

Lustre had never heard of such tea, but he accepted it to avoid giving any negative impressions. He reached out and took hold of the teacup. He was still a bit dazzled by the whole situation, and something didn't feel right. He had that feeling, an anxiety-inducing sense that something was off. After quickly trying to figure out what it was, something hit him. His stomach began to churn, and a chilling thought went through his mind. He quickly dug his hand into his pocket; there was nothing. He silently began to panic. Lustre reached into his other pocket. A wave of relief flushed over him. The jewel was still there. He wouldn't even know what to do if it wasn't.

"So, how did you end up unconscious in the Crimson Forest?" Winston asked, sparking a new conversation.

Lustre's head shot up, completely unprepared. He stuttered, trying to remember the answer. "Umm…Oh yes! I was searching for a man called the Crimson Chalice." Winston's eyes widened, "Oh…I have heard of him…" He answered avoidantly.

"Really? Where can I find him?"

Winston's gaze veered up to the ceiling as he leaned back in his chair. "Oh…I don't know if you can."

"Why… Is he dead?"

Winston began to chuckle; his laughter filled the room. "Oh! No! Not yet, anyway." Winston snickered.

Lustre raised an eyebrow. "What do you mean?"

"He's me. I am the Crimson Chalice. It's the name of my market stall back at Bandeira," explained Winston.

"Oh! Really?" Lustre gasped.

"Of course, so why were you looking for me? Did you want to buy a potion?" Winston continued. To be honest, Lustre had forgotten the answer to that as well. To give him more time to think, he sipped Winston's tea. He regretted that decision almost immediately after it entered his mouth. It was the most bitter and sour-tasting liquid he had tasted so far.

Lustre was now trapped in an awkward situation. He couldn't spit it out, which would be rude, and he couldn't swallow it. But he needed to answer Winston, so he reluctantly swallowed it. "No, I wasn't looking to buy any potions." Lustre paused to cough. "What was in that tea? May I ask?" Lustre said, trying to be as polite as possible.

"Oh…Well… Crushed hazel nut, water obviously, mint leaves, crushed crimson berries, salt, sugar, lemon juice, aztel fern, and blood orchid pedal," listed Winston. All those ingredients didn't sound disgusting. Crimson berries were Lustre's favourite fruit. Maybe just combined, they were disgusting. After almost throwing up, Lustre changed the subject. "What I came here for was to ask you some questions."

"Yes…And what might those questions be?" Winston replied, taking another sip from his teacup.

"About… Like… Gemotroplis era: 1st." This question caught Winston off guard.

"Well…era: 1st was a dark and ancient time for Gemotroplis. There were a lot of strange creatures that trekked the island. I can tell you a story if you wish?" proposed Winston. A smile grew on Lustre's face, stretching from cheek to cheek. His eyes twinkled as he spoke. "Please do!"

Winston stood from the table and hobbled toward an old bookshelf in the corner. The bookshelf held many large books. They varied in size; the only thing they had in common was the dull leather cover that bound the pages. A blanket of dust layered across them as they sat undisturbed for what looked like many rots. Lustre watched Winston drag his fingers along the books, row after row, before landing on a faded title written in crimson ink across the spine.

'*The legend of the Arachna-vire, the mother wavire - a terror of era: 1*st*.*'

He withdrew the book from the bookshelf and carried it back to the table. After blowing the dust off the cover, he resumed. "All right, this book here is the story of the Arachna-vire. The…"

"Archna-what?" Lustre interrupted.

"The Arachna-vire, the mother of all wavires."

Winston carefully opened the book and turned the first page. The musty but comforting smell of bibliosmia filled the air. Nothing was more pleasing than the smell of the vanilla pages of an old book.

"Anyway. We can read until the blizzard subsides," said Winston as he cleared his throat.

"*Once, at the dawn of time. A young and immature Peroa experimented with her magic. This resulted in the birth of many creatures, including the Arachna-vire.*" Winston then took a further sip of tea.

"*Peroa named the Arachna-vire, Wendy. Only the size of the familiar wavire, Wendy crawled her way into the mountains, as her outer shell wasn't enough to protect her from the blistering cold. Wendy created a sustainable living space in a cavern, eating small rodents and animals trapped in her den and seeking shelter from the cold. Humans included.*"

Lustre's eyes widened. "Humans?" He gasped. Winston peered up, nodding ominously. Lustre shuffled forward in his chair, keen to hear more.

"*She stayed in the cavern for hundreds of rots, growing colossal. Since she couldn't fit within her den any longer, she ventured out of her cavern and stretched out her previously cramped body. She stood almost thirty feet tall, with her eight legs capable of stretching out over ninety feet wide. She was hungrier than ever. So, she migrated up north alone, toward the Banderian Village. She had never seen so much food in one place. All the people were terrified to see such a gemotro towering over them. They had never seen a wavire, nor one being so large.*" Winston paused to turn the page.

The room was filled with anticipation.

"*She devoured the folk and demolished huts. Her huge body cast a dark shadow over the ruins. Peroa saw the Arachna-vire destroying her creations, and since she can't kill, for she is the god of life, she simply cursed Wendy with poor sight. It was said there was a blinding radiance of white light that washed over Bandeira. When the light dissipated, Wendy was left stunned; she cowered backward, fearing what had happened. After realising she was part blind, she was seen retreating south to the mountains where she was first born...*"

"What happened next?" Lustre said, leaping up from his chair. Winston smiled at Lustre's enthusiasm before turning the page.

"Well, what happened next is still a mystery, as she was never heard from again. Some say she died of starvation in the mountains as she couldn't spot her food. Others say she was recalled back to the infernal realm by Peroa to face the consequences of her dark actions. Most folks say she is still out there, surviving over a thousand rots for her next opportunity to strike."

Lustre was baffled. Winston folded the book closed and stood up from his chair.

"That was a creepy story," Lustre remarked.

To that, Winston replied, "Oh, I have many tales more chilling than the Arac-vire. To name a few, there's the herpeta-mosa, the Heart of Gemotronia, and the list goes on." Suddenly, Lustre's attention snagged on what Winston had just said. He spun in his chair.

"Wait, repeat that last part," said Lustre with a sense of urgency.

"Um... The Heart of Gemotronia," repeated Winston, wondering why the boy was so interested. Lustre turned back around, scratching his chin fretfully.

"Do you want me to read that story?" Winston asked. Lustre nodded.

"Okay." Winston again smiled.

He slid the book back into the vacant slot on the shelf before exchanging it for another similarly sized book. He brought the book down to the table and relaxed in his chair. Lustre's eyes twinkled with curiosity. After taking another sip of his tea, Winston cleared his throat.

"*The Heart of Gemotronia*," Winston read, admiring the cover closely. He opened the book and flicked through the first few pages. "Okay. To warn you, please listen carefully. As this may be a little confusing..." Winston advised.

"*Once, before our time, there were three gods. They sat comfortably in the immortal realm, a peaceful place reserved for only those gods. It is thought to be a vast oasis deep within the clouds. Daradero was a cold-hearted male god of death, and Peroa was the god of life, a kind-hearted mother with the looks of a beautiful golden-haired lady. Finally, there is Queen Gemotronia, a mature woman jealous of Peroa's beauty; she is the god of magic. The three gods of Death, Life and Magic are the three crucial pillars of creation. Gemotronia ruled as Queen, with a heart that held all of her magic and sorcery. She could use it to cast any spell she desired. But one day, Peroa created all living things, things that had the desire to build, create and develop. Gemotronia wished to share her magic with them. But Daradero interjected; he feared that if Gemotronia gave the humans magic, they would grow too powerful, become greedy and selfish, and want the power for themselves.*

So, Gemotronia and Daradero agreed. She could grant the humans magic if she put herself on the island in mortal form. That way, she was vulnerable. If the humans killed her, it would prove Daradero right. The Queen's confidence made Daradero uneasy. But right before they shook hands, Gemotronia made a critical exception.

'Wait.' She said, 'If I die, you have to make it possible for a human to give their soul to resurrect mine.' She argued.

'Why would anybody do that?' Daradero laughed.

'It would prove some humans still aren't selfish and greedy. If at least one is willing to sacrifice themselves for me, that would prove you wrong. If at least one is pure enough to sacrifice themselves to save a god, you will be wrong.' She announced.

'Fine, I know that won't happen. If it does, I am confident you can banish me to the infernal realm! I am confident they will kill you for your magical powers within the first octave. I bet my life on it.' Daradero smirked at his sister and Queen.

Grudgingly, they both accepted, and they shook hands. Gemotronia summoned herself to the island and granted humans magic." Winston paused to turn the page.

At this moment, Lustre asked. "So, her heart contained all the magic, right? So, what did it look like?"

Winston peered up, stroked his beard, and said, "Oh. It was said to be a beautiful, colourful gemstone about the size of a human heart."

Gradually, everything began to click together like a giant puzzle. Piece by piece, everything was taking form. Lustre was in awe. Winston read on.

"*When Gemotronia summoned herself, all the developing civilisations worshipped her as queen. She was queen over the heavens and Gemotroplis. She gave them every form of magic possible. Healing, taming, defence, firemaking, illusion, destruction, and everything else. Soon, Daradero began to grow anxious. All the humans had no intention to harm her. He knew that betting his life was a terrible decision. After the first few days, Daradero knew he had to take matters into his own hands...*"

"What happened? What did he do?" Lustre shouted.

Winston chuckled. "I will continue reading after supper; you must be starving?"

Lustre was keen to hear more, but also couldn't resist food. He hadn't eaten anything for days.

"I just need to make the broth for grombler stew." Winston got up from his chair and hobbled to the corner to get two plump breadsticks. He carried them back to the table. The bread's tough, golden crust looked so appetising. Lustre circled his tongue around his lips.

Winston returned to the corner, carrying a heavy steel cauldron. With a struggle, he managed to place the pot over the fire. It was so heavy because it was full to the brim with water. "Okay, Lustre, a favour. Could you go fetch that sack of ingredients sitting on the pile of old furniture in the corner?" Winston asked.

"Of course," Lustre said politely. Gradually, Lustre stood up from his chair, holding the table for balance. He limped over to the corner and grabbed the sack of ingredients. Before he returned to Winston, his curiosity meant he had to peek inside. He loosened the rope and stuck his nose inside. He saw a huge jumble of colourful ingredients he could recognise, but some strange herbs were also within. Satisfied, he brought the bundle over to Winston. Actually, if this entire journey had taught him anything, he was expecting something disgusting.

"Thanks," Winston said. Winston tipped the sack upside down and shook it aggressively. The contents splashed into the small cauldron, scattering throughout the water. In addition to the ingredients, Winston added a pinch of salt to improve the final taste even more.

Lastly, Winston lifted the cauldron and hooked the fire crane within. A fireplace crane was a long steel bracket nailed to the back wall of most chimneys. It was used to hang pots easily.

"There we are." Winston exhaled.

Winston made his way back to the table.

"It shouldn't take long. Maybe ten minutes," assured Winston.

While they waited, Winston asked.

"Hey, Lustre, could you please quickly fetch my knife? I need to cut the bread."

Reluctant to get up again, Lustre suggested an alternative that didn't involve him leaving the table. He remembered the dagger he had used back in the forest. Even though it wasn't the cleanest, it was much more convenient.

"Hold on, I have a dagger," Lustre said, reaching down to his belt.

"Oh! Okay then, we'll use that," replied Winston.

Lustre unsheathed his dagger and carefully handed it across the table.

"Oh, it's nice," commented Winston.

He raised the dagger to his eyes, admiring how the firelight glinted off it. Winston stroked the blade's edge with his finger to test the sharpness. Surprisingly, it cut, even drawing a small drop of blood. Winston quickly brought his finger up to his mouth and sucked the blood off. "Ouch, it's very sharp."

Lustre nodded.

"Lustre, do you mind if I test it?"

"What do you mean?"

"Can I test the dagger's durability?"

Lustre shrugged. "Sure, I guess."

Winston smiled and drew the dagger high above his head, carefully aiming it down at the table. Then he plunged it down. The whole table rattled as the blade sank deep into the wood. It had gone so deep that it took a few seconds to withdraw it. Winston drew it back above his head once again and repeated the process. With each stab, the blade bit deeper and deeper into the table. After about the fourth time, Winston was done. He pulled it out from the table and examined it closely.

There were no signs of a fracture, blunting or chipping despite the punishment it had just endured. Even the blade tip, which had experienced the most battering, was still pin- sharp. Winston was beyond impressed. "This is one quality knife! I feel like using it for slicing bread would be an insult to its craftsmanship. It is made for hunting. Never mind, let's cut back to the bread." Winston chuckled.

Lustre laughed softly at his joke, even though it was not funny. Winston began to slice up the bread. The dagger sliced clean through the crust, revealing the bread's white, spongy centre. After slicing up the first breadstick, Winston noticed something. "Jackie Fletcher?" Winston said, staring closely at the inscription.

"Oh yeah, I found this dagger in the forest. I am pretty sure that's who it belongs to." Lustre explained.

Winston paused for a moment. That's when Lustre noticed a shift in his expression. His face was racked with confusion. "That's strange…" uttered Winston.

"What's wrong?" Lustre asked nervously. Instead of answering, Winston asked firmly, "Where did you say you found this dagger?"

"Uh, I found it in the Crimson Forest, inside an old chest."

Winston gazed back down at the dagger. "That name... Jackie Fletcher. That's my brother."

Lustre's mouth fell open in disbelief. "Really?" Lustre asked. Winston nodded with a sleek smile.

"My brother is a hunter. He comes up to the White Plains every second octave. He normally only stays for an hour or two. Long enough for him to have a cup of hazel tea and chat with me. He exchanges his findings for a few potions before returning to the Crimson Forest. He was the one who brought that grombler meat. You should thank him. Otherwise, we wouldn't have that wonderful stew," explained Winston. "Which reminds me..." Soon, a warm smell filled the room.

The ingredients bled their flavour into the water, giving the broth a beautiful orange tint. Lustre turned his attention to the cauldron and watched it bubble vigorously, occasionally spilling over the edge and sizzling in the hot coals below. "Okay, I think it should be ready by now."

Winston stood up from his chair. To avoid burning himself, Winston then used a rag to lift the cauldron off the crane and onto the table. He then fetched two large spoons, two bowls, a ladle, and, most importantly, a bright smile. He handed Lustre a bowl and spoon and stirred the stew with the ladle.

"Smells great," Lustre commented.

Winston nodded. "Indeed, it does."

Lustre held his bowl up close to the cauldron to avoid spilling. Winston ladled a generous amount of stew into Lustre's bowl before his own.

"Tuck in," said Winston with a smile.

Lustre couldn't wait. Immediately after the go-ahead, he reached across the table and tore off a piece of the bread from the unsliced breadstick. Inside his bowl, Lustre saw the chunks of grombler meat, flecks of cabbage, handfuls of peas and corn, and a sliced carrot all floating in a pool of delicious-smelling broth. Lustre eagerly picked up his spoon. Winston was shocked by his manners, but he was contented by the speed at which Lustre scooped the stew into his mouth. It showed how hungry he was. The broth was a little spicy, but it didn't bother Lustre. It was too delicious for him to care.

"You must be starving!" remarked Winston.

Lustre smiled gratefully, wiping his sleeve across his mouth. "I sure am."

"So, when did you last see your brother?"

After swallowing, Winston replied. "Oh… It was quite a while ago, actually. I think maybe a few octaves. He came over wounded with an arrow in his shoulder. I brewed up some disinfectant and gave him some Muzzle Mud, and he was healed. Then he set off again out into the forest."

"Hang on… I remember that…Mazzle…Mould. I remember somebody saying something about that," mumbled Lustre, tying his tongue into a knot.

"Muzzle Mud!" said Winston, correcting Lustre.

"Yeah…"

Winston leaned back in his chair. "I will get you some Muzzle Mud later for your leg."

"Okay then," Lustre said, scooping more stew into his mouth. After a few minutes, Lustre wasn't hungry anymore, yet he still found himself licking the empty stew bowl. The taste alone was an excuse never to stop eating. Complemented by Lustre's love for the stew, Winston stood up and spoke.

"There's plenty more if you want some later."

"Oh, okay!" replied Lustre.

Winston carried the heavy stew cauldron around the table and placed it beside the fireplace to keep it warm.

"All right," uttered Winston contently, before grabbing the previous book and sitting back at the table. "Where were we?"

He quickly flicked through the pages and resumed the story.

"Where was I up to? Oh yeah, *Daradero knew that betting his life was a terrible decision. After the first few days, he knew he had to take matters into his own hands... So, he decided to create a weapon... A weapon so powerful that it would be deemed the most powerful weapon a mortal could ever wield. The blade of Daradero... Using his power, he cursed the blade for moralising the immortal, overpowering the most powerful, and destroying the indestructible.*

Initially, he considered making the blade out of Rituratium, the most durable and indestructible material known. However, he quickly realised that this material is impossible to forge, as it cannot be shaped, melted, or sharpened into a blade, even at the highest temperatures.

So, he found the next best thing. The substance he inevitably used to make the blade was the metal, pure Demorite, the most durable material that can be softened at many thousands of degrees. The metal is also incredibly rare and almost impossible to find in the island's crust. It took three eras for even the first nugget of Demorite to be found miles deep in the ruby mines.

After one day, the blade was complete. Daradero summoned himself to the island of Gemotroplis. He disguised himself as a human, but everybody failed to notice his twisted intentions. When he was close enough, he stabbed Queen Gemotronia right in the heart, physically and poetically. Her only heart shattered into eight pieces and scattered throughout the island. As her sister requested, Peroa created a small island off the coast of the Emerald Nation to house a specific spot for the unlikely resurrection. Her mortal worshippers obeyed her wishes and built a large temple. However, Daradero interfered with the construction of the temple; he convinced and influenced her subjects to add booby traps and defences for mortals. He also ensured the resurrector must be pure of heart, or the ritual would fail. Daradero then convinced Peroa to guard the temple. She decided on a monstrous beast, the Trio–Septeria".

Lustre gasped. Winston turned the page.

"Right after the assassination, Daradero returned to the immortal realm. But he forgot to bring the blade back with him. All the humans who once adored Gemotronia had witnessed the assassination. They all crowded around her lifeless body, confused and traumatised. They eventually agreed to destroy the sword, but after attempting to smash it, they soon became aware of its unnatural durability. One human even picked the sword up and swung it into a boulder. The blade sliced into the stone, shooting sparks with a crackling twang. It was impossible to withdraw from the stone, and humans soon forgot about it. After two hundred and one rotations, it remained fused within the boulder, and the sword was rediscovered and shattered by the more advanced humans of Gemotroplis."

"Wait!" Lustre interjected. "How did they destroy it? It's indestructible!" He pointed out.

Winston smiled cunningly. "They destroyed it using an ancient and powerful weapon they created themselves. The Obsidian Axe forged deep in the heart of Obsidian Nation." Winston slammed the book shut conclusively. What a taunting and twisted cliffhanger Lustre was left with.

"Obsidian Nation? There is no such place." Lustre sneered.

Instead of arguing, Winston remained calm.

"Are you so sure?" he said.

Even though Lustre was confident in his geography, Winston's tone convinced him otherwise. He didn't want to be a fool, but still held his argument.

"Yes! There are only four nations," said Lustre.

Winston smiled. He got up from the table and went back over to the bookshelf. After searching each row, he returned to the table, holding what looked like a paper scroll.

Assuredly, he unravelled the scroll before Lustre.

"Oh, it's a map. I had one similar!" Lustre said. After staring at the map for a few seconds, Lustre noticed some unfamiliar labels and shapes that weren't on his other map. He squinted his eyes and blinked with confusion.

"What's that?" Lustre exclaimed, pinning his finger down on the map.

"Exactly," Winston said, leaning back with a smug expression. "That's the Obsidian nation. The long land stretch wedged between Topaz Nation and Sapphire Nation."

"Okay then… What's that then?" Winston leaned back and forward. "That small island north of Sapsasacria is the Diamond Nation," Winston explained.

"Diamond Nation!" Lustre screamed. Winston nodded.

Lustre was baffled, yet still very sceptical.

"If these nations are real, why haven't I known about them? And why aren't they on every map?" Lustre pointed out.

Winston paused for a moment. "Well, not many people know about them because of the…Things that inhabit those lands. Obsidian Nation is a vast forest infested with strange and terrifying gemotros. These gemotros are nothing like what we have here." Winston elaborated.

"Are there people there?" Lustre asked.

That's when Winston's face grew pale. The very thought must have scared him. "We-Well," he stuttered. "Yes. But they aren't exactly…Human. They are considered more…Humanoid. They're said to be…Vicious, agile creatures with pasty white skin and coal-black hair. They're like…Living corpses. Nobody knows because, ever since era: 1st, all emperors have agreed not to tell their subjects about it. They altered maps to have huge vacant areas where they once were. And they never spoke of them again."

"How do you know about them, then?"

Winston stuttered, unprepared. But he did make a somewhat convincing answer. "Well, I was told by…Err…The Emperor."

Lustre rolled his eyes. "Come on…At least make up a believable answer." Winston gave Lustre an irritated gaze before sighing. "Fine. Just wait there. Let me put this book away, but first, I'll show you something." Winston pushed himself back up from his chair and ventured away from the table, leaving the book behind. Winston continued to the next corner, where he found a tall glass cabinet standing proudly. He carefully opened the cabinet door, a pane of grimy glass with an intricate wooden frame. Upon opening the door, a plume of musty air was expelled from within. Lustre turned his head curiously.

Winston then admired all the old ornaments, bottles, and relics on the inner shelves, but one thing stood out to him. "There it is." Winston grabbed an artefact. Lustre gasped; he was at a loss for words. Sitting delicately in Winston's hands was a golden crown.

"This was Emperor Cranium's crown. It was forged within a furnace two eras ago in the Topaz Nation," said Winston, offering the crown to Lustre.

Lustre carefully took the crown out of Winston's hands and admired it. Lustre could see that it contained an argent wavire pendant at the front, which was accompanied by two rubies on either side. The gold band of the crown was also not left plain, decorated with mesmerising patterns that covered the whole exterior.

"It used to be a beautiful crown, symbolising the emperor's power and authority." Winston again sighed.

"I think it's amazing," Lustre remarked. Lustre thought the crown was cool, even though time had faded it into more of a bronzish colour rather than gold. But after closely examining it, Lustre noticed a rust patch forming around the wavire pendant. Gold didn't rust, so Lustre began to question its authenticity.

"If gold doesn't rust, why is there rust on this crown?" Lustre asked, raising an eyebrow.

"Oh, that's not rust. That discoloured patch is just scratch marks from when I tried picking out the rubies with a knife," replied Winston. "By themself, those huge rubies would be worth a lot, but when they are attached to that filthy gold ring, nobody wants to buy it." Winston was resigned, sinking back into his chair.

Even though it wasn't the prettiest, the crown still deeply impressed Lustre. "I have never held something so beautiful. The closest I've come would probably be... My friend's hand." Lustre chuckled at himself. Even though it was a joke, Lustre would still ponder the truth in that statement, even after he left Winston's cottage.

"Me and my friend Rusty are from nowhere. We're both homeless orphans working in the ruby mines in Bandeira. We don't ever see anything so priceless." Offended, Winston immediately snatched the crown from Lustre's hands and threw it back into the cabinet.

"Woah...What did I say?"

"It's not priceless. It's just a relic, a bad memory."

"I don't understand... Why is it a bad memory? Why does nobody want to buy it? Shouldn't the crown be priceless?" asked Lustre.

Winston sighed deeply. "Don't you know what happened to the emperor... before our current one?" Lustre shook his head nervously. "Well... Elder Maroon was declared emperor about thirty rots ago, to everyone's dismay, and has been a foolish emperor ever since. But before that, our emperor was a man named Cranium."

"Wait, Elder Maroon!" Lustre knew about these ruby fakes from the mines.

"Yes, that's why playful lads named them fools' rubies," Winston confirmed.

"What about Cranium? Was he named after a skull? Creepy." Lustre asked.

"Yes, Emperor Skull was... I mean, Emperor Cranium was desperate for power and wealth. He wished to expand the Ruby Nation outwards, invading other nations to increase his wealth. His threatening actions started the Ruby War; he was also a fool, but in a different way," explained Winston.

Lustre's eyes widened.

"The Ruby War? Yes, that's why Rusty and I mine for rubies. The nation has fines to pay. Is that right?" Lustre asked.

"Yes, let me read." He returned to the book and turned to a different chapter. "*It was the largest war in history. Ruby Nation, Topaz Nation, and Emerald Nation were all involved. It started when Emperor Cranium ordered the Ruby Army to march into Ravena. There, they expected to begin their expansion. Apart from the many gemotros, it was a perfect place. A vast field of basalt without any steep terrain. His army wore heavy steel armour, making climbing the steep terrains and the volcano almost impossible.*

Soon, the Topaz Nation became very anxious about the Ruby Nation. They began to send out scouts, who informed the Topaz emperor of the Ruby Army gathering at the edge of Ravena. They could see that Emperor Cranium was plotting something."

Lustre was fascinated. His mind was overflowing with new information.

"*So, after getting confirmation from his scouts, the Topaz emperor, Emperor Irindor, ordered his army to stand on the opposite edge of Ravena. Both armies remained hidden in the bordering forests until dawn, when they met in the middle with a devastating clash. Arrows blocked out the sky, and blood stained the ground.*

What was strange was that Emperor Cranium was fighting as well. Instead of discussing tactics and strategies at the Ruby Palace, he led the army as a past military man. He believed he was a hero, leading his enormous army to victory.

He convinced himself that he was Ruby Nation's saviour. He said he wanted to fight for honour, bravery, and courage, but none was true. His main reason was to go down in history.

Unexpectedly, Emperor Irindor had a plan. He knew that the old ways of fighting were always stalemates. He raised his trusty longsword, the Dazzldern, and ordered what was left of his foot army to retreat into his forest, letting his cavalry mow down the last of the Ruby Army.

The Ruby Army briefly celebrated when they saw the Topaz soldiers retreating, but it didn't last long. During the celebration, a storm began to brew high up in the clouds. Setting the mood for the Ruby army about to meet the wraith of ferinthor cavalry, the gemotros ablaze in their fire and blinding light."

Winston paused reading as Lustre began twisting his tongue around, trying to pronounce that last phrase. His constant interruptions challenged Winston's patience.

"Cavalry ablaze…Wait, blinding light… Hold on. Ferinthor? That's a tongue twister!" Lustre stated. Lustre had many questions, which Winston did not need to answer. A ferinthor was like a large war horse with fur at maturity that blazes into fire and light to scare off its predators. Though this fire didn't emit heat, it was still bright and scary, perfect for cavalry charges.

Knowledge of the ferinthor was common, as they were a part of folk stories and children's games. Ferinthor-carved toys can be bought in markets. Lustre knew this but, chose to play dumb to annoy Winston.

"Are you finished?" Winston groaned, picking up on the trickery.

"Fine," Lustre relented.

"Okay, where was I? Oh yeah, *huge black clouds circled the crater of the volcano. But Cranium didn't give up. The sight of the approaching cavalry was enough to strike fear into anybody's heart. Rain began to batter the ground, creating another problem for the army.*

The rain made the basalt slipperier than mud, and with the addition of their heavy armour, retreating was almost impossible. The helpless Ruby army could only watch them race closer and closer until the cavalry trampled over them with blinding force. It was a horrible sight for Cranium. At the same time, the Topaz soldiers on foot were recovering undercover in the forests of Emedella; the Ruby soldiers were getting slaughtered by cavalry.

Even with most of his army dead, Emperor Cranium was determined to win the battle. With what was left of his army, Emperor Cranium told his troops to stand at the foot of the volcano for their finale.

The Topaz cavalry quickly switched course and began advancing toward the volcano. Emperor Cranium put himself out in front of his army to maintain an image of bravery, if he was to be trampled first. 'Time to show those reatrits what Ruby Nation is made out of!' Cranium proclaimed.

All at once, the soldiers thrust their hands at the approaching gemotros.

'Wezdorth Dazzagar!' Some shouted. A blinding radiance filled the air, accompanied by a huge crackle of thunder. Lighting crackled through the air, exploding at impact. Most flew off course, missing the Topaz completely. But some did manage to impact close enough to knock them off their ferinthor gemotros. Even though it was a pleasing sight for Cranium, it wasn't enough. In the distance, Cranium began to spot soldiers wearing bright green uniforms emerging from the forest. The Emerald Army had arrived to break the stalemate.

Emerald soldiers flooded the fields of Ravena in massive numbers, charging toward Cranium's last hundred soldiers.

'Kill them!' Cranium ordered. None of his men wanted to move.

'Did you not hear me? I said kill the Emerald scum!' Cranium yelled again.

None of his soldiers listened.

'It's suicide!' they argued. Then, right before him, Cranium's army unarmed themselves, dropping their weapons. They did the most humiliating thing Cranium could imagine. They all held their hands up in surrender. Cranium was disgusted by what he saw.

'This is treason! This is cowardly!' He bellowed.

All the Emerald soldiers surrounded them, pointing their spears inward. Cranium felt betrayed, vulnerable, and lost. He refused to join his army in surrender; he was the only one still holding his sword. He tried to threaten the soldiers to back away, but they were undeterred.

Finally, he gave in and dropped his sword, BlunderBee.

Right then, two men stepped out from the crowd of Emerald soldiers. One was wearing a green robe but no armour, and the other was wearing a yellow robe but no armour.

This showed that Cranium didn't threaten them; they were comfortable being vulnerable in his presence.

The man wearing the yellow robe began to speak.

'I am Emperor Irindor. Ruler of Topaz Nation.' He introduced.

'And I am King Jackale, ruler of Emerald Nation.' The other added.

'Cranium, you have broken an era of peace throughout Gemotroplis all because of your greedy and unworthy behaviour.' Emperor Irindor stated.

'Who are you to call me unworthy?' Cranium beckoned.

'Don't try to argue with me. King Jackale and I have allied with the Sapphire Nation. Our armies will unite and overrun your nation if your actions repeat themselves. You are no match for our combined power. Finally, we all have agreed that you shall be stripped of your royalty and power and no longer be the Ruby emperor.' Irindor explained.

Emperor Cranium felt stranded inside his mind. He couldn't run, he couldn't hide, he couldn't fight. He was so humiliated by himself that he found that the last option was to end himself, which was never the answer. But he knew no better.

Suddenly, he reached up to his neck. The sharp, abrupt movement was enough to startle both Irindor and Jackale. They were quickly pulled back into the crowd of soldiers in case Cranium reached for a weapon.

But he wasn't, and he was reaching for vile poison hanging around his neck. He had the poison just as a precaution. He never actually thought he would use it. But now it was necessary. He snapped the necklace off and gulped the poison down.

Instantly, his mouth began frothing up, and his eyes began to roll loosely in their sockets like marbles. He fell backwards, landing with a painful thud. All his soldiers and enemies watched him as he lay there until confirming his death a few minutes later." Winston concluded.

"Woah." Lustre was stunned. "What did they do with his body?"

Winston pondered his mind for a second. "I'm pretty sure the Topaz Emperor Irindor forced the remaining Ruby soldiers to carry his corpse up the volcano and dump it inside," Winston replied.

Lustre's expression dulled with sadness at the thought of the Ruby soldiers.

"Those soldiers were helpless, forced to fight, only to be trampled like reatrits on the battlefield," Winston added. "But don't worry, Emperor Cranium's son, Emperor Maroon, is very cautious now. He knows he will lose if he attempts something stupid again." Winston was assured.

"So, how did you get the crown?" Lustre questioned.

That's when Winston grew noticeably sad. He gazed up at Lustre and spoke with a quivering voice.

"Well. Umm."

"Lustre, the crown was given to me by my dad because..." Winston said proudly. Lustre could see Winston was progressively getting sadder as he spoke. Before he continued the story, Lustre asked. "Are you okay? What happened to your dad?"

It was a stupid question. Lustre could already predict the answer from Winston's expression alone.

"He died... He was part of the army on that day. He was forced to fight by the emperor. So, he pickpocketed the crown after the battle and gave it to me. Now, every time I see it. It reminds me of him." Winston sighed.

"I mean, I hate his memory; it just makes me upset. I could make a potion to forget about him, but I also don't want to forget him. It's really... Difficult to explain."

Winston's gaze wandered wearily to the floor after a few seconds. He snatched up his empty teacup and Lustre's full teacup and carried them away from the table. He also took this opportunity to throw another log on the fire as it began to die out again.

"Alright...I will grab some of that Muzzle Mud you wanted me to show you. Then we can heal your leg," said Winston, wrapping himself in his snow coat.

"Oh, okay... But I thought it was already healed."

Winston chuckled softly. "Oh, that was just disinfecting it. That only prevents it from getting infected. Muzzle Mud is a potion that will stop the bleeding and heal the body. Sadly, there are dangers in assuming the potion will cure an infection."

Lustre smiled gratefully. "Oh! Okay..."

After sliding grombler leather gloves over his hands and buttoning up his coat, Winston trudged to the front door and swung it open. Immediately, all the warm air escaped in one gush, and the battering cold flooded the room. The fire flickered desperately in the cold, only to linger a few seconds before the wind blew it out. Winston quickly stepped out and pulled the door shut. The harsh wind stopped as soon as the door closed. But, without the fire or any other light source, the whole room was shrouded in darkness.

It didn't seem like much of a problem, but it was sure an issue for Lustre. Even though it may not have been apparent initially, Lustre was scared of the dark, especially when alone. Usually, his brain would hold back this reaction in the mines, like when a torch blew out. But since he wasn't with Rusty this time, he began panicking.

Outside, the moonlight could barely seep into the cottage through the cracks in the walls and the frosted windows. Knowing where the door was, he knew where to find the fireplace. After calming himself down, he felt his way around the room. Lustre kept his hands before him in that awkward anticipation when you expect to hit something. But his hands didn't stop the first thing he hit.

WACK

Lustre swung his foot right into the leg of the table. A stinging pain shot up his injured ankle. "Ouch!" he shrieked. He continued. "Come on! Where is that fireplace?"

Eventually, Lustre's hands touched the warm cauldron of stew, then something made of stone. He felt it for a few seconds, determining its shape.

"Yes! Finally," cheered Lustre. It was indeed the fireplace. He kneeled and positioned himself before it, aiming his hands inside. "Hope this works." He whispered, "Paxta-holla."

Then there was a spark of light. It illuminated the room for a split second before vanishing. The fire didn't relight. Irritated, Lustre tried again.

After repeating the charm, "Paxta-holla", another spark lit up in his hand. This one lingered for a bit longer but ultimately died as well. The fire was unchanged. "Come on! Please, I hate the dark."

He tried one last time. "Paxta-holla!" The spark lit up in his hand once again. Lustre held it out to the fireplace with his final hope. Then it caught on and crackled to life. Its comforting orange light projected across the floor, as before. Lustre breathed a massive sigh of relief.

"That's better." To be extra precautionary, Lustre reached over to the pile of kindling beside the fireplace and tossed on a handful. Satisfied, Lustre returned to the table and sat down. Moments later. Lustre gasped as the door sprang back open. Standing amid the spearing blizzard was Winston's trembling silhouette. He stepped inside, his footsteps sounding abnormally heavy. It took a moment for Lustre to realise he was carrying a large bucket. Winston kicked the door shut behind him and dragged a bucket over to the table.

The bucket was heavy, and Winston struggled to put it down in the centre of the table. It landed with a thud. Winston then threw his coat and gloves to the corner and sat down, breathing vigorously.

Chapter 7

Muzzle Mud

After catching his breath, Winston replied, "That's my bucket of Muzzle Mud. You can see for yourself if you wish." Lustre stood up and peeked into the bucket, and then a horrified expression fell across his face. The first thing Lustre found was the reeking stench that radiated from within. It was a strong metallic smell, combined with the odour of a dead decaying reatrit. This forced Lustre to gag.

He could see a dark blue gloop, like mud, inside the bucket, which was fitting. However, the strangest thing Lustre noticed was that the gloopy stuff seemed to be bubbling and squelching around like it was alive. "Gross! What is that?" Lustre asked, disgusted.

"It's Muzzle Mud, like I told you. It's the blood of the gemotro, the muzzle-myer, maybe also feather and a berry or two," explained Winston.

"Myers are tall creatures with a tree-like appearance. They are so convincing that people have mistaken them for trees many times. The only way to tell them apart is that they're shorter than the average tree without leaves, and of course, they walk." Lustre sat back down in his chair. "Oh...Okay, so what are you going to do with that?"

"You see, Lustre, the blood from a muzzle-myer can heal any wound. It's a potent elixir. If you drink even just a spoonful, you can be healed of blindness, wounds, cuts, broken bones and even stress! If you drink some, it will fix up your leg," advised Winston.

It would be an understatement to say that Lustre was a little sceptical. I mean, it sounded far too good to be true. The Muzzle Mud potion in the Banderian marketplace did not look that disgusting. His instincts were telling him no! So, he began to interrogate Winston before he drank anything. He was not about to drink some, just for Winston to yell, 'Ha-ha! I got you!'.

Lustre knew about pranks like that; he used them on Rusty all the time. Once, he tampered with Haley on the platform to make it seem like they both had missed their ride. Those were good times. "If it's such marvellous stuff, why isn't anyone talking about this?" Lustre asked suspiciously.

"Well, it's reserved only for soldiers. This stuff is so valuable it is almost impossible to take into public without somebody pickpocketing it," Winston explained. "Also, muzzle- myers are dying out because they only breed every few hundred rots. There are only about twenty left in the whole forest. So, it is incredibly rare. They are being hunted and killed for their marvellous blood." Winston knew his potion stall depended on them surviving.

"That's horrible. But I understand why people are hunting them." Lustre remarked.

"Yes, Muzzle Mud is so valuable. There is an old water well about twenty feet from my cottage where I keep my stash of Muzzle Mud inside it," revealed Winston.

"Wait…What? Inside it?" Lustre exclaimed. Winston nodded.

"It's quite ingenious, actually. I hook the bucket to the chain and wind it down to the bottom. It's the perfect hiding spot," said Winston proudly.

"Oh…I see."

Soon after, Winston scurried away from the table to retrieve Lustre's teacup. After emptying the hazel tea, he brought it back to the table.

"So…Are you sure this will cure my leg…For real?"

Winston smiled assuredly. Even though Winston seemed to know what he was talking about, Lustre was still unconvinced. Lustre replied, "Okay then…"

Then, using the ladle, Winston scooped up a huge dollop of the Muzzle Mud and plopped it into Lustre's teacup. "There you are, drink up," Winston said. Lustre stared down at his teacup hesitantly. The smell made his stomach churn with disgust. He nervously lifted the teacup and brought it to his lips. What made Lustre uneasy was that Winston kept watching him. Lustre felt awkward at that moment. Winston silently waited patiently until Lustre finally took a sip. Lustre's tongue cowered to the back of his mouth, fearful of the impending taste. And as predicted, it was disgusting. It was so bitter and horrid.

"How is it?" Winston asked. Somehow, Lustre's revolted expression wasn't enough of an answer already.

"Oh, it's so nice. Tastes better than sweet crimson cider." Lustre snarked with his mouth full.

Winston chuckled. "Oh, I know it tastes bad. I didn't want to mention it before you drank, or else you would never have."

Lustre let out an annoyed groan, to which Winston responded. "At least you drank some. Even though it's not much, it should help your leg heal faster."

Winston rose from his chair and retrieved his coat and gloves from the corner. "I will just take this bucket back to the well outside. I won't be long." With a struggle, Winston lifted the bucket and carried it towards the door. It was so heavy that Winston had to pace his slow walk to avoid a spill. The contents were far too valuable. As soon as Winston's back was turned, Lustre spat out the Muzzle Mud into the cup. Winston was unaware. Lustre had been holding it in his mouth for the past two minutes. Lustre stared down at his cup, whispering, "He really thought I was going to drink that crap."

Winston put down the bucket to put on his coat and gloves. Once again, the heat left the cottage and was replaced with icy wind. Winston quickly picked up the bucket and stepped outside. As soon as he entered the blizzard, he stumbled off balance. After another little stumble, Winston continued walking. A few seconds passed, and Lustre watched Winston stumble off balance for a third time. That was the moment Winston began to regret his decisions. With the sound of the storm blurring his voice, he called out. "Peroa! The blizzard is getting worse!"

He then switched directions and started retreating toward the cottage. Winston fought desperately against the wind, making maintaining a straight walk almost impossible. Lustre watched in discomfort. He thought he might do something, but Winston was wise and experienced and could handle this. Then there was a loud crack. It was distant but noticeable. This was the point when Lustre decided to get up from his chair. He scurried over to the door and peered outside. The cause of the sound was initially unclear, but Lustre only had to wait a few more seconds.

For out of nowhere came a large branch, thrown in the wind. It must have snapped loose from a tree. The speed at which the blizzard carried it was alarming. Before Lustre could react, the branch flew into vision, striking Winston from the side.

He was bowled over, knocked out cold. He landed with a thud face-first in the snow.

Lustre shouted, "Mother Peroa," into the wind.

"Are you okay, Winston?" he cried out. There was no response. Winston lay motionless in the snow, the bucket tipped over beside him. Lustre panicked. He had to do something. An option went through his mind. He couldn't go out there without protection, and he couldn't wake Winston up from inside the cottage.

"Winston! Wake up! Winston!" screamed Lustre. The blizzard was far too loud. Lustre began to scavenge around the room for anything that could help. After a few minutes, he returned to the door without a plan. He had only his dagger, a single shot of Gone Gazz, and the jewel. All those weren't helpful right now.

"Oh, no." He could not think, but he just had to do something. Without consideration, Lustre forced himself through the door and into the blizzard. The wind immediately speared him. His skin burned, yet he still ploughed on through. With each step, he slowly realised how stupid this decision was, but he couldn't turn back now. "Winston!" he screamed out.

Once arriving at Winston's frozen body, Lustre was left trapped. He hadn't planned this far; he hadn't planned at all. He had to devise a plan immediately to get Winston inside while being battered by this blizzard. He reached down and took hold of Winston's wrist. His skin was pale, and he felt as cold as ice. Lustre gripped hard and dragged him through the snow. He only moved Winston a few inches before he was exhausted.

"His coat and heavy clothes are weighing me down," Lustre then realised. Riskily, Lustre shed Winston's coat and continued dragging. Without the extra weight, Lustre began to make progress. Over a minute, Lustre dragged Winston two feet closer to the cottage door. His energy was now completely drained. He needed to get back inside quickly, before exhaustion overpowered him. He couldn't stand the blizzard any longer, and his whole body was already numb.

Then, something terrible happened when he tried to let go of Winston's hand. Once he released his grip, he felt his hand tug. He glanced behind, seeing his hand still interlocked with Winston's. He was so confused. He quickly tried to yank it free, but the cold had fused his hand to Winston's wrist. Lustre started to panic. He had no energy to tow Winston anymore, and moving forward with a human anchor glued to him was impossible.

After trying to separate his hand, Lustre finally dropped to his knees and fell forward into the snow. It was truly a horrible yet humorous way for them to die, a sight of two frozen corpses lying only yards from the refuge. Lustre had no idea how long he had been lying there, but for some reason, he woke up. Unfortunately, he wasn't lying in bed. He was still lying in the snow.

The door was right in front of him, wide open. He pushed himself up from the ground with a sudden energy spike and took one decisive step forward. Winston was dragged through the door, and then Lustre collapsed once again. Lustre had never felt so relieved by the feeling of a wooden floor.

With Winston still glued to his hand, Lustre kicked the door shut and dragged them to the fireplace. The fire had died out, but it still had plenty of firewood. He saw the old water canteen. Lustre used his free hand and splashed the crimson oil over the firewood. He then uttered, "Paxta-holla." His voice was weak, and his teeth wouldn't stop chattering.

WOOF

The firewood exploded into flames; he shocked himself as his hair and eyebrows were now fire-singed. But at least the fireplace was roaring, and a small face burn was nothing compared to the comfort and satisfaction that now flourished in Lustre's mind. He lay there for almost fifteen minutes, letting the heat thaw his skin. He felt it soak into his face and gratefully prayed, "Thank you, Mother Peroa."

Once again, for an unexplainable reason, Lustre had cheated death against the most incredible odds.

Chapter 8

Stolen Heart

The frost melted off his clothes, forming a puddle beneath him. He slowly sat up and gave his hand a firm yank. To Lustre's joy, it finally broke free from Winston. He wriggled his swollen fingers in discomfort.

"Ouch." He then turned to face Winston, who was lying beside him.

"Oh yeah, I almost forgot about you." Lustre quickly stood up and grabbed his cup of Muzzle Mud.

"This is why you shouldn't lie, as if you die now, Winston, it isn't my fault," Lustre rationalised. Lustre turned to Winston, kneeling before him. He lifted his head and carefully poured the Muzzle Mud into his mouth. At first, there was no response; Lustre's heart sank. "Come on, wake up."

But then, slowly but surely, Winston's eyes fluttered open. His skin brightened to its original colour. Winston let out a deep sigh. He gazed up at Lustre, a look of gratitude in his eyes.

"Thank you, Lustre," said Winston, his voice delicate and sincere. Lustre nodded, feeling a mixture of relief, pride, and shock that the Muzzle Mud worked as Winston had advertised.

"Why did you save me? You could've frozen out there!" He said through clattering teeth.

Lustre smiled serenely. "Why wouldn't I? You did the same for me." Winston grinned at the truth in that. Lustre helped Winston up off the ground and guided him into a chair. Lustre then sat down in his chair.

"Your bucket of Muzzle Mud is still out there, knocked over," Lustre reminded him.

"Oh yes. That's okay. I will go put it back when the storm settles." Winston said. "Well. It's good we're both alive. Suppose you hadn't done anything. You would be sitting alone right now. Could you pour me some more hazel tea? The kettle and teacups are just there, by the fireplace. I need something to warm my throat."

"Of course." After getting up from his chair, Lustre poured Winston a cup of hazel tea and placed it before him. After smiling gratefully, Winston said, "You're a good friend."

Lustre took this as a compliment, even though he knew it was a lie. Winston brought the teacup to his lips and took a sip. It was so simple, yet this one sip removed the quiver in his voice.

"That's much better." Winston rubbed his throat. "It's like magic what this tea can do for me."

That was when Lustre remembered something: the jewel. The story of Gemotronia shook Lustre; its description perfectly matched the jewel. What Ryan and Winston had already told him made him wonder if it was the Heart of Queen Gemotronia, even though that would be impossible. The thought fascinated him, and he had to ask. "So…Um, Winston."

"Yes?"

"Me and my mate Rusty found this…" Lustre stopped; just then, a gust of wind brushed past his ear. Through it, he faintly heard a voice. This voice sounded familiar to him, and it said three familiar words.

"Don't tell him."

Lustre could have sworn he heard this phrase before. Last time, he assumed it was the wind playing tricks on his mind. However, a coincidence can only occur once before it isn't a coincidence. Lustre's face turned pale. "What was that?" he asked.

Winston looked confused.

"You and your friend found what in the mines?"

"Oh...Yeah." Lustre said. He continued his story with a sense of uneasiness.

"So, me and my mate found this jewel in the mines. It has done so many strange and unexplainable things. Like magic. And I am pretty sure it's that heart of Gemotronia, just like in your story."

Winston burst out laughing, ignoring the seriousness in Lustre's tone. "Oh, don't be silly, Lustre. That would be impossible. There is only one heart, and it was shattered a thousand rots ago into eight shards."

"But it is just as you described!" Lustre argued.

For proof, Lustre reached into his pocket and pulled out the jewel. He held it out to Winston.

"See?"

"A beautiful, colourful gemstone, about the size of a human heart. Is that not a beautiful, colourful gemstone? Winston? Is it not about the size of a heart?"

Winston stuttered at its image. His mouth fell open. "Well, yes," he admitted. "But it can't be. The Heart of Gemotronia grants all forms of magic. Not just Ruby magic, like you."

Lustre gave Winston a confident grin. "Yes, it can..."

That was when Winston stood up from his chair. He scoffed loudly. "Ha! No, it can't!"

Lustre held his position on the matter. "It can!"

Winston was baffled by Lustre's confidence. He didn't want Lustre to embarrass himself. So, he gave him a chance to accept that he was wrong.

"Come on, Lustre. Just admit that I am right."

Shockingly, Lustre shook his head. "No, I have seen it cast foreign spells before!" He stated. Winston was out of ideas, and Lustre really believed that the jewel he was holding was a thousand-rot-old heart of a goddess. It would be unexplainable if Lustre was correct. It would dispute the whole legend of it being shattered if it were here, fully intact.

"Prove it then." Winston suggested, "You're Ruby by birth, so cast a spell, one that wraps me in vines! I do not know a Ruby spell that can do that."

Lustre took a step back and prepared himself. He pointed the jewel out to Winston and squeezed his eyes shut. There was a brief silence that grew awkward quite quickly. Winston stood there with his arms crossed, unimpressed. After waiting at least ten seconds, he gasped sarcastically.

Even with Winston mocking him, Lustre still believed in himself. He kept whispering to himself. "Please work...Please work."

After losing patience, Winston began advancing toward Lustre. "Come on, Lustre, just accept that I know more than you."

Every time Lustre had cast a foreign spell, it was at times when he was either not in control or only partially in control. And it was only in desperate or necessary situations. Lustre had no idea how to do it at will. He had to learn quickly. With his last shred of confidence, he uttered to himself. "Please..." The unknown words 'Emede Vinato' entered his mind.

In Lustre's hands, the jewel began to swell with light. That alone was enough to make Winston stop. His mouth dropped in absolute disbelief. Out of the blue, a loud chime echoed throughout the cottage, like a single ding of a church bell. The sound bounced off the walls and into their ears. Accompanying the sound was this radiant glow, shining in rays of green from Lustre's hand. Then, everything fell silent. The jewel simmered into a soft glow rather than a blinding radiance.

In a sudden flash, a green light beamed not from the jewel but from beneath the cottage. The light shunted upwards and dabbled through the floorboards. They both glanced downwards, Winston still trying to comprehend what was happening. Then, as quickly as it began, the light vanished. They both waited for what was to happen next. Ominously, neither spoke for at least ten seconds before Winston stuttered.

"Okay... How is-" Before Winston could finish, the floor began to rumble and crack under their feet. The floorboards began bulging upwards as if something was pushing them from beneath.

Furniture began to move on the uneven ground, specifically the table, which began sliding towards the fireplace. Everything on top of the table was either broken or now on the ground beside it.

"What in Peroa's name is happening?" Winston yelled.

The whole floor was mangled, the floorboards were sticking up in every direction, and a cavity of exposed dirt surrounded the centre where Winston stood. Then, to conclude the chaos, vines burst from the ground and tangled themselves around Winston. It all happened so quickly.

Lustre was relieved and astonished. He didn't look like a complete fool. Instead, Winston was.

"There you go. Proof! See! I don't lie!" Lustre cheered, waving the jewel above his head. Much to Lustre's satisfaction, Winston looked embarrassed at the position he found himself in.

"Peroa, what have you done?"

"I used this jewel to cast a foreign spell, just like I said I would." Lustre smiled smugly.

"Okay…Fine, I admit I was wrong. That is not a normal rock." Winston mumbled through the vines that covered his face, making it difficult for him to talk, physically and mentally.

"Can you please get these vines off me? I can't move!"

"Fine." Lustre sighed. Using his dagger, Lustre sliced the vines loose.

"Thank you," said Winston. He wriggled his feet free and stepped out.

"So, what do we do now?" Lustre asked.

"Umm…Let's see. There is a huge dirt crater on my floor. Next, you knocked over all my furniture, including my table. So I think the next step may be cleaning all this mess up."

"You started it," argued Lustre.

Winston groaned loudly. "Well, at least the walls are still intact, or else we would be freezing right now," he remarked. Winston then turned his attention to the floor, quickly trying to salvage what he could from the mess. "I should be able to fix this up in the morning. Let's flip the table back to you and sit down for now."

"All right, agreed."

Lustre helped Winston move the table back to the centre of the cottage where it belonged. It was positioned directly over the pile of dead vines from before. Then, after retrieving both chairs, they both sat down.

"Okay, Lustre, I don't understand how all this happened. Unless this is all a trick, that jewel may be… a heart of Gemotronia," explained Winston.

"I know, wait…What do you mean?"

"I mean, there has to be two. Because one is shattered, and the one you have is intact."

"But… There was only one in your story. Why would there be a second one?"

"I don't know! It just doesn't make any sense! There is only one Queen Gemotronia, and she only has one heart. I have no clue where this one could have come from." Winston leaned forward onto the table, holding his head in his hands. "Where did you say you found that thing?"

Lustre shuffled forward in his chair. "Oh…the mines. The ruby mines down south in Bandeira." This still didn't explain anything.

Suddenly, Winston's eyes widened. He stood up from his chair and scurried over to the bookshelf in the corner, which was still standing despite the uneven floor. He rummaged through the books, tossing them over his shoulder. He could only find one book relating to the Heart of Gemotronia, he scanned through its pages. Yet none of them mentioned anything about two hearts of Gemotronia. There was only one.

Winston was stuck and beyond confused. He returned to the table, clueless. "Can I see it, please?" he asked Lustre.

Lustre took it from his pocket and placed it in Winston's hand. He stared at it for a moment. There are two types of people. The first type is the person who gets stressed and frustrated over things they can't explain. The second type is the person who does not get stressed about the intrigue. Both want to learn, but one type lets it get to them. Lustre was born as a curious person without stress. And it didn't take long for him to realise that he didn't share that stressed trait with Winston. His panic and stress to learn about this jewel seemed unnecessary to Lustre.

Even after closely examining it, the jewel's origin remained unanswered. Winston's forehead sagged downward toward the table.

"I am lost, Lustre. I am completely clueless. But I do know that until we figure out this jewel, you can't show it to anyone." Winston pleaded.

"What? Why not! I need to show it to the emperor so I can-"

"No! You're not showing it to the emperor." Winston snapped, slamming his fist into the table.

Lustre gasped; the outburst was out of place. "Why are you so angry?" Lustre demanded an answer.

Winston sighed deeply. "Lustre, I don't think you realise how much power this… jewel possesses. The very wielder could be anybody! No matter what their intentions may be. I couldn't even begin to think what would happen if you gave this to the emperor. Nobody can be irresponsible or immature with such power."

"Irresponsible? Immature?" Lustre snapped.

"I'm not referring to anyone," Winston said as an excuse. This statement insulted Lustre. Lustre grew aggravated. "Can I have my jewel back?" he asked sternly. Winston hesitated. He gazed at Lustre for a few seconds, thinking it over.

"It's mine! Pass it over." Lustre said, reaching across the table.

"Uh, fine," Winston said, grudgingly handing the jewel back. Lustre was beginning to mistrust Winston. He knew now would be a good time to bugger off before anything bad happened.

"All right." Lustre stood up from his chair. "Look, thanks for the stew, disinfectant and muzzle mould."

"Muzzle Mud!" Winston's frustration was now showing.

"Yeah, yeah…Whatever. I reckon I should be going now. You have tended to my wounds as I tended to yours. You have also provided me with mountains of new knowledge. I must continue my journey towards the palace." Lustre said.

Winston quickly stood up from his chair and jammed his foot in the doorway, preventing it from opening.

"What are you doing?" screamed Lustre.

"Umm… You can't leave! The blizzard is still too harsh." Lustre groaned. "Please get out of the way."

Winston shook his head. "I can't let you freeze."

"I don't care! I am leaving, Winston, and whether I freeze or not is not your problem," Lustre argued. Winston paused for a second. Suddenly, his expression shifted as if he had an idea. "Well… How about this? You stay here in the cottage until morning. The blizzard will have passed by then." Sadly, this made sense.

Lustre considered it for a second.

"You can sleep right next to the fire, all cosy and warm. It wouldn't hurt to stay a few hours longer," proposed Winston.

Lustre didn't have to rush back down south; he accepted.

"Okay, I suppose I could stay until morning, and then I will be leaving. Deal?" said Lustre, offering his hand.

"Deal." Winston smiled.

Lustre turned away from the door and sat down beside the fire.

"I am just going to lock the door, okay? The wind always throws it open at night, but locking the door stops it."

"All right then."

Winston then turned to face the door. Just below the brass doorknob was a keyhole. Winston reached into his pocket for the key. It was a long brass key made to match the doorknob. Winston slid the key into the keyhole; it nestled into place. Winston then twisted it, ending with a satisfying click. After withdrawing the key, Winston twisted the doorknob to confirm the door was locked. He grinned before dropping the key back into his pocket.

"Okay...That should stop the boy," he whispered.

After a few minutes, Lustre tried to make himself comfortable. A timber floor wasn't that comfortable, but it was certainly better than sleeping on the gravel floor back in the mines. He lay down on his side, watching the fire crackle. He could hear Winston snoring in the corner. He slept beside the book cabinet, with his coat and gloves pillowing his head.

For what felt like hours, he lay there, lost in thought, watching the fire dance before his eyes.

He slowly drifted off to sleep, the cosy warmth of the fire wrapping him like a blanket. The soft crackling lulled him into a deep sleep. His eyes slowly shut...

What felt like moments later was at least an hour. Lustre's eyes shot open, awoken by a loud thud. He sat up, squinting around the room. There was a bright silver light interrupting the room. Lustre waited for his vision to focus before realising the door was wide open. The wind must have thrown it open, just like Winston warned.

"Winston, the door is open," groaned Lustre. Without any response, Lustre stood up, soured with annoyance. "I'll shut it. Don't worry; you can stay asleep." He grumbled. Lustre stumbled over to the door. The outside cold ruffled his skin. He gripped the doorknob and pushed it closed. Satisfied, he returned to the fire and settled back down.

"Seriously, this wind doesn't even want me to sleep."

Lustre tried to fall back asleep, but there were so many interruptions. Winston's snoring beckoned in the silence. The loud howling of the blizzard was also battering the cottage walls. Lustre tried to ignore them. As he lay there, he began to think.

"Hold on." His mind echoed. "Wasn't the door locked? How could the wind beat it open if it was locked?" He asked himself.

The question made him sit up. He stroked his head in confusion. As he tried to answer, another thing popped into his mind. The realisation was that he couldn't hear Winston's snoring anymore. "Winston?" He called out softly.

There was no response. Lustre stood up. The fire glow couldn't reach the corners, so where Winston slept, it was too dark to determine if he was still there.

"Winston? Are you still asleep?" Lustre called out a little louder.

"Where could he have gone?" Lustre moved around the cottage, searching for Winston. Honestly, there weren't many places to search; the room was not that large. Before long, Lustre stopped at the table in the centre. "Did he go out?"

Lustre quickly answered himself. "No, the blizzard is too strong." Lustre was so confused. "Where could he have gone?"

A horrible thought struck him. He was doubtful that Winston would do something like that. But he still had to check. He dug into his pocket, his whole body trembling with fear. There was nothing. He reached into his second pocket. He felt around to be sure he wasn't making a fool of himself. But then he felt something; a wave of relief washed over him.

"Oh, Peroa, thank you. I almost had a panic attack." He sighed. When he pulled his hand out, he gasped. He was holding his last potion of Gone Gazz. "Wait…What!" He quickly shoved his hand back into his pockets. He dug around for a few seconds, but eventually, nope, his pockets were empty. The jewel was gone. Lustre was lost for words. He didn't know what to do. Panic filled the room. He scuttled around, holding back tears.

"Winston!" He beckoned.

He had to do something. He thought that he could use his potion. It seemed like the right time. However, he still hesitated.

He knew he couldn't stand around just contemplating in the cottage. He quickly peeked his head through the door. With the white void before him, Lustre noticed a trail of deep footsteps leading outwards into the snow. Lustre could only guess who they belonged to. This proved that Winston had left the cottage and showed Lustre exactly where he had gone. However, he had to act quickly, as the blizzard was rapidly erasing evidence.

Lustre began to scavenge around the cottage. He didn't expect to find anything, but conveniently, Winston had left his snow coat, gloves, and water flask. He must have forgotten them when he raced out through the door. This was critical for Lustre.

He bundled them up and stood by the door. He couldn't repeat what happened last time, only making it a few yards before collapsing. His heart was filled with contemplation, and he was about to risk everything. He gulped down his fear and stepped out of the cottage, plunging himself into the blizzard. His feet sank into the soft, fresh snow, which caught him off guard. The snow had piled much higher since last night. It wasn't a good start; he almost lost balance on the first step. His ankle stood up to the challenge; he realised the mouthed Muzzle Mud must have helped.

Unlike before, he had a coat that gave his skin a layer of protection. He only had to trek a few yards outsides before he spotted something, a discoloured patch of snow. It was so out of place; a curious Lustre had to investigate. A random patch of snow with a dark blue tint wasn't natural.

"Oh, that must be where Winston spilt the bucket of Muzzle Mud."

The bucket was gone, but the spill remained. Lustre continued past it. Before long, he saw a small stone structure. Lustre altered his path toward it, again curious.

As he approached, the structure became recognisable. It had a slanted roof, similar to the cottage, supported by two wooden beams. Below the roof was a stone basin and a water well.

Lustre edged nearer and peered inside. He saw his distorted reflection staring back at him from the depths. But most importantly, he saw the bucket dangling far down. The bucket was suspended by a rope with the winch at the top.

"Woah," he uttered. "This must be the well Winston was talking about. Where he hides his muzzle mould." Lustre thought for a second. "Maybe…"

He grasped the winch and began to wind it around. It was more difficult than he thought. He circled it around, pausing briefly to catch his breath every half-turn. Gradually, the bucket ascended. After it reached the top, Lustre grabbed the handle and pulled it toward him.

"He stole my jewel, so I can steal his muzzle milk…I mean muzzle mould-DAMMIT! Why can't I pronounce anything?" He groaned.

After emptying the crimson oil out of the water flask, Lustre scooped up some Muzzle Mud, spilling the contents into the flask. He tightened and licked the lid, then strapped it to his belt.

"Okay, just a little medicine." He grinned.

Lustre continued past the well. "So much for a secret hiding spot, Winston," Lustre said to himself.

Only a few steps later, Lustre found that he had re-entered the Crimson Forest, proven by all the trees surrounding him. Although they partially shielded him from the blizzard, Lustre had to keep walking. The cold had just compromised his coat and gloves. The cold wind and snow had already started seeping through his skin, causing him tremendous discomfort. He buried his hands in his pockets, hoping to see sunlight soon.

Being in such temperatures expends your energy quickly, as the body must work harder to keep warm. Lustre had learnt this from last time. He needed to rest his legs, or he would collapse like last time. He veered off to the right, dropping at the foot of the nearest tree. The tree put a wall between him and the wind. He pulled the collar over his mouth; he couldn't keep inhaling that icy-cold air any longer.

"Cold…" he prattled.

Lustre knew he had to keep going, though his mind begged otherwise. He fought the urge and stood back up. "Come on… Almost there," he convinced himself. Somehow, he was right. After walking for about fifteen minutes, he felt a noticeable change in the blizzard; the storm began to weaken. The wind degraded into a breeze, and the snow no longer obscured his vision.

Lustre then dropped to his knees as he felt a speck of sunlight touch his skin. The sky turned crystal blue, and the tree branches were no longer draped in snow. Though the ground still had remnants of blizzard frost, it was long behind him.

"Ahh! That sunlight is so fresh." He sighed.

Lustre threw off his gloves and coat and just let the skin enjoy the warmth.

"All right, back to problems." He stood there, the vast forest enticing him forward.

"Winston can't have got far," Lustre told himself. Lustre began his journey back down south in search of his traitor, Winston.

* * *

Meanwhile, to the east, within the Ruby Palace, a crisis was forming. Emperor Maroon sat on his throne, his blood-red robes draped over the armrests. Torches lined the throne room walls, with many banners and flags of the Ruby Nation hanging from the arches. The flags were crimson red with a black wavire centre symbol. He watched his servants, guards, and other courtiers bustle like ants up and down the illuminated red carpet. They all were chattering, and the emperor did not join in the conversations; it was beneath him. Instead, he found his mind more occupied than ever.

While he sat there, angered, watching his precious red carpet get dirty, a sudden commotion broke out in his palace hall. The courtiers fell silent, all turning to face the entrance doors as a group of guards burst into the room. They marched down the carpet with muddy feet, their armour clanking loudly.

The emperor stood up, his heart pounding. "What is it now?" he called out. His voice echoed throughout the room.

The guards stopped and dispersed, revealing the scrawny man between them. The man seemed very nervous. The guards gave the man an encouraging prod with their spears, moving him toward the emperor.

"Um-hello, your majesty. I am here to deliver this letter to you. It's from the Topaz Emperor, Sage," he stuttered.

The emperor peered over the edge of his glasses. "Very well...Hand it over." He tore open the envelope and glanced down at the letter. He silently read line after line, visibly growing angrier each second.

"What!" the emperor boomed. He adjusted his glasses to make sure he wasn't misreading. He added, "A ten thousand large rubies tax. By tomorrow?"

He stared up in disbelief. Quiller stood there, his head bowed. Quiller was the royal advisor, the main right-hand man working for the emperor. He was unlike most advisors, who liked to be sharply dressed and valued image. He presented as more like a head butler and wore a simple dark robe. He was severely underpaid and treated like dirt. Whilst in the throne room, the guards regularly intimidated him into obeying the emperor's every demand, even though he had a higher seniority. But his one job, his golden rule, was not to upset the emperor, and he had done just that.

He knew what had happened to the people who had upset Emperor Maroon. Thrown into the dungeon forever, as they lay in darkness, alone and forgotten. The emperor gestured to the courtiers and guards to exit the room. Leaving Quiller to stand alone.

"Your Majesty, reparation fines to Topaz Nation are agreed upon. Ever since the Ruby W-"

"I know! They are taking the piss!" interrupted Maroon. Then he beckoned, "Our ruby mines haven't dug up that much in rots. They can barely cough up a few large rubies an octave. We only get small ones. Where in Gemotroplis am I gonna get ten thousand?"

Quiller shook his head nervously.

"I am sure we will figure this out, Your Majesty." All of a sudden, the emperor got an idea. He smiled, leaning forward on his throne.

"Quiller! Write a letter back to Topaz Nation," he ordered.

Quiller nodded. "Of course, Sire. I will write down anything you say."

"Dear Topaz Emperor…Whatever your name is. I am unfazed by your demands and threats. In fact, I find them humorous at times. I will not obey. They are completely irrational. If you, foreign scum, ever dare send me another letter, I'll… Umm."

The emperor paused for a moment. "I'll…No, you'll regret it! That's it, you'll regret it! Honestly, Emperor Maroon." He finished with a snort.

After scribbling down the emperor's every word on a scrap of paper, Quiller replied, "Sire, there we go. I will deliver this letter straight to the Topaz Emperor Sage."

Quiller then scurried back down the filthy red carpet out of the throne room. The emperor sat alone.

"Those pesky reatrits think they can order me about," he pondered. "If only I had something on them. Like a weapon or hostage. Then, they wouldn't be able to boss me around anymore. They need to be scared of me. If only..." He sighed. Finally, he yelled across the throne room, "Get my bloody royal carpet cleaned!"

* * *

Meanwhile, Lustre was back in the Crimson Forest, and he had no map or any way to navigate. He only knew he was going south. He had no clue where Winston could be. As a result of the silence of Crimson Forest, Lustre's mind began to slip in and out of concentration. Lustre dreamt of Tether's Tavern, a memorable place full of singing and drunken laughter.

He strolled up toward the counter with utter satiety. He stopped at the barrel labelled 'Fresh Crimson Cider'. With his mouth watering, Lustre twisted the handle above the faucet. The bubbling red liquid poured out into his stein below.

"One ruby, please, Lustre. It's discounted," Tether, the beautiful barmaid behind the counter, said.

"Of course!" Lustre couldn't wait to drink his cider. He searched inside his pockets before handing the barmaid one ruby.

"Thanks, Lustre," she said. Her smile made Lustre feel a strange happiness or a confusing desire inside.

"No problem, Tether. Have a great day."

Lustre turned around and returned to the table where Rusty was waiting. "I got my cider. Let's eat our grombler stew now." Lustre sat down at the table.

"Oh wait, Lustre!" Tether called out.

"Yes?" Lustre said seconds before taking his first sip.

"Just one more thing."

"What is it?"

"HELP! SOMEBODY HELP US!"

A curdling cry interrupted Lustre's fantasy daydream. He snapped back into reality, his eyes darting around in confusion.

"Woah! What! Who said that?"

Before long, he noticed a strange object looming in the distance. Intrigued, he began to walk towards it. At first, he thought it was a natural formation of greenery, but as he got closer, it looked more out of place than ever—a huge jumble of vines jutting from the forest floor. What on Gemotroplis?

"Oh, thank Peroa! I'm saved!" Lustre heard a voice cry.

From within the vines, Lustre saw the dappled appearance of a man. The twisted green fingers coiled around his body. Strangely, the man looked just as confused as Lustre. Rightfully so, Lustre couldn't even begin to comprehend the bad luck the soldier was in, and he was up the creaky vine without a paddle.

"Who are you?" Lustre asked.

"My name's Ryan. Please help me."

Lustre gasped. "Ryan, the guard? It's me, Lustre!"

The man had a spike of excitement, and he smiled with relief. "Oh! Lustre! It's you! I don't want to be trapped here forever."

Lustre quickly drew his dagger and began cutting Ryan free without hesitation.

"What happened?" he asked.

"I'm not sure. It was all a blur. One moment, I was strolling through the forest with Bear on official orders to track down some hunter who had been murdering Ruby soldiers, and then there was this sudden flash of green light. Next moment, I'm trapped in these bloody vines!"

"Where's Bear now?" Lustre asked.

Ryan didn't answer; instead, he just glanced upward. From above, Lustre heard a peeved voice groan from above.

"Here."

Lustre tilted his head back. Through the awning of crimson leaves, he spotted an annoyed man dangling from the trees. It was Bear, wrapped around by a single vine, like a yo-yo toy. He stared downwards, a face of fear, confusion, and anger mixed into one. It was truly impressive how those vines could reach such heights and support the weight of a fully grown man, even with all that bulky armour.

"Don't worry, I will get you down," Lustre said, trying not to let his laughter break out. Bear already looked frustrated, and laughing would only aggravate him further.

Once Ryan was free, Lustre turned his attention back to Bear.

"How am I going to get down?" screamed Bear.

"A ladder?" Ryan suggested.

Bear glared downwards, his face red with anger.

"Yeah! Go on, find me a ladder in the middle of the Crimson Forest!" he shouted back mockingly.

"How?" scoffed Lustre.

"I was being sarcastic!" shouted Bear. Lustre thought for a moment. As bizarre as the situation was, Lustre had an idea. However, he wasn't sure Bear would like it.

"Well...I think we would have to catch you..." suggested Lustre. Bear returned an exaggerated laugh, which quickly faded.

"Wait...You're not serious?"

Lustre nodded.

"You are mad! I'm thirty feet high! There's no way I am free-falling!"

"Well... I don't know what else to do."

"Ahh! I can't hold on for much longer! Just think of something else," shouted Bear. His arms trembled as he desperately clung to the vine. His grip slowly began to slip from all the stress and sweat building in his hands.

"We have to do something!" added Ryan.

While Bear and Ryan panicked, Lustre just stood there, calm, despite the situation.

"Lustre! He is going to fall!"

Bear gradually unrolled until he hung ten feet from the ground.

"Help!" Bear screamed once more, just before his grip gave way.

Then he slipped. Bear plummeted downwards, screaming insistently. He flailed his arms and legs weirdly, but any method now to slow his fall would be useless. He hit the ground, legs first, with a painful thud, along with the clattering of his armour.

He landed directly in front of Lustre. Immediately, a concerned Ryan rushed over.

"Are you okay, Bear?" Ryan was clearly concerned.

It took a moment, but they eventually got a reassuring yet slightly angered response.

"I'm... okay."

Bear's whole body was still shaking from the surge of adrenaline. He gazed around, dizzy. His hair was tousled; all his armour was dented. Lustre stepped forward, not a drop of concern on his face. Lustre may have come off as insensitive to Ryan, as he didn't panic when Bear fell. But it wasn't intentional;

Lustre knew that it was the only possible way he would get down.

Lustre was terrible at understanding how other people may see him. He was bad at understanding feelings, which may be why he could take things too far. This has been proven on many occasions, just like now. The very next thing he said was, "Did it hurt?"

Bear glared up at him.

"NOO! IT DIDN'T. IT WAS THE BEST THING I HAVE EVER ENDURED."

This time, Lustre knew it was sarcasm; usually, it wasn't that obvious.

"Why didn't you do anything?" complained Bear.

"What were we supposed to do? Catch you?" Lustre argued back.

Bear stuttered, "Whatever, at least I didn't snap my legs." Bear held his arm up to Ryan, and with a smile, Ryan grasped his hand and pulled him up. Bear slowly arose, steadying himself.

"All right then…"

After ensuring Bear was okay, Lustre returned to the matter at hand. "So, did you see anything…Or what did this to you?" Ryan's face looked furrowed in concentration. He silently repeated the question, hoping it would jog his memory.

"I am not sure…" Ryan answered.

Lustre sighed. "What about you, Bear?" Lustre asked.

Bear blurted out the same response, except he didn't even bother to consider the question properly. Understandably, he was still upset about the fall. Lustre didn't have time for it, however. He needed to find Winston. He repeated the question, hoping to get a better response from Bear.

"Come on, Bear. Please, what did you see?" repeated Lustre.

Bear groaned loudly. "Fine. I think it was a man. He ran up towards us, and those vines came out of nowhere and bound us up. Then he just ran away."

Lustre grinned, much more satisfied. "Which way?"

"Umm…I can't remember," replied Bear.

"Why? Which way did he go?"

"Come on! I was shocked, confused, and UPSIDE DOWN, thirty feet in the air! I wasn't paying attention to where he was going." Bear snapped.

Lustre chuckled.

"All right, all right." Then Ryan stepped in just before Lustre and Bear erupted into another argument.

"Okay, thank you for the help, Lustre. But I think we'd better get going. We need a drink!" Before turning, he privately whispered to Lustre, "He was the Crimson Chalice."

Lustre nodded. "Okay then."

After waving goodbye, Lustre continued. Ryan had confirmed that Winston was the culprit. It made sense; Winston must have used the jewel to cast the same spell Lustre had before.

But Ryan's response lacked the one thing Lustre needed: the direction Winston fled. Lustre realised he had no chance of finding Winston on foot, so he stopped and tried to assemble a plan.

"Uh…Okay. This is going to be tricky." He laid out all of his belongings on the ground. "The dagger is useless right now," Lustre concluded. He moved it to the side. "So is the flask of Muzzle Mud." He pushed the flask aside as well. He was left with one item before him—the last vial of Gone Gazz. Lustre stared at it for a few seconds. He was unsure if it was helpful or not. "I don't know… Winston can't have gotten far."

Leaned back, glancing up at the trees. His eyes wandered, searching for hints or clues that could spark a new plan. Instead, his mind began to recall some of the things Winston had said.

Winston's voice echoed in his head, repeating sentences and phrases from the books he had read, questions he had asked, and parts of his backstory. *"Gemotronia had a heart which held all her magic and sorcery."*

"It's just a relic! A bad memory!"

Almost all were completely irrelevant and didn't help Lustre think at all. But one…One thing stood out. *"I am the Crimson Chalice. It's the name of my market stall back at Banderian Village."*

Lustre sat back up. "He must be going to sell it…at Bandeira market! Take all the credit, all the rubies, and all the fame! That greedy reatrit didn't take it for good, and he didn't take it for power! He didn't! He took it for profit, and he stole my fortune!"

Lustre snatched the Gone Gazz off the ground after gathering the rest of his belongings. He popped off the cork and raised it to his mouth. The vial paused at his bottom lip for a few seconds; the fumes leaching into his nostrils. Hesitation filled his mind, even though he was certain this was the right decision.

He took in a deep breath through his mouth. "He stole it from me, so I am stealing it back. It's only fair," he muttered.

Then he drank the potion in one gulp. Right after, he tossed the empty vial out of sight and announced the words. "Take me to the Band…"

Right then, a small yellow figure entered his vision. It scuttled around with such speed that Lustre only managed to catch a glimpse before disappearing. It was so brief, but it was enough to startle him. As a result, he completely muddled his words. Instead of 'Banderian', as intended, Lustre screamed the word 'BAD-AHHH', along with various other curses and shrieks.

"AHH! Reatrit! Peroa mother of..."

Lustre had a serious musophobia. He was scared of reatrits. Usually, the only time he would hear the word reatrit, it would always be someone else cursing. But, when there was a reatrit, Lustre would completely freak out.

They were horrible, scrawny gemotros scampering around in dark and damp places. Also, in folk's houses, they nibbled on furniture and chewed up every morsel of food left on the floor. They also had disgusting yellow hair, sometimes with spines like porcupines, except their hair stunk of everything they ate: rotten meat, decaying plants, and pieces of paper and wood.

Only seconds later, Lustre vanished from the Crimson Forest. He thought that he could re-announce the spell after collecting himself. But no, he teleported somewhere. For some reason, the word 'BAD-AHHH' was a place.

* * *

Lustre had no idea where he had gone. His new surroundings were an unsettling darkness, so dark that he had to double-check that his eyes weren't shut.

"Hello?" he called out. His voice answered him several times, echoing back to him. He had to be in a large, dark room with little furniture to have such a severe echo. He began to walk around, feeling for anything in front. After a few steps, he hit the first wall. It had a rough, rocky texture, so he could guess it was a brick wall. He followed along the wall, looking for corners. He had to find the corners to measure the size of the room.

He kept walking...and walking. "Come on...How big is this room?" he muttered to himself. After what felt like fifteen minutes of walking, he still hadn't arrived at the first corner. The room he was in had to be gigantic. The walls had to stretch hundreds of yards because he still hadn't found where they intersected.

Suddenly, sunlight filled the room. Lustre was briefly blinded, as his eyes were already accustomed to the darkness.

"Oi you! What do ya think you're doin' down there?" A loud, gravelly voice bellowed. Lustre was so confused.

He found himself standing in a chamber no bigger than Winston's cottage. But what shocked him was that the chamber was cylindrical. The walls were curved into a perfect circle. The ground was a simple, boarded floor, and the walls were dull stones, cut to achieve curvature. Lustre turned to see a soldier dressed in armour peering through an open door. The door was raised about ten feet above the floor, the defining feature of the enclosure where he stood.

"What are you doin' in here, boy? Why were ya walkin' in circles?" The guard growled. Lustre just stood there, flabbergasted, too confused to respond. The guard quickly lost his patience and ordered him towards the door.

"Come here!"

With no other options or exits, Lustre stepped towards the door. The guard grasped Lustre by the wrist and yanked him to the ledge. Lustre stumbled outside, the sun beaming upon his face. He raised his hand to his forehead, shielding his eyes from the sun's glare. He sighted a large flat field on what looked like Bandeira. When he turned around, he was shocked. He was just inside a tower.

The door was level with the grass from the outside, but it was ten feet above the floor from the inside, for a steadier foundation. The guard slammed the door shut and turned to face Lustre. "What were you doing in the tower?"

Lustre stuttered. "Umm…I was…"

He knew the excuse of 'exploring' wouldn't get him out of this one. He had to think of something else fast. "Lost…"

The guard seemed to have bought it. "Lost, eh?"

Lustre nodded unconfidently.

"Well then…What's your name, boy?"

"It'sLustre."

The guard took an eager step forward. He showed an inquisitive smile before saying. "Okay…Mr Lustre. Do you know where you are?"

"Oh! No, I don't. Could you please tell me?"

The guard grasped Lustre by the wrist. "Certainly," he responded. Lustre was led around the tower until they stopped at the other side. The guard pointed towards the horizon where the sun was rising in the east, peering over the hills. In the distance, there were several watchtowers identical to this one. The towers occupied the whole span of his vision, stretching miles along the horizon. Lustre gasped.

"What are all these towers for?" he asked.

"Son, can you see that stone wall lining the horizon in the distance?"

Just beyond all the towers was a wall. It was too distant to make out any finer details. It simply appeared as a smaller black line snaking across the hills.

"Yeah," Lustre replied

"That wall separates green and red. It's called the yellow wall, as when the sun sets, it has a gold-yellow glow. Also, because yellow is the product of red and green, it's pretty genius." The guard explained. Lustre returned his eyes to the guard with a bewildered stare.

"Red and green make yellow…what? What are you talking about?"

The guard let out a disappointed sigh. He leaned in towards Lustre, pointing to the wall once again. "Let me put it in a not-so-metaphorical way. See just beyond that wall? That's Emerald soil. We are on Ruby soil. That wall is where the two collide."

Then, it clicked. Lustre gasped as the realisation hit him. "We are at the border!" He announced.

"Finally." The guard sighed.

"It all makes sense now. I messed up the words when I drank the Gone Gazz, and it sent me to the border," blabbered Lustre.

Unknowingly, Lustre had subconsciously admitted out loud to using a Gone Gazz potion only permitted for guards. Potions were prohibited for citizens in Ruby Nation. It was a law by Emperor Maroon, so subjects couldn't flee the nation easily. You are fine as long as you don't get caught using it. But Lustre had just admitted to using it while in the presence of a guard. This was pretty dumb.

"Gotcha," the guard announced. With no other words said, Lustre's hands were forced behind his back.

"Aye! What are you doing?"

"I knew you weren't lost! You teleported! Gone Gazz is illegal for a peasant like yourself." The guard chuckled.

Lustre was escorted onward, the guard laughing hysterically behind him. The guard moved him forward towards the border wall in the distance. Despite pleading constantly, the guard ignored him. Lustre knew he couldn't worm his way out of this consequence, and no excuse could save him.

"Just let me go!" Lustre demanded.

The guard scoffed mockingly. "And why would I do that? You just admitted to using an illegal potion!"

Lustre thought maybe the guard would be merciful if he told him the merchant who sold the potions had forgotten to mention that they were illegal for folk.

"I didn't know there were illegal potions!"

"Yeah, right, now you know! Muzzle Mud, Gone Gazz, Fazz Fire, Black Essence and all the other potions and stuff are illegal for peasants! If we catch you with them, you're done! Straight to the dungeon, or perhaps maybe the Bandeira Jail, depending on whether you behave," explained the guard.

Lustre stuttered, "Well…Could you at least tell me where you're taking me now?"

"I am taking you to the Captain of the Guard so we can figure out what to do with you."

Before long, they walked a few hundred yards to another tower. They saw a soldier dressed formally in a black uniform with a crimson and black wavire armband. A red robe was draped over his shoulders. He sat on a wooden crate at the foot of the tower, accompanied by two other guards. They all held beer steins, similar to those found at bars like Tether's Tavern.

All three men appeared very cheerful, chatting to each other with cackles of drunken laughter between sips. When Lustre and his escorting guard came into view, the laughter dissipated. They panicked and scrambled to their feet, quickly fixing their uniforms and straightening their posture.

As they all stood there, salvaging their professional appearance. One of them realised that they were still holding a beer stein. They quickly hid it behind their back before tossing it aside.

"Heil Corporal, you surprised us," spoke the red-robed man in the black uniform.

"Sorry Captain, I came here to speak with you."

The man in the black uniform gestured to his accompanying guards to scram. They nodded before gathering their equipment, including the beer steins, and dashing off to the neighbouring watch tower. The captain then enquired, "Who is this…Boy?"

Instead of the guard introducing him, Lustre decided to introduce himself. This would be a lot more genuine and respectful, potentially winning over the captain's respect. It would also prevent the guard from making any false statements about him.

"My name is Lustre, sir," he greeted. Typically, Lustre would offer his hand out to shake, but on this occasion, he couldn't. The captain let off an offended expression and spat. "You will address me as captain, not sir, boy!"

The guard behind Lustre even had to make things worse with an additional teasing remark. "Yes, and you will address me as corporal only, peasant!"

Both angered Lustre. He knew he shouldn't, but he couldn't stop his next phrase slipping from his mouth. "You won't address me a peasant, you reatrit..." he uttered under his breath.

Unfortunately, the captain of the guard heard the curse despite Lustre suppressing his voice.

"Did you just call me...?" The captain now showed clenched teeth. The guard behind Lustre inhaled, also realising how big a mistake Lustre had just made. But instead of fear, the guard felt a smug satisfaction. Lustre didn't respond.

"You little reatrit, do you know whom you're talking to?" the captain shouted, slapping Lustre across the face. He turned to face the corporal and said, "Did you bring this reatrit here just for him to insult me?"

The corporal began to explain. "Oh, he was caught using a prohibited potion. I need your advice. Do I take him to the Bandeira Jail? Or..."

The captain had heard enough and cut the corporal off.

"No, no...Don't take him to jail. Kill him, right here, in front of me..."

Lustre gasped; fear struck. He jerked his body forward, trying to break free from the corporal's strong grasp. He hoped that it would catch the corporal off guard. But no, somehow, the corporal was prepared. With a kick to the back of Lustre's leg, he broke his balance, allowing the corporal to wrestle him back.

"No, you don't." The corporal grinned. After failing to escape, Lustre resorted to pleading. "NO! Please! I am sorry! I didn't mean…"

"TOO LATE!" The captain grinned with a sly smile. Then there was silence. The captain stood before Lustre, staring at him with a cold satisfaction. Sweat ran down Lustre's forehead. He never imagined that this was how he would die.

SHING

Then he heard just about the scariest noise he had ever heard, a faint but shrill sound of a metal blade. This was followed by an evil chuckle from the corporal behind him. Suddenly, Lustre was pulled in closer, a wrapping elbow around his neck in a headlock. This restricted Lustre's movement even further.

That's when a dagger caught Lustre's vision. It appeared at his throat, gently at first. Then the corporal pushed the flat side of the blade firmly into his neck. Not to draw blood, but enough for Lustre to confirm he wasn't bluffing. Lustre squeezed his eyes shut, preparing for the inevitable cut. Strangely, instead of a slice, Lustre felt nothing. He felt the blade lift off his skin. He heard the corporal laughing hysterically, as well as the dagger sliding back into his sheath.

Lustre reopened his eyes.

"Ha! You should have seen your face, boy." The corporal snickered.

The captain of the guard was not laughing. "What are you talking about? Why didn't you cut his neck open?" The captain hissed.

Immediately, the corporal started laughing, then switched his tone. "Wait! Are you telling me this isn't a joke? You want me to kill him?" Lustre noticed the new sense of concern, an uneasiness in the corporal's voice. He wasn't pure evil after all, and there was a speck of mercy in him.

"Yes!" his captain yelled, losing his patience.

"What! I thought it was just to scare him! Do you really want me to kill him? He's just a kid!"

"YES!" the captain boomed.

The corporal couldn't develop an answer before the captain lost his patience. He just fumbled, with his higher-ranking officer beaming at him with frustration in his eyes. "Give me that dagger!" He shouted, lunging forward towards the corporal. His captain reached for the dagger. The guard could not disobey. It was an order! All guards are required to obey those of a higher rank.

Lustre was out of hope, with the captain now wielding the corporal's dagger. There was absolutely nothing he could do now. Just before Lustre was to be killed, the captain paused momentarily to say. "Goodbye, peas-"

Fortunately, he couldn't finish as he was interrupted by the distant cry of his soldiers. It wasn't clear what was bellowed at first, but it was in an alarming tone. Lustre turned his head to see what was happening. Standing on top of the neighbouring watch tower, Lustre saw a guard pointing out over the border wall.

"What now?" the captain called back.

"SACRO SLITHERS!" yelled the guard. Lustre turned his head to see what was happening. A guard was standing on top of the neighbouring watch tower, pointing out over the border wall.

That's when everything erupted into chaos. The captain gasped, dropping the dagger.

The air grew thick and cold with the heavy scent of eel. The atmosphere shifted around them, and the whole field collapsed into shadow. Clouds began to brew just beyond the border wall, their edges tinged with a sickly green hue. Suddenly, the clouds split open, and giant serpents descended toward the towers. This was the first time Lustre had seen these gemotros in such large numbers.

The corporal who had been restraining Lustre had moved on. Instead of worrying about Lustre, he was rallying his troops in the field, frantically screaming. "Everyone Move! Move! Move! To your stations!"

An eerie sense of dread settled in around Lustre as the serpents glided closer and closer towards him. Hundreds of guards emerged from the towers like ants, flooding the fields, wielding shields, spears, and crossbows. Some even stayed in the towers, manning the ballistae mounted at the top. Sacro slithers were much more intimidating in larger numbers. The captain standing before Lustre silently hesitated and said in an emotionless tone.

"How lucky... can one boy be? Your pending death awaits!" The captain cursed while pointing to the flying serpents, then scurried off to join his troops.

Right then, Lustre took his opportunity to run away. Behind him, he could hear the blood-curdling screeches of the serpents, gaping their jaws. The cries of the captain rallying his army of guards could still be heard.

Lustre hadn't reached a safe distance, but his curiosity still couldn't resist looking back. He stopped and turned at the exact moment the sacro slithers arrived. They swooped down, their movements sharp and precise. One by one, guards were carried off their feet into the jaws of the giant serpents.

The guards' screams and helpless cries motivated Lustre to keep running. Ballista bolts began to whizz through the air, and a few guards cried, "Wezdorth Dazzagar," casting lightning bolt spells; most were missing. Some guards abandoned the ballistae, realising the reloading process was far too tedious and slow against such creatures.

Another reason to abandon the towers would soon be apparent, as one sacro slither scathed a tower on the descent, being a victim of the few lucky ballistic bolts. The base of the tower cracked, shifting off balance. The guards on top shrieked with fear and rushed to the ladder. Unfortunately, they wouldn't make it in time. With the foundations weakened, the tower quickly began to tilt. It tipped further and further over until it reached the point of no return. It collapsed, sending a cloud of dust and stone cascading down. It landed with such a loud thud that it rumbled the ground and echoed for miles. It even made Lustre stumble, allowing him to take another glimpse. He only looked for a split second, enough to see all the chaos. Lustre didn't want to look again; it was too much to handle. The brawl of death and destruction baffled his mind.

The majority of guards were now fleeing along with Lustre. The rest were yet to succumb to the realisation that fighting was suicide. The sacro slithers were simply too swift and powerful for humans.

Unfortunately, the sacro slithers noticed the fleeing guards. They picked them off one by one with devastating speed. Their armour glinted in the dawn sunlight, making them easy to spot. Amongst them was Lustre, out in the front. One sacro slither spotted him and dived to snatch him off his feet. Strangely, mid-dive, the sacro slither must have seen that Lustre wasn't wearing any armour, so it was curious rather than furious. So, the gigantic serpent landed right before him instead of scooping him up like the rest.

This stopped Lustre in his tracks. He was startled with fear and had the urge to scream, but he kept it in. Whilst keeping direct eye contact, Lustre slowly reached downwards, ensuring every movement was fluent and calm. He felt around his waist for his dagger. Just as Lustre gripped the handle, the sacro slither lurched forward in a sudden rage. Lustre drew his dagger, but to no use. He was now clamped, trapped between teeth. The gemotro had only nipped him, a saving grace from the weight of its crushing jaws.

However, Lustre was now trapped, but his arms and legs waved freely in the air as they ascended towards the heavens at incredible speed. Lustre watched the field below shrink and shrink with each passing second. Throughout this ordeal, he kept a firm hold on his dagger. Without hesitation, he plunged it down between the beast's eyes. It let out a shriek of pain before losing control.

The celebration was cut short when the very next problem struck him. He and the serpent were now free-falling, spiralling down from what he thought was a terrifying height. He wished he was dreaming; the situation was a true nightmare. Luckily, the contorting gemotro, in agony, released Lustre from its mouth. The ground raced towards him. He could only await his doom until it happened.

THUD

Everything blurred.

His chest and arms ached so bad it woke him from the brief oblivion. Never had his body felt so sore. He couldn't even move without his muscles screaming back at him. He lay on the ground, and a strange calmness took over him, the last moments before death, how his journey had come to an end.

He managed to turn his neck enough to spot the canteen of a Muzzle Mud potion beside him...

Chapter 9

The Crimson Village

The fall had put a gaping crack in the canteen, and Muzzle Mud was spilling from it at an alarming rate.

With his previous recollection of the taste, he knew it would be foul. But he didn't know what to expect as he had never fully drunk it. Hopefully, it would heal him just as it did Winston. He lay there with no other choice, his lungs aching, each breath hissing through his teeth in sudden shallow gasps.

Without other options, he forced himself to endure the horrible taste. In one go, he reached and poured it into his mouth. His expression flinched with sourness as soon as it hit his tongue, but he forced himself to swallow.

He waited… And waited, his body convulsing in agony. From all he knew, he expected an immediate relief of pain, yet no pain relief happened. He was still in agony. Out of nowhere, his muscles tensed. A sudden burning sensation washed over his skin. His nerves tingled, darting up and down his spine. He felt as if his whole body was on fire.

"AHH!"

Lustre writhed on the ground with excruciating pain. The only sound he could hear was the pounding of his heart, along with his voice, muffled with pain and noises from the ongoing battle. His forehead veins bulged, and his face contorted in agony. Finally, after what felt like hours, the pain subsided. He exhaled.

Slowly, he rose. He didn't have enough energy to stand fully, so he crouched there for a few moments to let his body recover. "That was hell," he wheezed.

Fortunately, the Muzzle Mud had a good aftertaste. His whole body was no longer aching. He could even move his legs again. It had worked; the painful part had to be the healing process.

Lustre slowly built up the energy to stand. Because Muzzle Mud was so valuable, and he only stole a finite supply from Winston, he salvaged the punctured canteen, patched it up with some old cloth from his shirt, and stored it in his pocket.

"All right, now where's my..."

During the fall, Lustre had lost his sheath. The buckle must have come loose and fallen from his waist. Fortunately, he found it only a few feet from where he hit the dirt. After reattaching it and securing his dagger, he continued his escape from the border wall.

His journey resumed west. He passed debris and the bodies of many deceased guards, all scattered in the chaos. He tried to avoid looking, particularly after witnessing the decapitated captain. "Just deserts!" thought Lustre. He started a laborious walk across the vast field west; soon, he lost sight of the border behind him. Due to the horror he had witnessed, his senses were numb. Poor Lustre was in a trance, suffering shock from the recent events. He had walked for hours, and he had walked through the night. He had lost all sense of time. The sun rose and set; he just did not care or realise.

He was walking through vast fields of wheat and barley, swaying gently in the breeze. The scene reminded him of the farmlands Rusty and Lustre played in when they escaped the Banderian Forest. His mind turned to a dream state. The air was also fresh and cool, filled with the sweet scent of wildflowers. The colaies chirped peacefully, but Lustre could not sense these beautiful things due to his state of mind.

His body jolted, like snapping out of a dream; he could now see the silhouette of a windmill surrounded by a golden wheat meadow. Lustre adored the countryside. It was so quiet, so peaceful. Each structure told a story and aroused his curiosity. Who owned this particular windmill, and why was it abandoned?

The windmill had seen many rots of age. Its white sails were worn and eroded, their edges chewed by the wind. Impressively, the sails were still turning, and the walls, although rotted and frail, held the windmill together. One wall had even crumpled, exposing the inner scaffolding and support beams. Lustre could feel the windmill's resilience. Little did Lustre know he could relate more to this windmill than he thought. He was abandoned. He now stood alone. His outer walls were shedding, but his sails were still turning.

"Hold on. Farmland is usually on the outskirts of a town, to support the people living there, right?" he thought to himself. "I have to be close to a town." As it turned out, Lustre was correct. Soon, after crossing a majestic, moss-covered stone bridge, which stretched across the rushing Great Ruby River, Lustre walked along a well-travelled road for what he thought was hours. He just was not sure. Guided only by road signs leading the way to Crimson Village.

Before long, the wind carried a new smell, the smell of chimney smoke and roasting grombler. The smell motivated Lustre to keep walking; he had to be close now.

He passed only a few travellers who did not engage in conversation. Just as well, as Lustre's throat was too dry; he just needed a drink of crimson cider or maybe a bite to eat.

They were simple thatched-roof stone-walled huts nestled at the southern edge of the Crimson Forest. Unlike at Banderian Village, the cottages were spaced more evenly rather than cramped together in disorganised clusters. The huts varied in shape and size, and a maze of dirt pathways connected them, most likely carved by the rots of walking.

Lustre smiled at its sight. "Ahh! Finally." He sighed contentedly, "The Crimson Village."

The first thing that greeted him was the sound of laughter and drunken singing echoing through the streets. The people causing the racket were guards, stumbling in groups. The song they sang was barely recognisable, but Lustre found it familiar, even with their voices highly out of tune. Lustre moved aside to let them stumble on by. As he waited patiently, he couldn't help but notice a small bundle dangling from one guard's belt.

Being in such a clumsy and vulnerable state, the guard wouldn't even notice. Lustre didn't have long to hesitate. So, he took the risk and snatched it. He sped down a village sideroad with the clueless guards still laughing and singing behind him. After arriving at a safe distance, he untied the bundle and marvelled at its contents. It was only a small bundle in a brown rag. But what was inside made Lustre grin madly.

A handful of shiny rubies. He counted about twenty tiny rubies.

"Jackpot." Lustre beamed. He quickly closed the bundle and stuffed it into his pocket.

"That should get me a hot meal and drink. I need to find a place."

Lustre wandered through the streets, his eyes exploring the cottages and taverns lining the dirt pathways. Everything was so calm. All the men were dressed quite commonly in brown slacks and white button-up shirts, either barefoot or wearing old clogs. Lustre had been to the Crimson Village once or twice before, but he hadn't been enough to know his way around. On the other hand, the women wore long, brightly coloured dresses, often overlaid with an apron and were accompanied by children. Lustre could fit right in with his clothes, which were almost identical in fashion except for his leather boots. All the villagers kept to themselves as they went about their daily lives, never initiating conversation, especially with guards.

"I can't remember the Crimson Village being so peaceful. The last time I came here, it was infested with pickpockets, market criers and drunk people."

A sudden commotion broke out of nowhere. A woman burst through the door of a nearby tavern, gripping a man by the ear. The man's face was drowsy and confused, while the woman looked angrier than ever. The beautiful woman gave the man a hard shove, causing him to tumble down the entrance stairs and out into the street.

"And stay out!" she scowled. She spat at the ground before stomping back inside. Lustre was clueless as to what had just happened. His glance veered downwards to the man. He lay motionless on the ground, letting out a moan of pain. "Are you all right?" Lustre queried. The man could only respond with a peeved moan. Lustre decided not to worry about him. Instead, he turned to face the tavern from which the man had been expelled.

Besides the porch and stairs, something caught Lustre's attention. Suspended just above the door was a wooden sign. A striking sketch of a beer stein with a bubbling foam was upon the sign. Below the image were the words '*Tether's Tavern*' and a catchy slogan.

'*Crimson cider is our provider*', Lustre was excited.

"Perfect! My favourite inn. I can get a meal here."

Lustre walked on past the man and invited himself into the tavern. Inside, the atmosphere completely shifted; his smile looked out of place. The room was dim and gloomy, with only a few patrons.

It wasn't how Lustre remembered Tether's Tavern. His first time at this tavern was three rots ago. He was with Rusty, who had convinced him to come inside. He'd never been inside a tavern, so he didn't know what to expect. The first thing that struck him back then was the raucous clamour of voices, laughter, and music echoing off the stone walls. The air was thick with the mingling smell of smoke, spiced ale, and savoury meats roasting over the fireplace in the corner.

The sound of cutlery and drinks clinking together and the occasional raucous cheer filled the room. Above it all, the most memorable part was the blaring music, the cheery sound of a squealing fiddle. The crowd clapped along with the fiddle and then roared with cheers when they soared into a new song.

Lustre remembered when they played his favourite song, '*Daradero went down to Ravena*'. He and Rusty danced together for hours, prancing around the tavern and singing along, until they both sat down and laughed at tales from an old book, '*Dark Ruby Spells*'.

Despite the noise and chaos, there was a sense of peace. It's as if everyone there shared a desire to leave behind the troubles of the outside world and revel in the pleasures of their friends, food, and Crimson Cider. Those were good times. Now, Lustre made his way to the front bar. The whole room was filled with a silent, uneasy ambience.

Lustre slowly made his way to the front of the room, passing a man and a woman sitting at a table, both observing him with an unsettling gaze. He gagged at the scent of stale liquor and musty wood; he didn't remember it smelling so revolting. The tavern's interior was lit only by scattered candlelight, one for every table. Lustre arrived at the bar, propping himself on one of the wooden stools.

As he sat, he couldn't help but feel a sense of uneasiness around him. He gazed around, admiring the many shields, weapons, and paintings that decorated the walls. He even saw the old bookshelf in the corner. It hadn't changed, except it was missing a few books. The tables and chairs were not as he remembered; they were rough, layered with dust, and prone to wobbling.

Despite the chilly atmosphere, Lustre still kept his spirits high. He coughed loudly to grab the barmaid's attention. Coincidentally, the same woman had just booted the man out. A beautiful young, blue-eyed lady with long chocolate brown hair wearing a white-blue dress. She turned to face Lustre with an intent gaze.

Nervous sweat built up on his forehead as he waited at the bar, dreaming of such a moment. The patrons, mostly gruff-looking men with beards and ragged clothing, turned to look at him. They were a rough bunch, their eyes scanning him up and down as if they were sizing him up.

Her gaze was unsettling rather than soft and enchanting, as anticipated.

Fortunately, Lustre knew her. "Hi, Tether," Lustre asked confidently. He hoped Tether would return a smile, but she didn't; instead, she moaned with annoyance. "Don't you remember me?"

"Look, kid. I see dozens of people every day, and I don't have the time to remember them all."

Lustre frowned, and his heart sank. "Okay then…I will have a glass of sweet crimson cider, please," he softly requested.

"Right, three small rubies," Tether replied.

Taking a deep breath, Lustre unravelled the bundle and counted out three rubies. He placed them on the counter before Tether. Tether silently scooped them up, tossed them into a drawer below, and then turned away to prepare the drink. Lustre waited with anticipation; his mouth was already watering.

After a few seconds, Tether returned to Lustre with a stein of fresh, cold crimson cider. Lustre eagerly picked it up. "I haven't tasted this in rots. Here we go." He was full of anticipation.

He raised it to his mouth and took a swig. Then he lowered it back down, wiping his sleeve across his mouth. He felt a mixture of emotions, but the main thing he knew was that he wasn't satisfied. For some reason, it just tasted off. It wasn't the glorious liquor he could remember. It was just a cold, bitter drink with a sour aftertaste. It felt like there was an ingredient missing. Lustre gazed around him. He felt so alone. The drink just didn't taste as good when he was by himself. He got up from his barstool, and for the first time, he didn't finish a glass of crimson cider.

"Well… I thought that would cheer me up. I suppose I'm not eating today." Lustre left the tavern disappointed.

The first thing he saw was the man still lying on the street. At that point, Lustre thought he should do something. Obviously, the man was too drunk to get up or even know where he was. His bewildered gaze as Lustre approached him told it all.

"Hey, mate. Are you okay?" asked Lustre, kneeling before him.

"W-Water...Please," mumbled the man.

Though the man's face was filthy and overcome with drunkenness, something felt familiar. It wasn't anybody he knew, but he could swear he had seen that face somewhere.

Lustre had no water. He didn't know how to help. "I don't have any water..." Lustre said.

The man gazed up at him. "Please...I need water and... Wav-va-wire stella lo-compo...blood orchids."

Lustre was puzzled; why would the man need blood orchids? "Huh?"

"Blood orchids!" the man repeated.

That's when Lustre noticed a dark red splotch on the man's brown shirt. Since his shirt was brown, it was hard to see at first. Lustre gasped.

"What...What's this big stain?" He unbuttoned the man's shirt. Beneath, he saw a gaping wound, the source of the blood on his shirt. The cut had been partially covered with a rag wrapped around his torso, likely a previous attempt to stop the bleeding.

"Peroa," Lustre cursed.

Everything made sense now. The man was not just drunk but delirious and severely wounded. He must have been trying to numb the pain with alcohol and blood orchids.

"Don't worry...I can help," reassured Lustre.

Without hesitation, Lustre reached into his pocket and retrieved the cracked canteen of Muzzle Mud he had been saving. He tilted the man's head back and poured it into his mouth. The man moaned with disgust at the taste, but Lustre kept urging the man to drink more.

Once the canteen was empty, Lustre waited for the pain to kick in, which he knew was a sign of healing. As expected, the man screeched in agony. He clutched his stomach and squirmed around. Lustre quickly pinned him back down with comforting words. "It's all right…It will be over soon."

Eventually, the man relaxed. Though the rag was still drenched in blood, the puncture wound beneath it was healed and no longer bleeding. The man's eyes darted in confusion until he saw Lustre's face.

Instead of gratitude, the man sprang up with sudden rage. He wrapped his hands around Lustre's neck, forcing him to stumble backwards. Lustre was utterly dazzled. Instinctively, Lustre tried to pry the man's hands off, but his grip was far too strong. Lustre was only a teenager; this man was a strong hunter and thirty-six rots old.

Lustre lost his balance almost instantly. He tumbled onto his back, the man still squeezing his throat. "You little reatrit!" The man shrieked. He forced his knee into Lustre's chest, restricting his breathing even further. Lustre's head was spinning, and his lungs were throbbing. His mind was tied in knots; the only thing it bellowed was 'Breathe! Breathe! Breathe!'

Yet when he tried, it only grew more difficult. Lustre knew he couldn't escape from this without fighting. He brought his hand up and shoved it into the man's face.

SMACK

Though breathing was impossible, he managed to punch the man in the nose. The man was launched backwards, freeing his neck. The first thing he did was gasp for air. Before he was caught off guard again, Lustre staggered and held his hands up, ready to cut the man in half with a Bifurcation spell.

Usually, Lustre would never even think of using such a spell; he never has, but he was prepared this time. Ruby magic held dark, powerful spells that were forgotten in time, except for just a few souls. There was an attempt to erase such dark magic spells from Gemotroplis' history during the era: 1st.

All records of dark spells were destroyed, and the teachings were forbidden. Dark spells were erased for Ruby folk, by era: 2nd, but strangely enough, he'd read such a spell from the old dusty book in Tether's Tavern, readily available to all patrons. Little did Lustre know that Bifurcation was forbidden dark magic.

After landing on his back, the man tried to return to his feet. He inevitably gave up halfway and dropped to his knees. Lustre slowly approached the man, very tempted to split him in half.

"What is your problem?" Lustre called out.

"I'm just returning the favour!"

Lustre was still absolutely clueless as to what the man was babbling about.

"What are you saying? I have never seen you before in my life!" Lustre said.

The man scoffed. "Yeah, and you have never stabbed anybody before, either!"

That's when it hit him. Lustre was shocked. "Wait…are you that guy that I…"

"Yes! I was the guy you stabbed in the Crimson Forest!" He continued speaking. "That isn't how you treat somebody who saved your life. I defended you from those guards. Instead of saying thank you, all you did was run off! When I came to check on you again, you stabbed me!"

"Hold on…You were the one who put out my fire, started attacking and shot at me! I stabbed you in self-defence!"

The man sighed with disappointment. "I restrained you because I saw that you had a knife. I put your fire out because fires attract wavires! Yes, I shot at you. Look, didn't you see my many warning signs? I put them up around the forest. Is my handwriting bad, or did you not take it seriously?"

"Messy," stuttered Lustre.

Before waiting for Lustre to respond, the man rose and began hobbling towards him.

"Look." He said, "We both have our reasons, but I am still mad because this dagger wound is still bleeding and probably going to maim me. So, I need-"

Lustre interrupted, "Uhh…No, it's not."

"What are you talking about?" The man glanced down at his stomach and gasped, "Hey! My wound, it's all healed!" The man cheered.

"See? We are even. I saved you, and you saved me." Lustre said.

The man's eyes twinkled with gratitude. "Thank you." He smiled. "Haven't we got off to a wrong start? Let me introduce myself." The man started, with a new sound of friendship, "My name is Jackie. Jackie Fletcher. I hunt gemotros in the Crimson Forest."

"Uhh…I am Lustre. I am a ruby miner back in Bandeira." The man reached out and spontaneously started shaking Lustre's hand.

"Ok, then. So, we are cool now? No more strangling, stabbing or stunning?" said Jackie.

Before nodding, Lustre devoted the next fifteen seconds of his life trying to pronounce that last phrase, "S-dangling, wait! Strangling…S-stabbing or stopping, DAMMIT! That's such a tongue twister."

Jackie chuckled, entertained by Lustre's struggle. Lustre laughed along with him until he remembered. "Oh, I almost forgot. Before I came here, I was looking for somebody. I thought he was down in the Banderian Village, but I got lost when I tried to journey there. I am on the run from the Ruby guards and have witnessed horrible things." Lustre shared a short story.

"Me too. Who was it?" asked Jackie.

"Oh…He is a grumpy old dirtbag who stole something of mine. His name is Winston."

Jackie's eyes widened. "Hold on…Winston? My brother is named Winston!"

"Really?" Lustre gasped, responding to this ironic fact.

"Yep. I have never seen him steal anything before. Where did you say he was?"

"I am confident he is at the Banderian Village," Lustre said.

"Well then, let's go there and find him. I will gladly come along with you." Jackie insisted.

Before anything else was said, there was a loud bang. Lustre felt a tsunami of heat wash over his body. Following the heat was a surge of wind from behind him. There was total silence for a moment.

Lustre had momentarily gone deaf. An immense ringing blared in his ears; the sound was so loud it was the only thing he could hear. Jackie stared behind Lustre, his mouth hanging open in disbelief. When Lustre turned to see what was behind him, he reacted the same.

A giant fire cloud shrouded the distant parts of the village. The fire burned brighter than the sun, even piercing closed eyelids. An eerie orange light washed over the village, giving everything a saturated appearance. Lustre was lost for words. He even blinked a few times to make sure he wasn't hallucinating. After a few seconds, the fiery cloud died in intensity, leaving a looming tower of smoke in its place. The fire had consumed half the village, reducing every hut in its path to charred piles of rubble.

Villagers began to flee from the village. "Terrorism!" they heard a passing woman scream. "We're under attack," they heard another.

"That's not a Ruby spell," Jackie stated.

Lustre turned around to face Jackie.

"Come on, Lustre. Let us get out there, and I need to help those people." Jackie tightened his belt before turning and racing towards the smoke.

Lustre wanted to flee. Yet, for some reason, he couldn't help but feel a hint of cowardice. All those helpless villagers needed assistance. What he learnt about the feeling of guilt many rots ago, it never leaves you. Lustre couldn't break the feeling and inevitably bolted after Jackie, directly disobeying his fear.

Once again, he found himself running towards danger in an almost identical situation to the one in Bandeira days prior. Except this time, it wasn't a misunderstanding with Rusty; it was actual terrorism. Lustre went through the village; the closer he got, the more the devastation was revealed.

The smell of charred wood and smoke still lingered in the air as Lustre passed the few surviving villagers slowly emerging from the rubble. Their faces were etched with shock, sorrow, and despair. Those who hadn't fled wandered around. Some wept openly, while others stared in stunned silence at what had become of their beautiful village.

The once-thriving streets were now reduced to a desolate wasteland littered with debris and bodies. Huts had collapsed, and fire was still flickering amongst the ruins. The village market square was at the foot of a huge stone cathedral, a hub of activity and commerce, and was now a torched wasteland with only the remnants of it remaining. The cathedral was the only structure still standing due to its stone walls.

However, the blaze had charred and blackened its exterior, making it barely recognisable. Lustre approached the town square, where he saw Jackie comforting a mysterious figure amongst the bodies. Before leaping into action, Lustre hid in the rubble, overlooking Jackie.

"How could you do this?" Jackie yelled. There was a flicker of light, and Jackie was thrown through the air by an invisible force before landing somewhere out of sight. This prompted Lustre to stand up, exposing himself to the figure. Lustre instantly regretted this, as he had been spotted.

The first spell that came to his mind was the stun spell re-tentro-mjana; however, he wasn't readily trained in that spell. It wasn't going to work anyway, as he was far too distant. So, he decided to use the second spell that came to mind, a lightning bolt, although he was unfamiliar with this spell as well. He thrust his hands at the figure, shouting, "Wezdorth Dazzagar!" Surprisingly, Lustre has no trouble with this phrase. Sometimes, he had moments of excellent verbal pronunciation.

Adrenaline rushed to his clawed fingertips, igniting a minor *CRACK* that rippled outwards through the air—the lightning shot from his hand, more of a light than a bolt. The ground before him splashed like water, shooting a cloud of dirt and loose debris into the air. The figure, whoever it may be, had little time to react before the hit consumed them. Lustre threw his hands up into the air in celebration.

"I can't believe I just did that." He gasped. "I just defeated a Topaz terrorist."

Before Lustre stepped out into the open to assess the damage, he was caught off guard by another flash within the haze, still settling from his work. Suddenly, gigantic tree vines shot up from the ground, entangling around Lustre's ankles.

"Peroa!" Lustre cursed.

Before he could grab his dagger, the vines snaked up his waist and snatched his hands. He was wrapped in place.

Oh, no, "Help!" Lustre cried.

Slowly, the figure emerged from the haze, seemingly unscathed by Lustre's spell. The dust and dim lighting obscured the figure's face, as all the smoke had completely blocked the sun. Lustre could only watch him walk closer and closer. Lustre attempted to break free right before the figure's face appeared. He tried to wriggle his hands free and even cried for help again, but it was in vain. Eventually, the figure arrived only a yard's distance from Lustre. Lustre glanced up to see Winston's smug face.

"Well, look who it is," Winston announced.

"WINSTON!" Lustre bellowed; the realisation gave him a surge of anger. He wanted to wrestle free from a vine to punch him in the face.

"Don't try to break free; I've found it's impossible. An Emerald spell, Emede Vinato, permanently binds your opponent with tree-strangling Emedella vines. You can only free yourself with a dagger or some weed-killer potion," Winston proclaimed.

"I don't care, you black-hearted reatrit! You better give back my jewel!" Lustre scowled.

Instead of being offended, Winston laughed. "You mean this jewel?"

He took the jewel from his cloak and held it high. He boasted with a taunting look, prompting Lustre to hiss, "Yes. That jewel! Give it back!"

"No Lustre! You don't understand. You are too young and immature for something this powerful. I took it from you because whoever possesses this jewel has the power of Gemotronia, a goddess! It cannot be in the wrong hands."

"How dare you call me immature!" Lustre spat. "How are you any more responsible than me? You just destroyed the Crimson Market!"

Winston stepped back defensively. "No! That was an accident! This jewel can be uncontrollable and play with your mind!" He argued. Winston momentarily turned away from Lustre, scratching his chin. He gazed down at the jewel in his hands and considered the situation. "I can't let the emperor know about this. The only way to destroy this thing is to throw it away somewhere where it will never be found."

He thought for a moment before determining, "I know! I could drop it down into a wavire burrow! Nobody would ever think to climb down and retrieve it there!" But then, an even more cunning idea struck his mind. "No, wait! I will travel to Ravena and throw it into the volcano. It will be gone for good. It would be an octave of travel, but I will do anything to stop others from wielding such power." Winston was talking to himself.

Unfortunately, Lustre heard only some of Winston's plot; the vines occupied him. "THROW IT AWAY?" Lustre shrieked, "It's mine! You don't get to decide anything, you elder-moron..."

Before Lustre could finish his curse, Winston tightened his fingers around the jewel, prompting it to expel more green light. Three more vines shot up from the ground and wrapped around his mouth, muffling his last word. Probably for the better, as what he intended to say would have agitated Winston further.

"But first, I have no choice but to kill you, Lustre, so you can never reveal anything. Also, because you are annoying," Winston said, aiming it at Lustre. "I am sorry, goodbye... Lustre."

Lustre almost choked on his tongue after hearing that last part. He tried to scream, but the vines covering his mouth made it impossible. The jewel erupted with light once again, growing rapidly in intensity. This time, its glow hued a bright blue. The light blinded Lustre, even flaring beneath his eyelids. It was too bright for his eyes to handle, like staring straight into the sun.

The light consumed his vision.

He couldn't move, he couldn't scream, he could only wait.

He was a goner, for sure.

He was dead…

He could not possibly escape this time.

SMASH

Out of nowhere, there was a loud, sickening sound of shattering glass. Then, the jewel began to dim back down. The jewel had temporarily blinded Lustre's eyes. While recovering from what he had just endured, Lustre saw that Winston had frozen. He looked disorientated and drowsy, almost like he had forgotten where he was. Inevitably, he lost balance and fell forward, face down into the dirt.

Standing behind Winston stood Jackie, holding the neck of a shattered bottle. Jackie's face was riddled with cuts and bruises, with one gash scored across his forehead. With blood trickling down his cheek, Jackie still smiled.

"I hope I didn't hit him too hard." He chuckled.

Lustre let out a cry of joy. Jackie could tell Lustre was overjoyed, even with the vines muffling his words. Jackie limped over and helped untangle and cut the vines.

"I thought I was going to die."

Jackie responded, "I thought so too!"

Now free, Lustre quickly scuttled over to Winston and snatched the jewel back. He grinned with satisfaction before stating, "I am not letting anybody else steal this jewel from me again."

Jackie turned back to face Lustre. "I still don't understand," looking confused. "How did my brother do all this? How did he cast foreign spells? I know he isn't Topaz, Emerald or evil at heart."

"No, he isn't. He was using this jewel. We believe it's the ancient heart of Queen Gemotronia," explained Lustre.

"Wait…What? Heart of Gemotronia? It was destroyed over a thousand rots ago!" Jackie queried.

"I know. I am just as confused as you are. But there is no time to explain. I need to head towards the palace. I didn't go there earlier because I feared guards would recognise me. It should be fine now."

"Okay then… I will go with you?"

"What about him?" Lustre pointed at Winston lying face down in the dirt.

"He will wake up soon," Jackie said, disgusted by his brother's actions.

"Okay then, as long as you know where you're going, Lustre, let's go!" Jackie motioned towards the village outskirts.

Lustre hadn't had the time to build any trust with Jackie; besides, he was a man who had shot at him in Crimson Forest and then tried to strangle him outside the tavern just moments ago. Not the kind of bloke one should travel with, he thought. It just didn't seem wise. However, Jackie just saved him. It was time to leave, and he needed to rush, so he agreed.

A squad of Ruby guards, now sober, presented themselves. They just stood frozen in the middle of the market square, in awe of the witnessed destruction, bodies of people lying everywhere. Still coming to grips with the situation, the guards did not notice the pair leave.

Before long, the two left the partly ruined Crimson Village. Winston was still lying in the street.

As they were entering the Crimson Forest. Lustre asked, "Why are we going back into the forest?"

"Well, at the moment, it's a safe option. But the forest is like a maze. I must check where I'm going. Let us find out," Jackie said.

Lustre raised an eyebrow. "How?"

"I have this genius method. Many rots ago, I left several hidden chests scattered around Crimson Forest. I filled those chests with gear as a precaution in an emergency." Jackie explained.

"Hold on..." Lustre interrupted. "I found a chest in Crimson Forest... And I found a map and this dagger."

Chapter 10

Friends and Foes

Jackie chuckled warmly.

"Well…You're lucky! Does this dagger have my name on it?"

Lustre drew the dagger from his waist and examined the handle.

"Jackie Fletcher! Yeah, it does."

"Well, what do you know?"

They continued a bit further into the forest until trees shrouded every direction. Jackie stopped with a gleam of confidence.

"Right here." He stopped with his hands on his hips.

"Where?"

"See that tree with the ancient symbol on it? I remember hiding a chest there." Lustre glanced at the tree Jackie was referring to. Carved into the bark was a large cross, obviously of a religious nature. "Ancient symbol? That's a cross! That probably means somebody is buried there!"

"Oh!" Jackie did seem surprised. "Whatever, that's where I hid the chest."

Lustre rolled his eyes and began scavenging around the tree, searching for a chest. The only thing at the foot of the tree was shrubbery. Interestingly, directly below the symbol was a cluster of blood orchids. They all seemed quite dull and droopy, the petals beginning to shrivel from a lack of water. Lustre noticed them but didn't pick them as they looked half dead.

"There's nothing. No chest!" Lustre concluded.

Jackie took a moment to think.

"Hmm, well, do you have a shovel?"

Lustre laughed sarcastically.

"Is that a joke? I am not digging!"

"We need that chest, or we'll remain lost," Jackie said.

"Yeah! You won't find the chest down there. You're probably going to find actual remains!" Lustre was thinking it was a grave.

Then out of nowhere, it hit him, literally. A small crimson seed must have detached from the branches. It fell from the tree and plonked right onto Jackie's head. Jackie moaned with annoyance, rubbing his head. He gazed upwards and saw something else.

The chest was wedged firmly between two branches, roughly twenty feet above the ground. The wood had been exposed to harsh winds and rain for so long that it had aged to a filthy brown colour, which blended into the tree.

"Of course!" Jackie glanced up. "It's in the tree!"

"How in Gemotroplis are we going to get up there?" pondered Lustre.

"Good question."

They both stood silently for a moment, developing a new plan. Jackie ended up going with the first idea.

"Are you any good at climbing?" he asked.

Lustre replied. "Not really. I'm not good at anything. I'm not a good fighter, swimmer, climber, or even a good friend-"

"Ok, I didn't ask for your life story." Jackie refused to look away from the chest in case he lost sight of it. "Surely there is a spell you can cast that can knock that chest down."

That's when Lustre got an idea. He took out the jewel and aimed it up at the tree. His eyes squinted, funnelling all his focus into his hand. Jackie was intrigued.

The inner light swelled, emitting a beautiful yellow. It glowed almost hypnotically, snagging Jackie's attention.

Gradually, the wind picked up. It was only a breeze at first, but it didn't take long to evolve into a storm. It came with violent gusts, sweeping the ground around them. Jackie's robe flailed as they watched the jewel glow ever brighter.

The wind grew strong enough to shake the trees. They all swayed back and forth, littering the ground with leaves. The tree before them rocked, but the chest didn't slip free; it was lodged tight.

Lustre was certain this would knock the chest down, but the tree proved him wrong.

"Why did you put it so high and difficult to free?" complained Lustre.

"Oh, I put it up there almost three rots ago; the tree was much shorter. It has grown since then."

After a few more seconds, Lustre gave up, annoyed yet impressed with the tree's stubbornness. The wind dissipated almost immediately, settling back into a soft breeze.

"Dammit!" Lustre spat.

"Hey, that jewel thing is very cool! What did you say it does again?"

"I am confident that it allows the wielder to cast spells of every type, no matter their nation."

"Woah, that's very powerful," Jackie replied in amazement.

"I know. That's the reason I'm travelling to the palace. To show the emperor and trade it for my friend's release and thousands of rubies! Maybe even a palace or two for me."

A few moments later, they both began to get desperate. Lustre had refused to climb the tree, claiming he was poor at climbing. The real reason was that he was afraid of heights.

So, convinced he could do it, Jackie attempted to climb the tree himself. He approached the tree and began his climb. He started by gripping the bark and pulling himself up. However, that approach was doomed from the start. The bark was too weak to handle his weight and only shed off and crumbled as he tried to lift himself. He thought a running start might be better. "Watch this," he said to Lustre, confidently sprinting towards the tree.

With the additional speed boost, he clambered six feet higher than before. But he didn't secure a strong grip and slid back down to the trunk, bark again flying. Jackie attempted this again and again, failing every time. After the fifth unsuccessful attempt, Lustre lost patience.

"Stand back. I am going to knock it down." Lustre walked up to the tree and held his hands before it. Sweat beaded on his forehead as he fixed his eyes on the trunk.

"Gamber Goth-Gorian." He whispered the incantation under his breath. Before Jackie could take cover, a fireball struck the tree, sending a blizzard of splinters whizzing in every direction like shrapnel.

The tree was completely engulfed in flames. As Jackie dived for cover, shielding his face, Lustre stood there with pride. The base of the tree took the impact, threatening its balance. Even with its incredibly sturdy roots anchoring it into the soil, it began to tilt.

The explosion shattered the outer bark, exposing the inner redwood. Though incredibly vibrant, this wood was also incredibly tough. Crimson wood was notorious for being virtually indestructible; some considered it red iron. But because it was so rich in oil, it would only take a few minutes to reduce to charcoal at the mercy of a flame.

Ultimately, the tree collapsed. Its base couldn't handle the stress any longer and snapped, leaving only a burnt tree stump. The whole top half plunged, landing with a deafening thud.

"Ha! Yes, finally." Lustre cheered, throwing his hands into the air.

Jackie stood up and dusted himself off. "I have to say, I am impressed. I never knew a knockdown spell could do that." He smiled.

After wriggling the chest free from the burning tree, Jackie kneeled before it, flipping the latch up.

Lustre felt a sense of anticipation rising within him as he stared over Jackie's shoulder. The old, rusty hinges groaned in protest as Jackie lifted the lid, revealing the contents hidden within.

The musty smell of time-worn fabric and aged wood wafted up to their nostrils, reminding them that this chest had not been opened in a long time. As they peered inside, Lustre's eyes were greeted by a collection of dusty relics, all bundled amongst the folds of moth-eaten cloth. An old, leather-bound journal, its pages yellowed with age, was among them.

"What's this?" Lustre said, reaching down for the journal.

Jackie was silent. Lustre examined the cover page, his curiosity sparkling at the patterns and designs decorating it. The cover featured a title written in a foreign language. Jackie replied, "It's just an old book," and placed it aside.

They also found a tarnished silver pocket watch and a matching silver chain inside. Its face was cracked, and its hands were frozen. It was made in Sapphire Nation, an inventive folk.

Apart from the second hand, which kept twitching if winded, it was trapped in a never-ending rhythmic struggle to move forward. Along with the watch and journal, there was a damp bottle of crimson cider, a small piece of rope, and perhaps most importantly, a map partially soggy from moisture.

Lustre picked the map up, satisfied.

"Well…There's the map I made," Jackie said.

Lustre slowly unravelled it, careful not to tear the damp paper accidentally. The only thing of use was the map. The rest of the junk was tossed back into the chest except for the journal, which Jackie kept for some reason.

Lustre held the map before his eyes, trekking ahead of Jackie. He pinpointed where the Crimson Village was to determine how far the Ruby Palace was. Fortunately, according to this map, it was only about thirty miles northeast.

* * *

The whole region of Crimson Forest was bounded by giant snow-capped mountains to the west, which arose from a vast rocky field. The mountains gave a source to the Great Ruby River. It carved its way through the hills, snaking across huge stone valleys and, in spots, giving the land a flush of greenery. The river was fast and powerful; its northern source was the place where it was strongest and most dangerous.

Because the river passes through the rugged mountains, it is full of jagged rock; anything caught in its flow is swept away or shredded up in the rapids. Fallen trees are carried down the great river through Crimson Forest, passing the village until finally weaving through the plains of Bandeira, ending at Crimson Bay. In folk tales, the people of Crimson Village discuss how they fought against the raging river and built dams and bridges. One famous tale exists about 'Olde Hickory' and how he built the ancient dam, which still stands outside Crimson Village. He calmed the Great Ruby River.

* * *

Using the map, they walked for hours. Jackie safely led Lustre through a maze of secret forest paths to an uncharted section of Ruby Nation, referred to as 'The Ruby Plains' or even simply 'the Plains'.

The wind was howling. Lustre could faintly see the winding blue river glinting in the distance. To break the silence of walking, Jackie sparked a conversation that Lustre was reluctant to take part in.

"So, how did you end up meeting my brother?"

Lustre responded with a peeved grunt. "I am trying to focus on the view."

"I know, but I have never seen Winston act evil."

Lustre attempted to change the subject. "So, why did you want to come with me? It is a long journey, and it seems strange that you are so willing."

"Oh…well, before you found me, I was wounded and lost my gear. I usually buy all my gear from this guy in Royal Ruby Town. Normally, I would use Fazz Fire to teleport without needing a map or anything. But I was all out. So, I thought I would go with you, considering we're together," Jackie explained.

"Oh…okay then."

The story seemed genuine, but Lustre wouldn't let his guard down yet. Maybe it was just an aftershock from Winston's experience, but he couldn't let anybody else, particularly his brother, gain his trust. For some reason, Jackie just kept tingling his senses. He had a gut feeling that something was off. Lustre had learnt from the last time. Once he was vulnerable, the instant he fell asleep, bang! He would wake up with the jewel missing from his pockets and Jackie gone from sight. He would not make the same mistake twice.

With each step, the terrain grew steeper and more treacherous. Jagged rocks jutted like teeth, threatening to trip them at any moment. They were now ascending some foothills. Lustre pressed on, determined to push through the harsh terrain, even if it meant ditching Jackie.

Jackie had started lagging as the sun began to dip below the border mountains, casting a fiery glow over the landscape. The strain of the journey was taking its toll, and his pace slowed. They both knew they would need to rest and eat soon, but Lustre knew sleeping next to a thieving Fletcher was stupid.

The dusk sky had become a vibrant canvas of dazzling oranges, purples, and pinks, all bleeding into one another. It was so beautiful that Lustre paused his journey to admire the picture below. He could see the treetops of Crimson Forest, the great river cutting through all the beauty of the landscape, right to the border mountains on the horizon. The sun was setting, and Lustre's reflective pause gave Jackie time to catch up.

As the day's light faded, shadows took over. The cliff peaks cast long, dark silhouettes. Lustre and Jackie looked tiny and insignificant when standing against these eerie shadows. The sun finally slipped away. The stars began to twinkle above, and a crisp, cool breeze blew.

"Wow, the sun went down fast," Jackie said. He was tired and suggested, "Maybe we should camp here for the night. My legs are killing me."

"No, we must keep going north."

Jackie called out with a face of drowsiness mixed with panic.

"Please, can we just stop for a few minutes? I can build a fire and find food! There are no wavires in these foothills of Ruby Nation."

Lustre moaned with annoyance, rubbing his eyes. "Fine, then. But we can't sleep. We will stop for maybe an hour, and then we must keep moving."

Jackie gave off a smile filled with gratitude. "Thank you."

Searching for a suitable resting spot, they found a small clearing beside a huge boulder. It provided a barrier from the wind and had no jagged rocks nearby.

After they had gotten comfortable, Jackie wandered off to gather some firewood.

"I must protect the jewel." Lustre reminded himself.

After half an hour, Jackie returned to Lustre, cradling a huge pile of sticks and a lepus, a large rabbit-like creature. He knelt and arranged the sticks into a tepee formation. Jackie had collected a handful of dry shrubbery, which made perfect kindling. He nestled it underneath the sticks and stood back. He skinned the lepus and began preparing to cook. Jackie knew it would be bland without salt or its substitute, the crushed flower, a fluro flutter. Lepus was no delicacy, but it had much meat, enough for two.

"Okay, Lustre, could you please start the fire?"

Lustre lifted an eyebrow. "Why? Can't you? The spell is paxta-holla"

"Yeah, I know, I'm tired; please do it!"

Lustre shrugged, "All right then."

He aimed his hands at the fire, "Paxta-holla!"

With a flash, the kindling flickered to life.

As the flames took hold, they began to crackle and hiss, sending sparks flying into the night sky. The wood slowly began to catch, the embers glowing bright red as they grew hotter.

The orange light emitted by the fire cast shadows on the surrounding rocks, reminding Lustre of being in the mines for some reason. It was like the glow of the lanterns flickering inside their tunnel.

Jackie skewered the lepus, allowing it to cook over the fire. He occasionally rotated it to ensure it was evenly cooked. The fire and a warm meal were a welcome respite from the cold hilltop air, and Jackie especially huddled close to it, soaking up all its heat. The fire burned steadily, giving Lustre time to rest his legs. They both sat there blanketed in its warmth, cutting and eating meat.

Lustre, now with a full stomach, broke the silence. "Gone Gazz would be useful right now. I mean, we could teleport to the palace."

"Oh, that reminds me. Do you mind if I brew over the fire? It's for my hunting," Jackie asked.

Lustre was always curious to see new things. "Sure."

Jackie rummaged through his cloak, pulling out a small pouch of herbs, a jar of clear liquid and a tiny glass tube. "These are the only two ingredients I have left." After placing the jar amongst the coals, Jackie explained that he was creating Acerbo-ironia. Lustre had no clue what he was talking about, but he was intrigued nonetheless.

He set to work sprinkling the pouch of herbs into the jar. The herbs began to sizzle almost immediately, releasing a bitter scent. Then, Jackie poured the tube contents into the jar, causing the jar to bubble and froth. After that, Jackie sat back down.

"So…What does this acerb…be…be-ironia do?" mumbled Lustre.

"Acerbo-ironia." Jackie corrected.

"Whatever, what does it do?"

"Well." Jackie cleared his throat.

"It is an acidic formula, not for drinking. It can melt through pretty much anything. If you pour just a little on any surface, it will dissolve right through, chewing away anything until it has formed a huge sizzling hole."

Lustre gasped, "That's incredible!"

"Yeah. The only exception is glass. It can't melt through any glass. This makes it storable. If it melted through glass, it would be useless."

Jackie let the fluid steam evaporate until only a small amount was left in the jar.

Using his cloak, he reached into the fire and extracted the jar. He then poured the concentrated liquid back into the small glass tube, and screwed on the lid tightly, which was also made of glass, and handed it to Lustre.

"You can hold the tube if you like."

Lustre, without thinking, put it into his pocket. "Sure." He was unaware of the dangers in carrying such a glass tube; he already had smashed a Gone Gazz vial on his journey. An injury here would be much worse than a cut finger.

After a few more minutes, Lustre knew they had to move on, but secretly, he didn't want to leave the fire.

As he stared into the fire, a random thought popped.

"Hey, Jackie."

"Yeah?" Jackie gazed up.

"Is it possible to turn somebody to stone? You know, with Ruby magic."

"Umm, I don't think so. I think that's a Topaz spell." Jackie replied.

"Well, this weird guy back at Banderian Village used this spell I have never heard of before to turn my mate into stone. He seemed to be with the guards."

"Strange." Jackie knew the Ruby guards hated foreigners.

Lustre stretched out and leaned backwards on a boulder. Though this wasn't the most comfortable thing in the world, the boulder gave him a beautiful, relaxed view of the night sky. Thousands of twinkling stars surrounded a silver- faced moon. Lustre hadn't even noticed the moon before.

He pillowed his head with his hands and crossed his feet. His eyes explored the various shapes and patterns amongst the stars and the moon, which watched everything that occurred beneath them. "Maybe Peroa is watching us," he thought. Indeed, one particular god was, along with one of his disciples.

Lustre felt just too tired after the meal. With all the chaos he had endured that day, he wanted to let his mind rest. Slowly, his eyes began to slip down. Lustre let his whole body relax. The soft crackling of the fire lulled him into a deep sleep.

He found himself sitting near a large pond surrounded by tall trees.

He didn't know exactly which forest he was in, but he didn't care. His mind was immersed in the pleasant sound of chirping colaies. He sat there, skipping stones across the lake. When he glanced behind, he saw Rusty's smiling face peering back at him.

"Rusty," Lustre called, fluttering with relief. "I thought you were turned to stone." Rusty didn't reply; instead, he moved closer to Lustre and grasped his hand.

Suddenly, a dark, unsettling figure emerged from the forest behind Rusty. The figure was Daradero, the god of death, who entered Lustre's dreams. He had a ghostlike body with a cloak of dark smoke draped over his skin. The figure reached its gnarled white fingers out and snatched Rusty's other hand.

"Peroa!" Lustre gasped.

The figure began to yank Rusty away, but Lustre didn't loosen his hold. He battled against the figure's force and pulled

Rusty back. Only seconds later, the figure made another effort and pulled Rusty more aggressively.

Lustre held on desperately, but he was overpowered. He couldn't hold on any longer, and their hands slipped. Rusty was dragged away. Lustre could only watch in absolute horror as Rusty disappeared, his face shrouded in the forest's darkness.

"No! Rusty!" Lustre cried out.

Then, the strangest thing happened. Lustre woke up to find himself drenched in sweat.

"Oh no! I fell asleep!" He instantly felt inside his pockets, confirming his worst fear. No jewel! He only had the vial of acerb...and the map. Somehow, he'd let it happen again.

Lustre shot up from the ground in a rattling panic. His first instinct was to race over to Jackie. He glared around in every direction before spotting somebody fleeing in the distance. It wasn't Jackie; he was lying fast asleep beside the campfire. Lustre just glimpsed the jewel's flaring glow emitting from the thief in the distance.

"Jackie! Wake up! Somebody stole the jewel from me again!" he beckoned, shaking Jackie violently.

Jackie slowly got up and squinted at Lustre, still half asleep.

"That guy! He is getting away!" Lustre repeated, pointing out in the distance.

"Lustre... there are no wavires... Just...talk to the crimson cider and..." Sleepy words were mumbled before Jackie collapsed back down.

Lustre was left with only one option. He abandoned Jackie and the warmth of the campfire in pursuit.

The absolute darkness of his surroundings meant he could not see the thief; he was only chasing the glow of the jewel. The light of Peroa shone that night. Without it, the thief would blend perfectly into the darkness.

"Stop you, thief!" Lustre called out.

Lustre's heart was pounding in his chest; his breathing grew ragged and sharp. At one point, Lustre darted past a jagged rock jutting out in his path. He narrowly managed to weave past it with only inches to spare. The thief was also surprisingly nimble, but Lustre was quicker.

In a moment of opportunity, the thief slowed down for a few seconds to catch his breath. This meant Lustre could catch up and finally tackle the thief to the ground.

The thief surrendered as soon as he was caught, holding his hands up in defeat, one of which was still clasping the jewel.

Lustre half expected it to be Winston again. The thief, with a long black scarf wrapped around his neck, was hiding everything but his abnormal grey eyes. They glowered at Lustre with an unnerving sense of joy, despite getting caught. The figure reached out to Lustre, unfurling his crooked fingers around the jewel.

"Who are you?" bellowed Lustre before quickly snatching the jewel back.

"Well, I am not Winston. If that's what you were thinking?" the thief answered ominously. Like Winston, the voice was deep and frail, but hollow.

"What… How do you know what I am thinking?"

The thief replied with something that made Lustre's skin crawl, "We are very similar, Lustre; I can enter your dreams. So, I know your desires and fears, and I even know what you're planning to do with that jewel. You know, you wouldn't have made it this far without me. Did you think that every time you escaped death was a coincidence? You should have died on the mine bridge. This journey you're taking, Lustre, I have to warn you, isn't going to turn out how you expect. So, forget him."

Then, without another word, the thief scuttled away into the darkness. Lustre thought about chasing after him, but he had already reclaimed the jewel, so he returned to the campfire.

"Well, that was strange. At least I got the jewel back."

On the brief walk back, Lustre couldn't stop thinking about what the thief had said. It seemed like a big jumble of nonsense. But as much as his mind nagged, he couldn't explain how that thief knew his name or thoughts.

"It isn't going to turn out how I expected? Forget him? Who?" Lustre kept thinking, "I am not letting anybody else get hold of it again, not until I reach the palace," he vowed.

When Lustre returned to the fire, he noticed the morning haze was just starting. Lustre admired the view momentarily as the mist rose from the ground and was trapped under the cliffs. Jackie was still fast asleep, oblivious to the chaos that had just occurred. Lustre squinted at Jackie, brewing with rage; he thought this was a good opportunity to get up to some mischief.

Before he did anything, he decided to give Jackie one last chance to wake up.

"Oy! Jackie! Get up now!" He kicked him in the stomach. Jackie sat up momentarily, moaning a load of gibberish, before falling back asleep.

"Winston, please just... Leave... your... crimson cider, wavire juice."

"I just chased a thief almost a mile in the dark! And you just snoozed?"

Jackie didn't answer.

Lustre stepped back and aimed the jewel towards Jackie, still sleeping soundly on the misty ground.

As Lustre had learnt, the jewel somehow knew the appropriate spell to cast for any situation, which was so convenient. It was almost like it had a mind of its own.

Strange words just entered his mind when he wrapped Winston in vines, back at the White Plains.

So, Lustre decided to give Jackie a little of what he deserved. A harmless prank. He knew it was cruel, but he sometimes liked getting up to mischief. Lustre held his breath, and the jewel began to glow. For some reason, it didn't change colour; it remained white. There were no words, which was all new for Lustre. He smiled with glee as Jackie's body slowly floated up from the ground, suspended by an invisible force. Surprisingly, Jackie was clueless as to what was happening, remaining asleep.

"Ha, Cool." Lustre chuckled.

Eventually, Jackie woke up. Lustre revelled in the exact moment when Jackie realised he was levitating ten feet in the air.

"Ahh! What's going on?"

Lustre was savouring the moment. Seeing Jackie flail in a panic. Arms and legs everywhere brought him great satisfaction. He couldn't help but laugh.

"Hey, Lustre! Stop this! I am awake!" Jackie squealed. Though it was incredibly funny, Lustre also felt a pang of guilt. Before the prank could go too far, he returned the jewel to his pocket, causing Jackie to descend softly. He had caused Jackie the necessary fear and distress to be satisfied, even though he did not deserve such treatment.

"That wasn't funny," Jackie grumbled, his face red with embarrassment.

"Yeah, okay."

Clearly angered, Jackie gathered up his equipment from last night's brewing and waddled ahead of Lustre.

"Let's get going, then," Jackie said. The sun had only just started to rise. It was still freezing cold; Lustre could even see his breath as he exhaled. As the campfire dimmed and finally died, they gathered their belongings and continued the journey.

Lustre kept checking over his shoulder to gauge progress. Every time, he overestimated the distance travelled. It was slowly annoying him, and his impatience was growing. The only sound around was the morning songs of the colaies.

Lustre tried to focus his thoughts on the jumble of unanswered questions that nagged his mind. He wondered what his dream last night was about or who that mysterious thief was. Lustre desperately wanted answers and hoped the emperor could provide them.

"Hey Jackie, how much longer until we reach the palace?" "I am not sure, an hour or two... Maybe even three." "Okay! I get it, and it is far."

There was a long walk to go...

One hour later...

The sun was now visible over the horizon. This time, Lustre's legs were aching, begging to stop. Jackie's cloak caught the flailing wind uncontrollably, like a brown flag. It slowed his pace tremendously, leading him to fasten it tight. Every minute, Lustre's motivation to keep walking lowered.

After a rocky decline, the ground returned to rolling hills, which were easy to walk on. This was a good indicator of progress, but it wasn't enough to motivate Lustre.

"I can't keep going, Jackie!" Lustre called out. "I have no energy."

He sank to the ground, leaning up against a tree, which was surprisingly uncommon where they were.

Lustre wiped the sweat from his forehead, still panting uncontrollably. It was only mid-morning, and he had finally reached his limit.

When Jackie peered over his shoulder, he spotted Lustre sitting with his face bathed in sweat. Jackie rushed back.

"I can't keep going." Lustre moaned, his eyes fixed on the ground.

Jackie knelt beside him, placing a hand on his shoulder in a gesture of support. "Remember why you started this journey?" Jackie said, offering him a flask of water. "Think of all the obstacles you have overcome, the sacrifices you've made. You've come so far already and can't give up now."

Lustre gazed up at Jackie, seeing the genuine concern in his eyes. He sipped from the flask, feeling the water quench his parched throat. As he caught his breath, he felt a renewed sense of determination. "You're right," he said, his voice shaky but resolute. "We will finish this journey."

Jackie smiled, patting Lustre on the back. "That's the spirit."

Lustre stood up, his muscles protesting with every movement. Yet even with the pain, he pushed through, drawing on Jackie's strength and urging him to keep going every step of the way. As they continued, the sun's heat was now gruelling, but at least they found it easy walking. Lustre felt a sense of pride and accomplishment, especially when they trekked up the next grassy knoll to see a spectacular view.

They stood on the edge of a small drop overlooking the Royal Ruby town and the palace in the distance. The palace's white sandstone walls dominated the view. With its towering spires, domed roofs, and ornate archways, it was truly a beautiful piece of architecture covered in intricate details and patterns.

Within the walls, Lustre could see the courtyards and gardens sprawled out like a verdant oasis; he could even see the faintest hint of fountains glinting in the sunlight.

A collection of huts and stone towers surrounded the palace; the town was even bigger than the Banderian Village. The town held the nation's riches and knowledge via the Royal Treasury and the Royal Ruby Town Library. These buildings lined the market square but were dominated by the massive centrepiece statue of Emperor Maroon in a heroic pose.

The Fletcher brothers regularly visited the library but avoided key buildings due to the guards' presence. Neighbouring the town was the glorious blue ocean, stretching as far out as the eye could see. Its dark blue waters were dotted with fishing boats and various docks protruding from the shore. Even though it was distant, Lustre could still hear the waves gently lapping in and out, a soothing sound everybody loved.

It was indeed the most beautiful sight Lustre had ever seen. As he stood there in wonder, taking in the breathtaking sight, Lustre felt a sense of familiarity. He could not place this feeling; it was a fairy tale scene from his youth. He felt a strange connection to Rusty.

The palace was genuinely stunning, displaying the power of the emperor.

"Woah." Lustre was the first to say.

"Yeah, woah." Jackie sighed.

"I have only seen paintings of the palace hanging inside Tether's Tavern," Lustre said.

Jackie laughed. "Well, it's much more stunning in person. No painting could ever capture walking those halls."

Lustre suddenly wanted to explore the village and learn more about himself. He was worn out moments ago, but now he fluttered with energy.

He was the first to start clambering down the cliff.

"Wait up! Don't leave me behind!" Jackie hurried after Lustre.

Soon, they found themselves standing before the arched gateway, the entrance to Royal Ruby Town, a maze of markets, huts, and bustling roads crowding the foot of the palace.

As they invited themselves through the gateway, Lustre was shocked to find an empty town. What should have been the most crowded township in Ruby Nation was lifeless and deafeningly silent, with not a single person in sight.

Dusty wind drifted between the houses, shrouding the streets in dirt. The town's unkept nature gave it an eerie atmosphere. Roadside market stands, wagons, barrels, and other clutter were abandoned throughout the streets.

The only movement that caught their eyes was the stray pieces of paper tumbling across the road, carried with each breath of wind. Lustre noticed that all the windows, doors, and entrances were hedged in timber barricades, and some doors were even obstructed with furniture. It was pretty suspicious; this town was the nation's capital.

To say the least, Lustre was nervous and confused.

"Where is everyone?"

"Hiding," Jackie replied ominously.

"What? Why? I'm not that ugly." Lustre laughed.

"No, it's not us, Lustre. Every morning, the palace guards come to the village and try to score an easy feed off these poor people. They abuse their power, and when the people try to defend themselves, they are either slashed with their swords, or if the guards have a speck of mercy, they are sent to the dungeon. The village is pillaged of their rations, potions, rubies, water, equipment, and everything valuable. The people try to recover, only for it to happen the next morning," said Jackie, peeping through one of the windows.

"That's terrible."

Jackie nodded.

"I thought that my life was bad back in the mines, but hearing this makes that life seem like a luxury."

"Yes, the palace steps are this way," motioned Jackie.

Lustre travelled up the street, the palace looming in the distance. He was confident his incredible journey would finally and restfully conclude at the entrance doors. He prayed that the many laborious miles would be worth it. Maybe he could finally help Rusty.

The palace's grandeur became more apparent as they approached the doors. Lustre could see the deep, rough texture of the sandstone walls, all adorned with intricate carvings and large crimson banners. The many red banners were complete with a large centred black wavire. The two paused momentarily to take it all in, their eyes widening with wonder and foreboding. The place was wonderful, but scary.

The grand entrance doors had two brass knockers and an arched portico. Standing before such gigantic doors, they looked small and insignificant, but their wait was short-lived as two guards met them, their armour glinting in the sunlight. Their stern expressions soured further at the sight of Lustre and Jackie. Instantly, they crossed their spears in front of them as an act of intimidation. The tall and imposing guards stood with shields made from sacro slither scales at the ready, barring the way and demanding to know their business.

"Halt! State your business," one shouted.

"Hello, good sirs! We seek entry to this magnificent palace," Lustre declared, his voice filled with youthful enthusiasm. One of the guards scoffed at his civility, as he didn't look like somebody who would use such formal language.

"Can you please let us pass?" Jackie asked.

The guards looked confused before one of them spoke. "I'm afraid that's impossible," he said, grinning. "This palace is only for guests, envoys, scouts, guards, and the emperor. You need proper authority to enter. If you have no official invite, scram!"

Jackie and Lustre exchanged a disappointed glance before Jackie stepped forward, a mischievous hint in his expression.

"But we are! My name is Sir Ja-Ja...James," he said, barely stringing his words together. Lustre, confused and clueless, tapped Jackie on the shoulder, whispering.

"What are you doing? You're not a sir."

"Shh! I know! They can't know my real name. Just follow along, okay?"

Jackie returned his eyes to the guards. "And this is my good friend, Lust-Umm…Lustful Liam."

Lustre scoffed under his breath. "That's the stupidest…" Before he could finish, Jackie nudged him once again.

One of the guards stepped forward, squinting ominously into Jackie's eyes. He had a face of confusion mixed with suspicion. "Hey…Sir James. Do I know you from somewhere?"

The other guard stepped forward. "Yeah, and you… Lustful Liam, do I know you from somewhere?"

Jackie and Lustre began to get nervous. Suddenly, one of the guards gasped in a sudden realisation.

"Wait! Lustful Liam, you're that kid who escaped from Bandeira a few days ago!"

Before the guards could react, Lustre pulled the jewel from his pocket and began to recite an incantation under his breath, his voice hollow with an eerie tone. Suddenly, Lustre's skin turned pasty and white, his eyes pure black.

The air around them crackled with foreboding energy as he unleashed a spell that sent a shadowy darkness rushing towards the guards. Strangely, the jewel went dark. Lustre had not seen this before; it was pure black. The jewel emitted no light; the dark shadows travelled through the air, swallowing all light around them.

The guards were frozen instantly; they looked like chess pieces. Their bodies transformed into statues that stood as silent sentinels before the grand doors, looking not out of place against a sizeable crimson banner with a black wavire backdrop.

Stunned silence filled the surrounding air, completely baffling Jackie. As the jewel returned to its original white colour, so did Lustre's skin and eyes.

They both stared at the guards, and their bodies had turned into black glass. Lustre had never seen anything like that before.

"What...What did I do? Did I turn them to stone?"

Jackie approached the two guards, inspecting them. After tapping them repeatedly with his finger, he heard the crystalline dinging. "No... You've turned them into obsidian—an unbreakable black glass. If you turn somebody to stone, their heart can sometimes still beat. But if you turn somebody into obsidian, they die instantly, right then and there!"

Lustre shivered.

"Forget about them; they probably deserved it," Jackie added, unafraid to waste a few more Ruby guards.

Lustre forced himself to laugh, but he couldn't hide the nervousness in his voice. He tried to renew his excitement, passing the now lifeless guards towards the palace doors. Before he pushed the doors open, he noticed Jackie was no longer following him.

"Are you coming in?" Lustre asked over his shoulder. He heard a deep sigh from behind him. Lustre turned back to face Jackie.

"I am sorry, but I'm afraid I have to leave you."

"What! Why?" Lustre gasped.

"It's been fun, but I need to head back to the village and pick up those supplies and maybe get a book from the library. I do need some more hunting equipment and brewing ingredients. I have brought you this far, but you must complete your journey alone. I am thankful for everything; having somebody to accompany me on my travels has been nice." Jackie finished his speech. This all seemed out of nowhere.

"You're leaving me?"

"Yeah, these Ruby guards and I are at odds; remember the Crimson Forest? I have a bounty on my head! I truly hope you can help your friend! Be careful, and don't trust anyone behind those doors!" With that, Jackie sighed sadly. He had no business behind those doors; it was an unnecessary risk.

Lustre felt a sense of guilt, thinking Jackie was leaving because he had mistreated, teased, and been rude. He couldn't believe they were parting, but Jackie showed the truth in his final words. Overall, he felt upset. During that journey, Lustre had built up a strange connection, a new friendship. Perhaps that was it.

Saying goodbye to another mate was too tough to swallow.

After waving, Jackie strolled back down the stairs towards the Ruby Town Library, leaving Lustre alone at a crossroads. Lustre still felt a mixture of emotions. Ultimately, he again thought about his lost friendship with Rusty. Lustre sighed deeply and returned to face the big brass knockers.

As he pushed the doors open, he was greeted by the smell of dirty carpet, which insulted his nostrils. The light illuminated the vibrant blood-red banners, wavire tapestries, paintings, and ornaments adorned the sandstone walls. A long, red, filthy carpet was stretched out, leading down an eye-funnelling corridor, both sides lined with arches and doors.

The heavy doors creaked until they fully opened, stopping at the entrance walls. Lustre tentatively stepped into the grand entry hall, his heart pounding excitedly. The air was thick with a heady mixture of burning candles, dust, and eroded fabric. The palace was designed by the same architect who built the ancient Cathedral of Peroa in Irindor, the capital of Topaz Nation.

A symphony of sounds echoed throughout the hallway, the gentle rustling of people, along with forced laughter and chatter that could be heard somewhere far in the distance. The palace seemed positive, pulsating with energy and a strange, mystical wonder that filled every inch. The roof was arched and decorated with bright chandeliers dangling from the rafters. Eyes widened, Lustre strolled down the hallway, exploring every nook and cranny.

As Lustre progressed down the red carpet, he noticed the many doors on each wall. They were all identical in shape and colour, except for the corresponding numbers labelled above the arched doorframes.

He counted them as he strolled by, "one...two...three... four...five...six..."

Then he stopped. Door number seven was different; it was slightly ajar. Curiosity getting the better of him, he peeked inside and was immediately struck by the grandeur.

The boardroom was massive and filled with furniture. The most prominent was the large, lengthy table stretched out in the centre, accompanied by a dozen plush chairs, each with a patterned wavire red cushion. Another chandelier hung from the very centre of the roof, casting a warm and inviting glow over the table.

At the far end of the boardroom was a raised dais with an ornately carved wooden chair, differing from all the others. This chair was much larger and more grandiose, with not just a blood red and black wavire cushion but a red cushioned padding incorporated into a carved wavire backrest. This one was for a leader or somebody in a position of power, giving an enhanced comfort and view across the table.

The boardroom walls were simple, each lacking the detail and furniture of the hallway.

Lustre felt a sense of awe wash over him as he gazed around the room. He wondered who owned the room and what important meetings were held there.

As he turned to leave, he noticed a small golden plaque on the wall near the door. He moved closer; it read, "Boardroom reserved for the Emperor Council." Lustre gasped in surprise, realising that he had stumbled upon the room reserved for the emperor and his council members. This must be the boardroom where new laws are discussed, and the emperor solves economic and financial woes. Lustre did not know; such matters hadn't improved in decades and were now at the pinnacle of despotism.

Feeling excited and nervous, he quickly peeked his head back in for one last look. Suddenly, Lustre heard somebody burst out laughing. It startled him; he jumped up, smacking his head on the door frame. He turned and glanced down the hallway, rubbing the top of his skull.

Due to the acoustics, voices carried, and he could see two guards chatting to each other much farther down the corridor. He began to panic almost instantly. It was a straight one-way corridor. He wouldn't be able to leave without getting spotted, and a filthy, washed-up boy from the streets would certainly look out of place here; he would look sketchy.

He could not run; that would look even sketchier, and he saw nowhere to hide in the boardroom or any other rooms, as the other doors looked locked. His only chance out of this would be to walk past the guards, so he started to stroll calmly towards them.

He then moved with a determined stride, purpose in his every step as if he were important or needed to be somewhere. If only he had a clipboard; now, nobody questions somebody with a clipboard. It was evident that this was a bad idea. The guards bought it for the first few seconds, letting Lustre slip past them confidently. Gradually approaching, he managed to overhear some of the guards' conversation.

"I can't believe it, they appeared out of nowhere."

"That's unbelievable. Can you describe the boy?"

"Well, he was rather tall, with a mop of black hair. I discovered him hiding in the tower. That was before those sacro slithers attacked us."

As Lustre passed the guards, he hastened, and his stride picked up to run with a trampling urgency.

"What about that kid over there? Could that be him?" When Lustre heard this, he broke into a sprint.

"Hold on, that's the boy!"

"Stop!" the guards ordered.

Lustre sprinted down the corridor, his ears filled with the thunderous echo of the guards' pursuing footsteps. Eventually, the guards had to slow down. Lustre thought he outran them, but it had more to do with their unwieldy steel armour weighing them down. Before Lustre arrived at the huge door marking the end of the hallway, one of the guards uttered between huffing breaths, "Re-tentro-mjana!"

In desperation, Lustre veered to the side, attempting to dodge the spell, but his nimbleness had been all used up. His muscles were drained of energy in a flash of red light, leaving him overwhelmed by fatigue and unable to support his weight.

As he collapsed to the ground, Lustre was unaware that a common stun spell had struck him. As the realisation came to him, he desperately tried to crawl forward, but the guards caught up to him.

"Cheap shot," Lustre spat, his voice seething with defiance.

"Silence, boy! I am taking you straight to the dungeon. Remember me!" said the corporal. This was an all too familiar tone for Lustre.

"Fine, you take him. I have better things to do than arrest some random kid from the border," the other guard said, retracing his steps down the corridor.

Lustre was left sprawled in the centre of the corridor with the well-known palace guard demanding that he stand.

"Get up!" he heard the guard shout. But Lustre, still incapacitated by the stun spell, couldn't comply. He then heard the guard grunt, followed by the ominous rattling of chains.

"I didn't want to have to play this dirty boy."

He felt the cold metal of shackles lock around his wrists, permanently chaining his hands together. "Right, get up, potion boy, now! Before I pull ya up," the corporal said, tugging on the shackle.

"I can't."

The guard had no mercy, yanking him up by the handcuffs. Lustre didn't know that some Ruby guards usually modify the equipment they give to make it even more unpleasant for their captives. They shortened the chain to restrict movement further, and perhaps the most horrific, they deliberately sharpened the inside of the shackles so that the unlucky person wearing them wouldn't want to squirm around. Lustre found this out when the corporal pulled. The sharpened edges sliced into and cut his wrists. Lustre screamed as blood began to trickle down from his wrists.

"I see you survived the sacro slithers," Lustre mentioned.

"Lost many mates. I am sorry, boy, but it's the dungeon for you now."

"Ahh! These handcuffs!" Lustre squealed.

"Shut up and walk!" He was now resolute. The corporal had to correct Lustre's posture every few seconds during the walk, as the spell still made balance very difficult for him. He ensured that Lustre didn't accidentally trample or dirty the marvellous red carpet rolled out down the centre of the hallway. This was probably so he didn't have to clean up the rug on his way back. Emperor Maroon prized his royal carpet; it made him feel grand.

They reached the door at the end, reinforced with a barred window above. "Password!" a muffled voice said from the other side.

"Crimson cider." There was a faint click, almost like a key. The door swung open, its hinges squealing loudly.

"I have got a boy here. He is a trespasser. I cannot stomach his sight," the corporal responded. He was taking some pity on Lustre as he didn't reveal the true nature of the crime; he was recalling the recent battle. He shoved Lustre forward through the door.

"Very well, sir, I will take him to the dungeon," said the jailer.

Lustre was handed over in a smaller room. This room had a table and chairs; it was a guardhouse. The walls were still sandstone, and the floors were still marble. There were food shelves, mugs of crimson cider, and a large chest for storage. These were all essential items to keep the jailers happy as they guarded the entrance corridor to the dungeon. A high ceiling was built entirely out of red glass, letting the sun's rays bathe the room in ominous blood-red light.

Lustre's footsteps resounded upon the polished floors, as did the jailer behind him. The rhythmic noise bounced off the walls as they entered a gloomy corridor.

The floor now turned to dirt. For some strange reason, this corridor reminded Lustre of the mines. Lanterns and blazing torches lined the walls like the ruby mines. He remembered the distinctive feeling of absolute joy when he would strike luck and the ruby of the day. Those were good times. Lustre could easily recount a hundred pleasant memories in the mines. Lustre did hope he could return to that life after he rescued Rusty. However, in his current situation, he was struggling.

As they progressed down the dirt corridor, the jailer noticed the blood dripping from Lustre's hands, so he gave the shackles another tug.

Seconds passed.

Lustre stumbled and almost collapsed again; his legs were still very weak. The stun effects lingered longer than anticipated. Again, he was hoisted back up by the shackles, the sharpened edges starting to dig into his flesh. Excruciating pain surged through him; he let out another cry, which echoed throughout the corridor.

"Quiet and walk!" the jailer spat.

"Where are you even taking me?" moaned Lustre.

The guard didn't respond, only telling him to shut up again.

"I just want to know." Lustre bugged.

"No, we are already here," the jailer spoke. Before them lay a heavy door embedded in the rock wall. It was made from wood, which was bland without any paint. It had a rusted iron frame with gnarled bolts protruding from their sockets. The door also had a window in the centre, a roughly cut opening closed off with prison-like bars. On the door, in white chalk, was written, "Did you say goodbye to your mother?" Through the bars, Lustre caught a glimpse of the foreboding interior. It was dark with a leaching smell of rot and decay.

Patches of mould consumed the lower section, flourishing in the puddle of water seeping from beneath. The mould had crept almost to the handle, painting the door green in its sticky embrace. The jailer briefly let go of Lustre's shackles to approach the door. It was a risky move, but in Lustre's current state, he knew it would be impossible for him to make a run for it.

"The dungeon; I haven't been here for a while." The jailer laughed, taking out a ring of assorted keys. They rattled vigorously in his hands as he searched for the right one.

After attempting to nestle multiple keys into the keyhole, one slid into place with a satisfying click. The jailer twisted it. The old door sprang open, unleashing a foul odour and a deep, unsettling cry of stale wind hissing up the stairs.

Only darkness could be seen through the door. The jailer snatched Lustre's hands once again and escorted him inwards.

After seeing the inside, Lustre finally put up some resistance. Still under the effects of the stun spell, he tried to plant his foot on the ground.

"I am not going in there. There could be reatrits!" Lustre screamed.

The jailer scoffed, "Do you think I care? Go in!"

"They are awful little gemotros. They scamper around in dark, wet, and rotten places. I am positive it will be full of reatrits." Lustre explained.

The jailer moaned with annoyance, "I don't have time for this…Worse things than rodents down here, boy!"

He gave Lustre a violent shove, enough to break his balance. He was forced forward into the darkness. It was so dark that Lustre couldn't see the floor, almost tripping over his first step. This was when he realised it was not on flat ground; he was walking downstairs.

"Stop! I don't want to meet a reatrit! Their bodies are covered in yellow fur that can be soaked in diseases! I AM NOT GOING ANY FURTHER! I can't have another reatrit scuttle beneath my feet again." Lustre yelled, putting up one last struggle.

As you may tell by now, Lustre was terrified of many things, including rodents, darkness, and being alone. He was currently enduring all three fears simultaneously.

Though the jailer may have thought Lustre was making up excuses not to be put in the dungeon, he was legitimately terrified.

Lustre's final struggle was in vain. They continued to walk further down the stairs. Soon, he saw dim candlelight. As he walked down more steps, he could see where he was. He had been walking down a spiral staircase. The steps corkscrewed down a stone pillar leading from the entrance into the abyss.

When Lustre reached the bottom of the stairwell, he stood in a damp, dark room lit by the dim lighting of large candles scattered around the floor. The chamber had an unnerving atmosphere, almost like the remains of a ritual or demonic procedure.

He noticed the uneven stone walls, like those of a cave. He had to be in a small cave or grotto. It looked as if somebody had stumbled upon this little cave beneath the palace and decided to use it for a dungeon.

Lustre slowly crept across the room, ensuring not to step in the pails holding the candles. Some were filled with hot, sticky wax. The jailer kept a firm grip on Lustre's shackles until they stopped in the centre, which gave Lustre a chance to view his new surroundings. As his eyes adjusted, something unsettling unveiled itself from the darkness.

CAGES

There were iron cages everywhere, all varying in size and shape. Most were empty, but the few that weren't held soulless had grey statues inside. Their faces were illuminated in the candlelight. They all stood in various poses, casting an image of horror in Lustre's eyes.

"Now, give me everything in your pockets!" The jailer guard yelled, breaking the silence. His voice echoed throughout the room.

Lustre panicked; he couldn't give up the jewel.

"I can't. My hands are shackled." Was the first excuse that he came up with.

Which was true.

"Smart ass." The jailer spat. The guard then quickly unshackled him, freeing his hands.

Before following any of the guard's orders, he brought his hands up to his face to assess the wounds.

Just as he imagined, there was a lot of blood. The shackles had sliced deep into his skin. "Ouch." He cried.

"Okay, empty your pockets now." The jailer repeated.

"I have nothing."

That was his second excuse, and he hoped it was enough. But no. The guard didn't believe it. He shoved Lustre against the wall, pressing his face into the jagged stone. He felt the guard reach into his back pocket.

"Ah-ha! What is this?"

"A shiny rock, a dagger. I think I will keep these!" the jailer laughed.

The guard let go of Lustre, satisfied with what he found.

"Give me the jewel back! It's mine!" Lustre snapped, spinning back around.

Lustre tried to snatch it back, but the guard was quicker. He waved it high above his head with a teasing grin, putting it just out of Lustre's reach.

After a few seconds, the jailer reasserted his dominance in the form of a brutal punch across Lustre's face. Lustre dropped to the ground with his head spinning.

He circled his tongue around his lips, tasting blood. The punch had scored a cut right across his bottom lip, splitting it in half like a trench. Blood drooled down his chin as he tried to get back up.

"Oh, that's gonna leave a scar," spoke the jailer. "Now, get into this cage."

Lustre didn't have a choice now. He stumbled into the cage to avoid receiving another punch. The guard grinned before removing the wrist shackles. He slammed the cage door shut and secured it with an iron padlock: "You're lucky. Everybody here is like a relic, a statue of their former self. Some have been here for over a hundred rots, forgotten. But in the end, you will all be here for the same amount of time, *forever!* Be grateful that you're not like them."

Before Lustre could respond, the jailer guard turned his back and strolled back up the staircase, admiring the jewel and dagger. Just before Lustre lost sight of him, he said, "Don't try to escape, or I will make sure you become one of them."

That was the last thing Lustre heard from him. Slowly, the clunking footsteps softened, and the guard ascended further upwards. The final noise Lustre heard before complete silence swallowed him was the screeching of the door as it swung shut. The noise danced off the hollow walls before dissipating.

He was now alone, his worst fear!

Lustre could have already been there an hour after he heard the door shut. He had no perception of time. Being confined in almost complete darkness gave Lustre a chance to think. Mostly just of ways he could escape this, but also other things. Lustre considered using a spell to blow the cage door open, but that would be very loud, possibly alerting the guard. Besides, Lustre's hands and general fatigue were not in the best condition. He also felt that the guard purposely put him in a cage way too small for him. He had to hunch his neck to fit, which quickly became uncomfortable.

He could only assess his surroundings as he pondered a new plan. Chills crept up his spine as he scoured the terrified faces each statue held. All their feelings, emotions and thoughts tied into one face seconds before they were transformed. The worst part of being in a cage was the noise. The sound of silence was unbearably quiet. The only noise that stopped Lustre from slipping into complete insanity or unawareness of his consciousness was the faint dripping of water. Lustre couldn't see where the water was dripping from, but it was like a sombre metronome, keeping his mind in touch with time. Each droplet fell about two seconds from the other, which he found somewhat entertaining.

He would count them.

Drip...

He could almost swear the two-second delay between the drips was speeding up.

Drop...

Lustre didn't want to think of anything else at that moment, or he would lose count.

Drip...

He wasn't going crazy. Yes, this is normal. Everything is fine.

Drop...

The dripping reminded Lustre of how damp this place was. It was the perfect habitat for reatrits.

Drip...

That's five drops so far...Or was it four? Lustre groaned with annoyance; he had forgotten. Even with complete concentration, he managed to mess up. It wasn't that difficult.

In the darkness, Lustre heard something—the distinct unsettling sound of paws skittering and scuttling around his cage. Claw scratching produced an unsettling chorus that reverberated through the cave. Something touched his skin, a terrible, uneasy feeling. The creatures let out various squeaks and cries as they brushed past. Shivers overwhelmed Lustre, and the horrible thought he feared most came to him immediately.

"AHHH! Reatrits! Stay away, you pests! Somebody help me!" Lustre screamed.

Lustre wasn't expecting an answer; strangely, his cry was answered. He heard a voice in the dark, a faint whisper, like an ethereal breath blowing past his ears. The sound was subtle, a distant murmur balanced on the edge of comprehension. Lustred strained to listen, soon realising that he wasn't alone.

"You will get used to them." Said a mysterious voice. The voice emanated from all directions, its origin veiled by darkness. It carried a wind that toned it in a haunting melody. It was low, gravelly, and filled with a sense of despair.

Lustre froze. "Who said that?" Lustre yelled back.

"Stop yelling. I am right in front of you," it said.

Lustre couldn't see anybody in front of or around him. He could barely make out anything through the darkness. There were only cages. "I don't see you," Lustre stated in a cold shiver.

"Oh, right; sorry, this is still new to me." The voice replied, with another gush of breeze scathing his ear.

Lustre was freaked out. The voice seemed so otherworldly, yet for some reason, it sounded familiar.

"Wait, I swear I have heard you talk to me before," Lustre recalled.

"Correct. I have been guiding you on this whole journey. That's a fact," the voice replied. "You want another fact? You see there? That cage in the corner. That was mine."

Lustre gazed into the corner of the dungeon; apart from the many puddles and cave walls, something else came into view. Previously cloaked in darkness was an old cage with its door wide open. It looked like the oldest cage in the room. Its bars were bent and mangled, and the iron frame was distorted and rusted. No other cage in the room was in such bad condition.

"Who are you?" Lustre asked.

To that, the voice replied with only three very unsettling words.

"The name's Cranium!"

Chapter 11

Re-Met

"Wait, are you… Cranium? Like the deceased Ruby emperor? Who died in the war decades ago?" Lustre asked, holding the cage bars.

"You know, you and I are very similar," the voice said.

Lustre snapped, "I don't want you talking to me! I have no clue what you're talking about! I must be going insane."

"I am not here to fight with you, Lustre. Instead, I wish to help you. I can guide you to what you desire most."

"What! You don't know what I want," argued Lustre.

"Yes, I do…" Cranium continued, "I have finally found somebody I can poss…I mean, guide. If you listen to me , I will give you the one thing you desire most."

After that last phrase, the voice fell silent, no longer responding to Lustre. He was more puzzled than ever. Cranium also realised that dealing with this boy would be a real challenge.

"My desires?" Lustre thought. His eyes wandered around the room again; three large dungeon candles in pails were placed along the wall, illuminating the many statues within the cages. Suddenly, one struck a bell. One statue stood out. Lustre leaned inwards, squinting his eyes, trying to focus on the statue standing in the cage opposite his. It was a small boy standing in a relatively calm pose with his hands locked by his side. His eyes glowed with innocence, accompanied by a warm smile. This one didn't look scared compared to the other statues in the chamber. The boy stared upwards; his neck was craned back like he was staring at something twice his height.

Lustre was in disbelief at how somebody could be so heartless to transform someone so timid. It took only a moment, but he came to a sharp, aching realisation in the gloom. He knew who this boy was. His heart drummed, pressing his face against the bars.

"Rusty!"

He couldn't decide whether he was relieved or terrified. He slammed his shoulder into the cage door; panic always results in poor decisions. "I am coming, don't worry, I am coming!" Lustre screamed, tears forming in his eyes.

No matter how much power he put into each shoulder charge, the bars wouldn't break. The door wouldn't budge. It quickly became known that the cage door was only secured by a single rusty iron padlock, which, from experience, he knew the shackle might snap off easily with some force. He reached his hand through the bars and began yanking on the lock.

"Come on! Break! Snap!"

Yet, the shackle was stubborn. It refused to snap off. The whole side effects of the stun spell had only now worn off, leaving Lustre still highly fatigued. Lustre wasn't thinking straight; seeing Rusty for the first time in what felt like octaves filled him with immense guilt and desperation.

Lustre was ready to give up, but, reaching into his cloak's deep inner pocket, a new spark of hope revealed itself. The bubbling, acidic liquid, the small glass tube of Acerbo-ironia, somehow went right under the guard's nose when he rifled through Lustre's pockets. Lustre unscrewed the glass lid and poured a generous amount of the acid over the shackle. Within seconds, the iron padlock began to deform. It sizzled and cracked, sending the gassy smell across the chamber. Finally, the lock snapped, dropping to the ground in a mangled mess. The acid had done it; it had quickly melted iron, just as Jackie said.

With the now-molten padlock lying on the floor, Lustre kicked open the cage door and crawled out. He crawled over to Rusty and stood, meeting him face-to-face for the first time in an octave. There was silence for a moment. Lustre couldn't believe what he had laid his eyes upon. Lustre reached his hand through Rusty's cage and grasped his stone hand. It was cold and lifeless. "I am so sorry, Rusty." He fell to his knees, feeling like a murderer.

Glancing around the dungeon, tears shedding, he began thinking of a new plan to turn Rusty back from stone.

"Obviously, there is no Ruby spell to turn Rusty back to normal, but if I could use the jewel, maybe there is a foreign spell that could do the trick? I have gotta find that jewel!" He wiped the tears away; he was now resolute. "Don't worry, Rusty, I will fix my mistakes."

"Hands in the air!" The jailer yelled, standing at the foot of the stairs.

Lustre had utterly forgotten how much noise he had made: the padlock hitting the floor, the crying, the cage door swinging open. Lustre threw his hands above his head, and tears again filled his eyes.

"You disobeyed me. I gave you a chance. Now you're gonna be a statue!" The jailer then yelled up the stairs, "Autumn, he is down here!" Lustre knew he had to make a run for it, but the jailer blocked the exit. He could not slip past unseen, and the jailer watched his every move.

Then, the thought of the dungeon candles came to him. "What if the jailer couldn't see?" He acted and let fate unfold; a failure would mean he would be turned to stone and placed in a cage, anyway.

Dungeon candles were thick and long, generally standing in a pail. Once the wick had burned down, pints of melted wax were in the pail. Sometimes, the guards threw this wax over the prisoners.

He executed his plan, or impulse, doubting that it would work. He bolted forward, clapping out the first two dungeon candles that lit up the chamber. They went out instantly.

"Hey! Freeze!" the jailer guard demanded, racing towards Lustre. Lustre changed direction and began running toward the last candle sitting in the corner of the chamber. This candle was now just a wax stump, the pail full of hot wax. Before the jailer reached him, he grabbed the pail and poured, sending hot, gloopy wax splattering across the floor.

It was now pitch black. Lustre had done it. The now blind jailer let out a cry of confusion mixed with fiery anger and pain. He stumbled around, then slipped over, squinting his eyes to spot Lustre in the darkness.

"You little reatrit! Where did you go?"

Lustre could see better than the jailer, since his eyes had adjusted to the darker conditions. He walked around the guard with mischievous joy towards the stairs, still carrying the pail half-filled with wax. But still, he wouldn't celebrate too early. The jailer now realised Lustre's plan, quickly regained his feet, and retreated towards the stairs. He used the little glow from the top of the spiral staircase for navigation. But Lustre was already one step ahead of him, already on the stairs, with a pail in hand.

Lustre poured the candle wax all over the lower steps, ensuring the remaining hot wax covered the steps as a barrier.

The guard tried to chase after him, but he found his foot glued in place. The wax hardened almost instantly against the cold stone stairs.

"Ahhhh! Hot! You little pest!" The jailer shrieked.

Lustre watched in joy as the guard struggled to free himself. Lustre then bolted up the stairs.

"No! Come back here!" the jailer demanded, trying to free his foot. The wax had bought Lustre some time. Lustre clambered up the stairs until he stood before the exit door. Heavy footsteps could now be heard, followed by much grunting. "I am gonna get you!"

Lustre was out of breath, but he couldn't stop. Still panting, he staggered toward the door and yanked down on the handle. The door was locked.

Initially, when Lustre reached the door, he expected the escape to end, but he hadn't planned this far ahead. Time was ticking, and his jailer was progressing up the stairs; it would only be a few more seconds before he reached him.

Lustre knew the only way to open the door was by using a specific key. Flashbacks of the key to White Plains Cottage swarmed his mind. He had to think very fast.

He could not use the tube of Acerbo-ironia; it was all gone. Brute force was the only option.

In desperation, he slammed his shoulder into the door, sending a loud echo down the stairwell. The door didn't budge. He took another step back and charged towards the door once again. He focused all his power on his shoulder and hammered the door. He created a crack this time, with the decayed wood just starting to fold.

"Come on!"

The following shoulder charge did it. The door collapsed inwards, shooting splinters and wooden fragments across the floor. The sudden transition from almost complete darkness to a torch-lit corridor blinded him. Lustre lay on the ground atop a pile of rotten timber and rusted iron. He couldn't move; every part of his body ached. To make things worse, the jailer has finally reached the top of the stairs. "Ha! Gotcha now." He heard a chuckle from behind him. The guard approached him slowly, walking through the naked doorframe with an evil smile.

"You're dead!" the jailer said.

Suddenly, Lustre gained a spike of energy. He rolled over, pointing his hand up at the guard.

"Gamber Goth-Gorian," he shouted.

The small fireball he summoned in his hands was bright as hellfire. He shot it towards the guard without seconds to spare, hurling him backwards through the doorframe. The guard tumbled back down the stairs, counting each step with a painful thud until landing in the dungeon chamber.

Lustre took this opportunity to get back on his feet. After dusting himself off, he cried out through the door frame. "Hope you get what you desire, a doctor…And a new nickname, Wax Feet! You big reatrit!"

Lustre felt he could be proud of that statement. He made it up on the spot, and it was pretty cool, considering the jailer said similar things earlier. With a newfound spirit, he ran down the well-lit dirt corridor back to the guardhouse. There, the blood-red light shone on the marble floor, the table and the chairs. Lustre was starving. There were no other jailers, no Autumn to be seen. He went to the shelves, grabbed some cheese and crimson cider, sat at the table and enjoyed a quick meal. Blood dripped on the table from his wrist, wounds caused by the shackles. He looked around and spotted the chest. "I wonder," thought Lustre. He opened it, and behold, it was his personal effects, the jewel and his dagger. He unlatched the guardhouse door with the primary objective of finding the emperor.

* * *

"Okay, I have to find the throne room," Lustre said. The problem that became apparent instantly was Lustre's lack of navigation. He had no clue where anything was. The palace was a maze of rooms, hallways, and corridors.

Finding the emperor would not be easy, to say the least. He rejected the idea of asking a guard for directions. He figured that if he just followed the red carpet, it would lead him to the throne room. The red carpet was reserved only for the emperor and permitted special guests; now, that would be him.

Whilst navigating the palace halls, Lustre's eyes explored the many paintings that decorated the walls. One of which stood out to him. It was a dramatic image of a knight mounting his steed and holding a jousting stick. Lustre always adored the concept of jousting. It was a competitive sport where knights raced toward each other on steeds and attempted to knock each other to the ground. Or, in even more intense situations, they would try to impale others.

Lustre wished to be a knight, especially to be part of a tournament. A few rots ago, Rusty and he visited a jousting event in the Bandeira fields, and he dreamed of competing. He had already planned out how it would happen: He would dress in gleaming silver armour, wielding a sword, spear, and shield while mounted on a glorious blazing ferinthor. Standing proudly, he would duel before a huge crowd that would erupt with cheers when he emerged victorious and covered with the blazing light of glory.

The audience consisted of thousands of village folk, many beautiful girls like Tether or, better yet, Haley Tinker.

GEMOTROPLIS: THE STOLEN HEART

That would be truly amazing. Lustre's plans for jousting had to wait, as he had problems at hand. The halls reminded him to stop daydreaming as he was about to walk into two giant, blood-red doors.

"Woah!" Lustre gasped.

The heavy crimson wood doors had guards on either side; that was Lustre's first red flag. The presence of guards meant that something important was inside. The doors were heavily decorated with spiralling patterns, but they must have added an extra coat of varnish to keep the natural blood colour from going dull.

The second red flag was... well... the red flag. The Ruby Nation's flag was displayed above the door, hanging high above, perfectly still, without a breeze to carry it. Lustre was familiar with the flag, as it was a centrepiece in every Ruby village. Its primary colour was also blood red, with a black shape in the centre depicting the silhouette of a fanged wavire, the most well-known Ruby gemotro and the symbol of wealth, power and the emperor's rule.

"This has to be the throne room."

Lustre began to approach the guards with confidence; it was a matter of time before he was stopped in his tracks once again.

"Hey, buddy, you are not allowed in here," one guard said, stepping out before him. Lustre had to play this one smart.

"Oh, no, that's not why I am here. I just wanted to tell you that your corporal fell down the stairs to the dungeon. I think he needs some help." Lustre explained, pointing down the long red carpet.

"Oh no! We will be right there." The dumb guards shrieked. They left their marks and rushed down the hallway, leaving the door unguarded and Lustre with a smile on his face.

"That was pretty easy."

With all his might, he pushed open the doors. They swung inwards, and a room bathed in golden light was revealed. It was a breathtaking sight. The sun gleamed through the stained-glass windows, enveloping the bright red carpet that led his eyes to a towering throne, sitting proudly on an elevated platform at the very end.

The wooden throne was covered in ruby, cut and polished to create beautiful patterns. Perched upon the throne was a man with crimson silk robes draped over his shoulders and a golden crown resting on his head. His crown was different from that of Cranium's crown, the crown Lustre had seen previously in White Plains Cottage. It was much more straightforward, with no jewels or unique design, just pure gold that glinted in the sunlight.

Stepping hesitantly into the room, Lustre was immediately greeted with a heady ambience. Ruby guards lined the walls; the air held a symphony of scents and fragrances that gave a sense of nostalgia.

The earthy aroma of dusk wafted through the air, mingling with the aged scent of dusty tapestries. The air hinted of lavender and vanilla, most likely from candles hanging high above him in the chandeliers.

The room also echoed with the soft murmur of a bubbling fountain; its melodious trickling was heard through one of the arches. Lustre caught a glimpse of the beautiful courtyard outside. It was a flat area of grass, home to many towering oak trees. Their gnarled branches reached for the heavens, sheltering flower beds that flushed the palace with vibrant colour, blood orchids, fluoro flutters, and various other exotic flowers. The stone fountain was the courtyard's centrepiece. Soft bubbling was accompanied by colaies happily drinking.

The scene put a warm smile on Lustre's face; it was a slice of heaven.

The reality of the situation was different from the perspective of Emperor Maroon.

"Who are you? I didn't call for a servant," the emperor roared.

Lustre stuttered, "I am not a servant."

"You will address me, Heil Emperor. Who are you then? A merchant? A peasant?" Emperor Maroon boomed.

Lustre could tell the emperor was not in a good mood. "Uhh, I am just a miner. My name is Lustre, Your Majesty."

The emperor leaned over the edge of his throne to get a better look at Lustre. Quiller, the Emperor's advisor, was standing by Maroon's side. "Sire, it's the boy from your breakfast briefing, the boy that escaped the Corporal of the guard from the Border Wall."

"Yes indeed," Maroon exhaled.

He most likely expected Lustre to bow or make some other sort of respectful gesture, as did everybody else. But Lustre didn't want Maroon to feel like he held all the power.

"I don't have time for miners to complain about their working conditions. Leave!"

Lustre wasn't about to leave, raising his voice. "I am not complaining! I am just here to show you something I found…"

The emperor raised an eyebrow. "Show me something. Eh?"

As Lustre walked closer, he reached into his pocket and slowly pulled out the jewel. The emperor peered downwards, intrigued. Guards in the room were now on edge.

"What is this…Rock?" said Maroon.

"It isn't just a rock! It's a magical jewel!" Lustre's voice did not change.

"Only I possess the authority to raise my voice! Cease your utterances, you insignificant commoner, or I will execute you!" The emperor's superiority was evident in every word. "Nevertheless, I find no interest in your rock. Leave my presence immediately! Begone! Peasant."

Undeterred by the emperor's instruction, Lustre stood his ground, seizing the opportunity to make one final plea, this time with a persuasive tone. "Emperor Maroon, I-"

"You can call me your Majesty peasant, nothing more!" the emperor interrupted.

"My apologies, Your Majesty. Will you please consider the true value of this stone? It possesses great power, nothing like any other item in Gemotroplis," Lustre explained.

"It is an artefact of history, buried deep beneath this nation. I uncovered it in the mines. It is the Heart of Gemotronia. By wielding it, you shall hold the might of any spell known across all nations!"

The emperor scoffed sceptically. "Nonsense, don't you know your history, boy? The Heart of Gemotronia was shattered into eight pieces a thousand rots ago; it is impossible that rock is authentic."

The emperor's patience dwindled with each passing moment, evident by his finger tapping on his throne.

"It's real! I swear, I don't know how; there must have been two hearts! I can show you…" Lustre pleaded. Before he could finish, the emperor stood up from his throne, crying out, "Guards! Seize this peasant boy immediately!"

In a flurry of urgency, a few Ruby guards stepped forth. Lustre was propelled forward by physical force, teetering him off balance. He kept a firm grip on the jewel. Desperate to regain composure, he flailed his arms amidst the chaos. It became evident that his efforts were in vain. He felt his hands being bound in front with rope, together with the jewel in his grasp. At least it wasn't those dreaded shackles again.

In an instant, Lustre found himself crashing to the floor, momentarily winded under the brunt of a guard's kick to his stomach. The agonising sound of the boot reverberated through the air. Pain surged through his body.

"Ahh! My ribs!" Lustre found himself in an agonising predicament, his arms now tightly bound and with a cracked rib.

To make matters worse, one of the guards who had tackled him had also lost balance, falling on top of him. The guard's knee dug into his back. The pain was excruciating, made even worse by the armour reinforcement covering the guard's kneecaps, a small spike. As the guards knotted additional rope around his hands, Lustre's face was so firmly pressed into the floor that his jaw could not move, rendering final efforts to plead or convince the emperor anything impossible.

After what seemed like an eternity, the guards finally released their hold on Lustre and pulled him upright.

"Please, give me a chance!" The emperor ignored Lustre as he was led towards the giant crimson doors. Throughout the situation, Lustre has kept the Heart of Gemotronia tightly in his grasp, even when tied. Just as Lustre was departing, he said, "I can cast any spell you want! Sapphire! Emerald! Even magic from your greatest foe! Topaz!"

To that, the emperor decided to make a final mocking statement. "Fine then, if it's real, turn my guards into stone!"

It was a tease, but Lustre had an opportunity. The guards stopped and released some slack on the rope. Lustre had one chance to prove himself. He swiftly manoeuvred, shaking his bound hands and the jewel above his head. "Please work."

The jewel's power suddenly hijacked his mouth, and Lustre began chanting a foreign spell.

"Loomapa-lingera!"

Instantly, a brilliant flash of yellow light emanated from the jewel, casting his silhouette forward. Light rays enveloped his body, creating an ethereal aura as if he stood before a blinding white flare. Everyone, including the emperor, shielded their eyes.

As abruptly as it began, the light faded away. When everybody slowly uncovered their eyes, they were met with a startling sight. Lustre stood amidst drifting clouds of yellow mist, while in front of him, two guards stood as frozen grey statues. Frozen in time, they maintained the same poses and expressions as they did just moments ago. It was nothing short of a miraculous sight that left the emperor astounded.

The emperor sat utterly speechless for a few seconds, his mouth hanging open as he stared at Lustre. Lustre's triumphant exclamation broke the silence. He shook his roped-bound hands in the air, saying, "Yes! It worked!"

In disbelief, the emperor shouted, Is this some Topaz Nation trickery? Are you a terrorist?"

"No! This is real! The jewel possesses immense power! It can cast spells of Topaz, Sapphire, and Emerald, even Obsidian and Diamond!"

Maroon's interest was piqued, and he descended from his throne, approaching Lustre. "Let me see that," he ordered, extending his hand. Lustre handed the jewel to the emperor without hesitation.

Curiosity sparked within the emperor as he held the jewel to his ear, listening intently to the faint sounds of bells and metallic chimes. "This is truly remarkable. So, with this jewel, I can cast any form of magic?" the emperor inquired.

Lustre nodded, a profound sense of relief now washing over him. Maroon appeared to regret his initial judgment as he now held the jewel eagerly. He was ready to deal!

"I came here to sell it to you," Lustre offered.

"Name your price," Maroon responded. There was an awkward pause. "Well…Land? Jewellery? A barrel of rubies? My crown? Or even an endless supply of bread, clothes, and water?" The emperor began listing as if a peasant boy did not have dreams.

Lustre quickly gave it some thought. Honestly, he hadn't fully decided yet; this was where his journey peaked. Travelling miles through perilous terrain and challenges, all funnelling down to this very decision.

His mind was cluttered with so many options. He could take the most obvious price, a barrel of rubies. The fortune would change his life, but would it be worth it? Instead, he could ask for a home, as he had been an orphan his whole life. Or he could even ask for endless crimson cider! "Umm, let me see…" Lustre thought.

Tension grew in the throne room. Everyone eagerly waited for Lustre to name his price. Even the remaining guards who stood around were curious.

"Uhm…"

A thought then popped into his mind. A price that somehow fit all the criteria of what he wanted. A real home, a great fortune, and the sweet taste of crimson cider.

"I want to sell this jewel… In return, I request the freedom of my friend. He was sent to the dungeon, and I wish he were released."

"Done," the emperor boomed, snapping his fingers. "Release him!" With that, a guard cut Lustre free. Emperor Maroon then reached out and began aggressively shaking Lustre's hand.

Rusty was his happiness. It was astonishing that it took him a journey across the nation to realise that life's simple pleasures are the best. He didn't need piles of rubies. True happiness was available! It was like the night in Tether's Tavern, when two friends danced around, overjoyed with what little they had, not caring about the outside world, and were happy. All Lustre wanted now was to return to that old, glorious life of being with Rusty, two orphans enjoying their freedom, joyous to the smallest pleasures life gave them.

"Can somebody please take Lustre to the dungeon to release his mate, Rust-tea?" the emperor ordered, clapping his hands.

"No, it's Rusty," Lustre replied.

"Whatever."

Lustre was escorted back through the doors and down the red carpet towards the dungeon. He was more excited, yet more nervous than ever. Lustre's hopes hung by a thread. The flickering torches cast distorted shadows on the walls around him, truly showing the turbulence in his heart. Every step they took was filled with anticipation. Rusty, his dear friend, trapped in an eternal petrified state, remained the embodiment of their shattered dreams. The weight of their past life, their cherished memories of the mines, pressed heavily upon Lustre's shoulders.

They arrived at the guardroom.

"Wait here," the guards said. "We will go and retrieve your mate."

Lustre, gripped by anxiety, again sat at the table and urgently interjected, his voice quivering. "Remember, he's a small boy, barely above five feet tall!" The guards walked down the corridor towards the dungeon and saw the remains of the broken dungeon door. They descended the spiralled stairs into the dark.

Time stood still in the brief silence, and Lustre's heartbeat echoed in his ears. He just sat there, waiting, eating cheese, and drinking crimson cider.

Finally, footsteps began ascending back up the stairs. This time, they sounded much heavier and had a much slower pace. Suddenly, the burdened figures emerged in the corridor, bearing a lump of stone. With a pause to catch their breath, the guards placed the statue onto the marble with a loud thud.

Lustre stood frozen, his heart sinking as he realised his oversight. The truth was that Rusty remained encased as an extremely heavy statue.

"Okay, I still need to see the emperor, just one more time!" Lustre told himself. A glimmer of determination remained within him. He needed to plead with the emperor again to grant him one more opportunity to use the jewel's power.

Anxiousness swirled in Lustre's gut as the guards passed him, laughing at his struggle, leaving him the almost impossible-to-lift statue of Rusty. With sheer determination, Lustre wrapped his arms around the statue's waist, seeking the sturdiest grip. Every muscle strained as he dragged his friend.

In a slow and laborious process, Lustre dragged his friend back down the red carpet, pausing every few seconds to catch his breath. "Come on. Just a bit further." Lustre encouraged himself.

Then, to his joy, Lustre saw Maroon advancing toward him with his entourage.

This was his chance. Carefully, he set the statue down and approached the emperor. It was like the emperor couldn't even see Lustre. As he strolled down the hall, his eyes were fixated on the jewel in his hand. Its radiance mesmerised him, making him oblivious to anything else around him.

This presented Lustre with a new problem, for the emperor was accompanied by his entourage of five palace guards, who marched around him in a ring formation. With a desperate plea, Lustre called out to Maroon.

"Heil majesty! Please! I need one more favour!"

Startled by the interruption, the emperor halted and turned his gaze toward Lustre. One look and his expression soured. From the Emperor's point of view, it appeared as though Lustre had discovered the unfairness of the deal. Realising he might have been caught in this duplicitous trade, the emperor ignored Lustre and continued walking, this time with more urgency.

"Your majesty! I need to talk with you!" Lustre cried out again. But Maroon was unfazed, acting as if the plea didn't even reach his ears. Yet, deep down, he knew he could not ignore the persistence of this boy.

Lustre found another way to get his attention. He needed to stop him in his tracks. However, the guards, staunch in their loyalty, would undoubtedly stop any attempt to let Lustre get closer to the emperor. Approaching him head-on would likely result in a forceful challenge, followed by a filthy insult, probably something like, "Back off your scrawny reatrit!"

It was a risky decision, but it was the only decision to make. Summoning his courage, Lustre dashed forward, putting himself directly in the guards' path. With an unwavering determination, he unleashed a resounding cry, "Halt!"

To Lustre's astonishment, the guards complied, and the group stopped. The emperor gazed up in utter confusion. "What are you doing? Plough through him!" demanded Maroon.

"How can a boy stop my royal guards?" The guards didn't act; instead, they waited for him to resolve the problem.

Maroon couldn't ignore this boy, so he stepped forward, groaning. "What do you want now? I thought we had a deal?" Lustre seized the opportunity to explain. This time, his tone was balanced with respect and formality, which he didn't use that often, so it sounded a bit off. "Your majesty, I humbly beseech your esteemed presence and grant me the privilege of using the jewel for a final endeavour. I forgot to mention in our previous agreement when I said I wanted my mate back that the restoration of my friend would encompass his restoration to…You know…human form?"

The emperor only gave a confused glance. "What? Rubbish boy," he grunted.

Lustre sighed deeply. "Can I use the jewel again? To turn my mate back to normal?"

Out of nowhere, the emperor burst into unrestrained laughter that pierced the air, and the royal guards joined in.

"Do you don't know? Being turned to stone is a permanent state. 'Loomapa-lingera' is one of the many irreversible spells among nations!"

After that, there was the ensuing silence of contemplation. Lustre couldn't process what he had just heard. His following words were shrouded in scepticism.

"You jest, surely. You're lying!"

The emperor closed the distance between them with resolute strides, his voice seething with firm conviction: "Emperors do not lie. Not a single spell within the realm of Ruby Nation can reverse that."

These words struck Lustre's heart with a jolt of desperation, and he clung to the idea of rescuing Rusty. He implored, "But… but you have the jewel! It can cast all forms of magic! Surely, there is a foreign spell that can restore Rusty from stone. Please!"

With an exasperated roll of his eyes and a weary groan, the emperor relented, his voice laced with agreement, "Very well." The jewel, grasped lazily in his hand, was pointed toward Rusty.

"Come forth, magic," uttered the emperor.

Lustre prayed as he watched each passing second. The jewel didn't glow any brighter nor change colour; it kept dwindling to a soft white glow. Seconds became an agonising stretch of time, each moment adding to the Maroon's declining patience. Yet, in the end, as if mocking the very idea of hope, nothing happened. Lustre was left with the disheartening realisation that Maroon was yanking his chain. Hearing Rusty's voice or seeing him again was a dream, shattered and irretrievable.

The silence that followed seemed to magnify the despair. Lustre's heart sank, an indescribable cold sadness seeping into his bones, weighing him down like chains. Yet somehow, a nagging voice in his head refused to take that as the truth. "You can't be right. Try again!" Lustre begged.

"Enough!"

"It is impossible! Now you can take your statue and get out! Or else I won't hesitate to turn you into a trophy," the emperor boomed.

Trembling with disbelief, Lustre struggled to gather his emotions, his voice quivering as he spoke. "So... So, you're telling me Rusty will remain petrified forever? There's no way to bring him back?" The emperor's response was callous and final.

"Yes! Now leave!" he commanded, his tone empty of sympathy or remorse. Guards stepped in, pointing their spears.

Lustre turned away, his head drooping with despair. With faltering steps, he made his way towards the statue of Rusty and knelt to pick it up. Unbeknownst to Lustre, the emperor smiled wickedly, relishing in the misery unfolding before him.

Despite the weight of his anguish, Lustre lifted Rusty, summoning an impossible strength in his current state. He didn't cry. Carrying his friend on his shoulders, he trudged back down the corridors, his face a mask of stoicism.

Passing through the hallway door and navigating the fork in the corridor, Lustre finally emerged at the palace entrance. As soon as he stepped outside, away from the suffocating walls of the palace, he sank to his knees, surrendering to the overwhelming surge of emotions that had been held back for far too long. Tears streamed down his face as he stared at the ground, the weight of his grief and the statue of Rusty crushing his spirit.

Lustre's heart felt like a barren void, aching with an emptiness that seemed impossible to fill. "I... I don't know what to do," he admitted; his mind was weak, his words travelling far in the desolate silence.

"Let me give strength and memories", the voice of Cranium whispered through the breeze.

Rusty needed a proper burial. And so, with a sorry heart and determination, Lustre was given the strength of two guards. He began his journey back through the market square towards the town gate, with his friend on his shoulders and not realising his strength.

Although the night was still young, a full moon having risen only a few hours prior, Lustre's world seemed shrouded in darkness and coldness, mirroring the bleakness of his heart. Each step felt like an eternity as he travelled outwards from the village. He turned in a trance down an old path towards the sea and the eastern edge of the Crimson Forest that neighboured the palace.

This old path was long and winding, forgotten by many, but for Lustre, it was a destined path to travel in the night. The salty soil near the coast prevented the growth of the crimson trees, which thrived in the richer soil further inland from the shore.

Lustre had traversed these woods, and he knew that now his memory had just been unlocked. He had some dedicated purpose again, as he believed that the perfect resting place for Rusty was now where their friendship had first met. For a few miles, by moonlight, Lustre carried his dear friend deep into the woods, down the old path, thinking how and why he did not know. He felt he had dishonoured Rusty. He felt ashamed.

Though Lustre's recollection of that place had faded, he knew it existed within the confines of a small clearing nestled amidst the towering trees. Two miles along the path rested an unmistakable centrepiece—an old water well. Unlike the one at Winston's cottage, this water well was nothing more than a hole in the ground, surrounded by a few weathered river stones. Its size was that of an average tree stump, deceptively easy to fall into. Memories only now cascaded through his mind, memories once forgotten. His mind started to paint vivid scenes of days long gone.

He kept trudging on through the night with Rusty on his shoulders, retracing his path in his youth. He felt a wave of nostalgia with each step. And there it was, the same clearing came into view, bathed in full moonlight. In the heart of the clearing stood the weathered well, a relic of time.

Lustre's gaze fixated upon the well. Lustre could now clearly remember how it all began, how their lives intersected.

Many rots ago, Lustre and his parents spent time in tents within this forest. His family was a travelling family, constantly on the move. His parents were hunters and gatherers. They would roam from place to place with their children, seeking refuge from the rest of the Ruby Nation by hiding in the forests. At nightfall, they would set up their leather tents, his father skilfully putting them together with hammered support poles and tightly secured ropes.

Meanwhile, his mother would kindle the fire. Lustre, eager to help, would venture into the surrounding woods to gather firewood but often strayed to search for blood orchids, his mother's favourite flowers.

One night, Lustre wandered a little too far from his parents' sight. During this journey, he stumbled upon the old well. A strange young boy knelt beside it, his threadbare shirt soiled and tattered, his pants caked in mud, and his worn-out boots bearing many holes. He looked like he had lived in the forest his entire life.

He gazed at the ground, whispering to himself as if in prayer. Lustre, drawn by curiosity, approached the boy, noticing the ruby he held in his hands.

"Please, make me fearless," the boy wished. Then, he threw a precious ruby into the well. He waited for the splash at the bottom before opening his eyes.

Startled by Lustre staring down at him, the boy said, "Oh! Who are you?" Lustre stood there, enveloped in a shy silence, trying to find the right words.

"I-I am Lustre," he stammered. "My family tasked me with gathering firewood."

"F-family?"

Lustre took a step closer, his empathy guiding his actions. "Yes, my family. And what about yours?"

A sombre hush descended upon them as the question's weight fell on the boy's fragile shoulders. "I don't know," he confessed,

Sympathy swelled within Lustre, compelling him to kneel beside the boy, gently resting his hand upon his shoulder.

"What's your name?" asked Lustre.

"Rustera, but you can call me Rusty."

"Well, Rusty, do you want to be friends?" Lustre offered.

A smile flickered across Rusty's face, but it didn't last long. "I've never had a mate before," he confessed, his voice filled with grief.

Understanding that Rusty was quite upset for reasons unknown, Lustre quickly diverted the conversation, seeking to raise his new friend's spirit.

"Okay then, what did you throw into that well?" probed Lustre.

Rusty remained in a shy silence. "It was nothing," he murmured nervously.

Lustre wouldn't take that for an answer, so he persisted. "Please, Rusty, tell me. Can you trust me? I won't tell if it's a secret," his voice laced with genuine concern.

Caught in the battle between secrecy and trust, Rusty hesitated. With his words hanging heavy, he said, "Okay, it wasn't nothing. It was a ruby. I tossed it into this well to grant wishes."

Lustre was suddenly struck with a brilliant idea, sending a wave of excitement coursing through his veins.

He reached into his pocket, eventually grasping a small, shiny ruby—the very one he had received for his birthday a few octaves prior. Clutching it tightly, he turned his attention to the well before him. With a mixture of anticipation and determination, Lustre took a deep breath and tossed the ruby into the well, shutting his eyes tightly. After hearing it splash at the bottom, he opened his eyes and said, "That was a ruby well spent." Lustre had a hint of satisfaction in his voice.

Rusty couldn't help but chuckle at the pun, even if it was cheesy. "You've got a sense of humour," he laughed.

The sight of Rusty's face finally lighting up filled Lustre with pride. Brimming with joy.

"Hey, why don't you come and meet my family? They'll be thrilled to meet you." Rusty's laughter faded quickly, replaced by uncertainty.

"How can I be sure they'll like me?" he asked. Lustre reached out and pulled Rusty up from the ground, a warm smile on his face. "Trust me, they'll love you," he reassured. From that moment on, Lustre and Rusty were on a journey of close friendship. They eventually found work at the ruby mines. The memory of their meeting would always be preserved in his mind forever, cherished and loved, one of the few precious memories he could occasionally return to. Well, it should have been.

However, amidst the memory, there was a lingering void in Lustre's heart and mind. Any other thought of his family was a blur. He couldn't remember anything else that happened to his parents or even if Rusty met them.

The absence of their love weighed heavily on Lustre, but he found that it was a fair trade. He lost his parents but was given a mate. Yet, now, he had lost that precious friendship and was left with absolutely nothing.

Lustre found himself standing again in the middle of the night at the well, where he had offered comfort to Rusty. Gently, he lowered Rusty's lifeless statue beside the well, his knees giving way beneath him as grief washed over him. He slept till morning.

The well remained unchanged, a silent witness to the past. Every detail seemed frozen; clusters of mushrooms and fungi clung to the weathered bricks while scattered debris lay undisturbed around it.

Morning came, and Lustre peered into the depths of the well, tears shedding from his face, disappearing into the dark abyss below. "I'm sorry, Rusty. I hope you find some rest down there," he whispered.

Lustre lifted his gaze, his face scarred with tears. At that moment, an inexplicable voice took hold of his mind, urging him to go elsewhere. The voice beckoned him forth that morning, forcing him to traverse away from the well deeper into the forest, leaving Rusty behind. With each step, urgency and desperation took hold, causing him to run. He raced through the forest as if an invisible tether propelled him forward. The towering trees blurred past him in a whirlwind of motion. He leapt over gnarled roots and weaved around the foliage, driven by an insatiable desire to reach an elusive destination.

Then, as abruptly as it had begun, Lustre halted. His feet planted themselves on the earth, refusing to carry him further. His strength suddenly vanished. A shiver ran through his body as the gravity of his surroundings washed over him in a chilling wave of realisation.

He now stood at the threshold of yet another small clearing, a desolate area covered with fallen leaves. In the centre of the clearing was a huge, tattered blanket made from what he thought was grombler leather. Nature had chewed it up, partially covered by forest litter.

The leather also bore many blackened marks, almost as if it had been burnt. Lustre also found an entanglement of old rope and wooden debris within the leather in the same charred condition. This clearing had a dark secret that Lustre could not place; he could feel a sense of déjà vu as he scoured through the debris. "What is all this stuff?" Lustre asked himself.

"Do you know where you are? Lustre?" A haunting voice whispered amidst the howling wind, barely audible yet unmistakable.

Lustre's heart skipped a beat as he recognised the voice, the very same voice that had plagued his thoughts within the dungeon. This revelation shattered his doubts about his sanity or strength; he wasn't going crazy.

"Who... who are you?" Lustre trembled.

"I have already told you. I am Cranium..." The voice replied, piercing his ears like a shriek of cold wind.

"I remember hearing you before; what are you? And why do you keep talking to me?" shouted Lustre. The trees around him swayed in response.

"There are things I must discuss with you, Lustre."

Eager for answers, Lustre mustered his strength and posed another question. "But who are you, really? Your words confuse me!"

"I know you have countless questions, perplexed by the old memories that haunt you. Like where you came from, and what path shall you follow next? Lustre, I have those answers," Cranium intoned ominously.

"I know you want to find out what happened to your parents, but once I shall, you must forget the past, and I will show you your future."

Lustre gazed downward for a fleeting moment, his mind yearning for answers. Yet, amidst the whirlwind of confusion and curiosity, he struggled to fathom how an ethereal voice could be talking with him. Thus, he questioned once more, "How can speak to me? How is any of this possible?"

Lustre wanted a good explanation, a respite from the riddles that threatened to consume his mind. Instead, he was met with a frustrating revelation.

"I am magic, all right?" Cranium responded, his tone bearing no solace.

Suspicion began to creep into Lustre's mind, enveloping him in its cold grip. He grew increasingly wary of Cranium's stubbornness, realising there was more to this haunting encounter than meets the eye.

"Very well, Cranium," Lustre challenged, his voice tinged with suspicion. "Answer all my questions. Why do you choose to speak to me now?"

Silence lingered in the air until a gust of wind returned Cranium's voice to Lustre's ears. Reluctantly, Cranium gave a more genuine answer. "Fine! I am Emperor Cranium," the voice confessed.

"I am a spirit, remembered only as the heartless ruler whose life ended in ruin and cowardice. After I died, I was not sent to the afterlife. I was reborn for some reason, not into a body. Now, I wander as a mere spirit, invisible and powerless, forced to witness the events of Gemotroplis as a mere spectator."

Lustre's thirst for understanding intensified, giving him the desire to know more.

"Wait, if you are but a soul, how can I hear your voice?" he inquired, desperate to untangle the intricate web of Cranium's story.

"I have witnessed your entire life, Lustre," Cranium revealed. I saw what happened to your parents, watched each day as you worked in the mines, and even saw when you lost your friendship. During that time, I have discovered that you and I, Lustre, are very similar. We are united by the devastating loss of all we loved. And now, I offer you a chance at revenge."

Lustre was filled with disbelief. His voice quivering, he said, "No... I don't want revenge. All I want is to have Rusty back." His despair weighed down his words.

Cranium's response was a sombre reminder of the cruel reality they faced.

"You know, deep down, bringing Rusty back is impossible. Once someone has been cursed and turned into stone, their fate is sealed forever," he reminded, reinforcing Lustre's sadness.

Lustre's gaze fell upon the ground, his spirit burdened by his loneliness.

"Fine then... I don't want anything. I want you to leave me be," Lustre pleaded, his fragile voice threatening to break into tears.

A sudden gust of wind enveloped Lustre, heralding Cranium's relentless presence.

"I knew you would resist my offer, so I brought you to this clearing to remind you of something..."

The following silence hung heavy in the air. Lustre could feel a sense of foreboding creeping into his skin. Then he noticed a shape concealed beneath the blanket of fallen leaves. Curiosity ignited within him. He walked over toward the shape and knelt before it. The shape seemed small, only slightly larger than Lustre's hand. He began to claw at the leaves, slowly uncovering the half-buried object. Once the top was revealed, its surface was smooth, filthy brown, and cold, reminiscent of stone.

As Lustre held it in his trembling hands, a sudden realisation struck him like a lightning bolt. He gasped and leapt backwards in horror, the object slipping from his grasp. "That... that's your father," Cranium whispered, the words cutting through Lustre's soul. His spine tingled as he cautiously approached the fallen object, his voice trembling with fear. It was a skull.

"What... what do you mean?" Cranium's response was laden with sorrowful revelations, his words weaving a tapestry of untold truths.

Cranium then gave Lustre a somewhat altered glimpse of his forgotten past. Only the parts he felt would serve his purpose. He was careful to ensure Lustre didn't see the entire memory. If Lustre knew the truth about his family, he would be less reliant on Cranium's guidance, as Cranium primarily fed off Lustre's loneliness.

"Lustre, that fateful day had far more than you see in your memories. You did not flee from your parents, but rather..." Cranium's voice trailed off, leaving Lustre to ponder the unfinished sentence.

Lustre blinked, returning to that day in the forest with Rusty. They had left the well, returning to the campsite, excited.

"I can't wait to see them," Rusty said, approaching the brown tents. Lustre called out eagerly, hoping to surprise his parents with Rusty.

"Mum! Dad! Guess what?"

But his cry was met with a disheartening silence. He tried for a second time. "Mum! Hello? Dad!" His voice echoed through the trees, searching for a sign of acknowledgement. Yet, none came. Cupping his hands around his mouth, he called out one last time.

Yet again, no response came. Even a simple "What?" would have been reassuring, but the silence persisted.

Just as despair threatened to consume him, a gust of wind barrelled toward Lustre, forcefully caressing his face. The haunting voice of Cranium once again found its way into his ears.

"Just focus."

In the distance, Lustre began to see a veil of smoke towering above the trees. At first, he thought it must just be the campfire, but a horrific sight came to his eyes when he got closer. The tent was in flames. Beside the tent, Lustre saw his father kneeling, his hands tied behind his back and a black scarf bound around his mouth.

Confusion and horror mingled within him, their arms tightening around his fragile being. How had it come to this? How had joy twisted into tragedy? Suddenly, two figures emerged from the shadows, their presence infused with malice. Lustre instinctively recoiled. Luckily enough, the figures hadn't spotted him. He overlooked two guards wielding daggers who began to surround his father.

"Who are these horrible people?" Lustre asked himself.

He could only watch as the men taunted and tormented his father, their grins twisted with sadistic pleasure. His heart pounded in his chest, urging him to intervene to protect his father. With a surge of adrenaline, Lustre rose from his hiding place, his voice trembling yet resolute. "Stop! Leave him alone!" Lustre cried out.

The men turned their gaze upon him, their eyes gleaming with amusement. But their eyes fell upon him, piercing right through his hiding place. "Is this the son of the Sapphire reatrit?" One of them sneered, their words laced with contempt.

Lustre's words hung in the air, momentarily freezing the scene in a fragile stillness. But the respite was fleeting, shattered by the mocking laughter from their lips. Lustre's breathing quickened as the guards closed in on him. Panic surged within him, urging him to flee, but he stood his ground in an act of bravery and what some may consider stupidity.

Inevitably, they grabbed hold of him. Lustre struggled against their grip, his body writhing with desperation. He could hear his father's muffled growls, "Get away from my sons, you black-hearted reatrits!"

This led one guard to trudge back over toward his dad, only to spit and slash him across the face with his dagger, scoring a huge cut along his throat. In a moan of pain, his dad collapsed forward, burying his face into the flaming wreckage of the tent. Lustre was traumatised.

He screamed in absolute horror, mixed with disbelief, only to be met with mocking laughter and jeers.

Suddenly, a sharp blade pressed against Lustre's chin, the cold metal biting into his tender skin. Fear constricted his throat, rendering him speechless. The guard's voice dripped with sadistic glee as he taunted Lustre with the power to end his life. "Stop squirming, or I'll kill ya, just like your dad. Say, you two look similar." The guard wielding the dagger laughed.

"Go on, kill him."

Lustre gulped as the dagger was slowly dragged from his chin to his chest. Once the guard reached his desired point at the stomach. He thrust it forward, pushing the blade deep into Lustre's skin. The searing pain kicked in almost immediately. The entire lower half of Lustre's body radiated with a horrible burning sensation, like a pot of boiling water had been spilled on him.

He let out the loudest and most blood-curdling cry his voice was capable of reaching. The guard quickly withdrew the dagger from Lustre's stomach, causing blood to begin oozing through his ragged shirt. Lustre fell backwards, clutching his stomach in agony.

"That will teach him." The guard chuckled.

Then, apart from Lustre's screams, the guards heard something else: a deep, low, and guttural growl. The sound reverberated through the forest, shattering the tension. The guards' faces paled, crumbling in the face of an unknown terror. Eyes widened as they gazed toward the depths of the woods.

Lustre's pain and fear were momentarily forgotten; he was, too, fixated on the unseen menace. What unseen force could inspire fear in those who had previously shown none? The answer eluded him, but he knew something beyond their comprehension was approaching.

"Wavires!" He heard the guards shriek. They both darted away into the forest, leaving Lustre on the ground beside his deceased father and the burning remains of the tent.

Lustre lay there, his body rendered utterly defenceless. At that moment, he surrendered to his cruel fate and accepted the inevitable. The thunderous footsteps of the wavire grew closer and closer, each trampling stride growing louder each second, reaching a peak of deafening volume before abruptly falling into an eerie silence. Lustre didn't dare to open his eyes.

He waited, expecting to feel the wavire fangs sink into his skin, yet nothing happened. After a prolonged few minutes of anticipation and being uncertain if he had already died, Lustre mustered the courage to peek and open his eyes.

As his gaze ascended, expecting to be met with the face of a wavire staring down at him. Instead, it was Rusty who stood before him. Hastily, Rusty knelt and tore off his sleeve to create a bandage.

"It's okay, not that bad," Rusty murmured.

He tightly bound the torn fabric around Lustre's waist with utmost care, securing it with a knot. Lustre sat up. "It's you."

A faint smile formed on Rusty's face.

"Yes, did you think I would run away?" replied Rusty.

Lustre gazed at Rusty, his eyes fixed upon him for what seemed like an eternity. "How... What... How did you do it?" inquired Lustre, his voice laced with disbelief.

"I just growled and stomped, and it was enough to frighten them away," Rusty explained.

"Thank you."

"Indeed, those guards are not the smartest," Rusty concluded, a tinge of amusement in his voice.

Finally, Lustre summoned enough strength to push himself back up with Rusty's help. As he regained his balance, a realisation struck him. "My parents!" his voice was filled with panic. Lustre limped back toward the tent, now in smouldering ruins. His eyes fell upon his father, motionless, lying face down. Hastily, he rushed to his side, falling to his knees. He rolled him over and saw his scarred expression. Running his fingers along the deep gash that marred his father's face like a bloody trench, it etched from his cheek to his nose.

"Dad!" Lustre cried out, shaking him by the shoulders. "Wake up!" he pleaded, tears welling in his eyes. "Please, Dad. I need you. Wake up..." he sobbed.

His voice cracked with anguish. Slowly, he lowered his head onto his father's chest. Rusty slowly approached him.

"It's okay, Lustre."

Lustre offered no response, his grief weighing heavily upon him. Deep within, Rusty understood the pain of losing someone beloved. He placed his hand gently on Lustre's shoulder, offering comfort.

"I've always longed for a friend, someone I could trust. We can stay together. We can be like brothers," Rusty suggested. Lustre gazed up at Rusty, and seeing his smile warmed his heart.

"R-Really?" Lustre said, his voice quivering.

Rusty nodded. "We can take care of each other, just like our parents. Always helping one another." Rusty smiled.

Suddenly, Lustre slipped back into consciousness, finding himself alone once again, kneeling before his father's skull, the remnants of tears still scarring his cheeks.

He stayed there for a few minutes, breathing heavily.

"That...That felt so real," he said.

A gush of cold air swept past his face. "That's because it was. A memory, Lustre." Cranium whispered.

It felt like a dream, like a hallucination.

"So...You're saying Ruby guards murdered my parents?"

"Yes."

As Lustre processed the shocking realisation, a wave of overwhelming emotions washed over him. "But what about my mother? Where was she?"

"You see, Lustre, your dad was Sapphire Nation. He couldn't be allowed to live in Ruby Nation. However, your mum loved him so much that she would be with him even if that meant they had to live their life in hiding, with the constant threat of being discovered haunting them. But she realised she loved something more than your dad when she had you. She wanted to be a good mother and give you a chance to experience freedom instead of always hiding. She hid the truth from you so you wouldn't fear. So, one day, she noticed guards roaming the forest nearby and decided to alert them. She wanted to abandon your dad and take you to live with her in a proper home with a proper life, but when she came to find you, you were nowhere to be found. So, she lost you both!" Cranium explained.

Lustre felt a deep betrayal, as if his whole world was crumbling around him. The weight of loneliness bore down on his shoulders, and he struggled to find the right words. "I can't believe it," he admitted. "I don't know what to do now. I was so foolish. I've spent my life mocking the things I am built upon without realising it. I destroyed my only friendship with Rusty, my parents lost me, and I no longer possess the jewel. I am worthless."

Lustre fell to his knees once again. Cranium could sense the aching dread in Lustre's heart and knew he had accomplished something.

"Listen, Lustre, you may not have any more friendships, parents, or power. But you know what you can have? Revenge! A sweet, satisfying revenge. Turn all the anger boiling inside you into justice. Forget your past and create a new chapter in your life."

Lustre was speechless.

"It's just…I don't know if revenge is the answer." He had had enough of tragedy.

"Of course it is! If you obey and follow my commands, I promise I will lead you to the revenge you thirst for." Cranium then boomed, "Revenge is always the answer!" his voice spearing Lustre with the wind. Lustre hesitated for a moment, pondering his mind for any other ideas. Without much else to do, he assumed Cranium was right. Revenge did seem like the only other option and purpose in his life.

"It's your decision, Lustre... You can sit here forever, sobbing over your losses. Or you can follow me, become a true power and find meaning." Cranium preached.

Grudgingly, he agreed, "Okay!"

* * *

Back in the Ruby Palace, Emperor Maroon discovered a newfound sense of confidence, joy, and excitement coursing through his veins. It was a potent mix that fuelled his new ambitions. He couldn't contain his enthusiasm as he pranced around the throne room.

"Quiller!" Maroon called out to his loyal servant. "Summon that bloke whom we hired from Topaz Nation. The one we pay to turn people to stone. I want to speak with him immediately!"

Quiller, taken aback by the emperor's unusual exuberance, quickly nodded and scurried out of the throne room. Soon enough, a man dressed in a bright yellow robe strode into the room, his expression offended. He stood before the emperor, his voice dripping with disdain.

"You have no authority to summon me, Maroon. You are not my leader. Besides, I have better things to do! You know I have two boys and a wife to care for! I can't just be doing your dirty work all the time! "The man said with defiance. Typically, such words would have swiftly earned him a one-way ticket to the dungeon, but instead, Maroon burst into hearty laughter. He laughed so hard that he nearly toppled off his throne, much to the astonishment of the man who stood before him.

Amid his uncontrollable laughter, Maroon managed to gasp, "Ha! Guess what, Buster? You're fired!"

He couldn't comprehend what he was hearing. He was expecting the emperor's wrath, not this turn of events. Through clenched teeth, he retorted, "My name is Autumn Rallian, not Buster. And what do you mean fired?"

Maroon's grin widened mischievously. "It means you're returning to Topaz Nation. We no longer need you!" Autumn was dumbfounded.

"But how will you turn your prisoners to stone without me? It's a spell only Topaz folk can cast," he questioned.

Maroon's amusement grew. "I'll take care of it myself."

Autumn's disbelief escalated.

"You? You're not from Topaz Nation. You don't possess the power to turn people to stone!"

Suddenly, the emperor produced the jewel from his pocket, its radiance capturing Autumn's attention. Maroon tightly clutched it.

"Then explain this!" A flicker of light erupted, momentarily blinding everyone in the throne room. Maroon lost control of his voice for a second, uttering unfamiliar words in a different tone.

"Loomapa-lingera"

Silence enveloped the room, and yellow mist billowed in puffs, shrouding Autumn until he disappeared. Gradually, the mist dissipated, settling gently upon the floor.

Maroon hastily returned the jewel to his pocket. Eagerly, the emperor peered over the edge of his throne, awaiting Autumn's reappearance. "Heh! This is too funny!" Maroon cackled with delight. Autumn now stood as a statue, frozen in an unflattering pose. The emperor found it entertaining that Autumn had been frozen in a moment of disdain. Out of respect, a final pose should reflect one's talents or legacy forever encapsulated. Autumn life was now a disrespected book, and only the cover was visible…

And for this statue, the cover was Autumn with a deeply unimpressed expression, arms defiantly crossed.

"Ah, that's a keeper," Maroon chuckled. "Throw him in the dungeon."

"Just wait until the other nations find out about this!"

Chapter 12

Cranium

"**E**xcellent," Cranium said, his tone gleaming with satisfaction. "Before anything, you have to ditch the vulnerability inside you."

"Vulnerability?" Lustre said, raising an eyebrow.

"Your insatiable curiosity, your kind heart, and that boy Rusty. You must forget them all; you can't start a new chapter if you still hold on to your past."

Even with that, Lustre couldn't just forget Rusty; before he could do anything else, he had to honour his lost mate with a proper burial. He began returning to the old well where he had left his friend. But, with each step, Cranium's patience wore thin, and frustration began to boil over in his voice. The wind whipped Lustre's face, and Cranium's voice firmly spoke his mind.

"Lustre, I have already told you." He declared, "For revenge, you must first forget your weaknesses, including Rusty!"

Lustre disregarded Cranium in that moment; it offended him. For everything Rusty did for him, he could at least do this in return. "No!" Lustre protested,

"I need to bury him, Cranium! I can't just abandon him! He could be stolen or destroyed, left out there in the rain!"

Lustre pressed forward with determination, hoping that Cranium would understand. But in response, Cranium unleashed a massive gust of wind, toppling him over.

"Lustre, forget Rusty!" Cranium bellowed.

Lustre was undeterred, pushing himself up from the ground and brushing himself off. Defiance ignited within him, burning away any trace of doubt.

"You can't tell me what to do right now, Cranium; I must bury Rusty!" Lustre asserted himself.

Cranium's patience had reached its limit, and the air around Lustre crackled with his anger.

In a surge of frustration, Cranium unleashed a bellow that could be heard for miles. "Enough!" he roared, his voice like a thunderclap that rattled Lustre to the core.

"I do hear your words, Cranium. I think I might not be ready for revenge," he confessed.

"No, you aren't burying Rusty. That would only stall your revenge."

Cranium did speak the truth, but Lustre still didn't understand his desires. He sat on the line between forgetting his past life and returning to it; both seemed impossible. Yet, somehow, he felt like he had already decided, urging him to speak with proper consideration. It was the panic that often led to poor words. In this pivotal moment, Lustre spoke confidently, as if this was the definitive choice despite his deep disagreement.

"I will follow you," he conceded. Cranium roared with triumph.

"Good! Fantastic!" Cranium's voice was laced with an insidious satisfaction.

"Now, the first step of my- I mean... We plan to join the army. The Ruby Army. I have seen this, and I sense something big will happen. Something that will stain history is on the horizon..."

Lustre was confused. "What do you mean? What's gonna happen?"

Cranium's response came in a whisper, as if revealing a forbidden secret. "I fear my son is a fool, has found something that will only lead to death on a grand scale," he confessed.

Lustre's eyes widened.

* * *

Meanwhile, Emperor Maroon was in a tense boardroom meeting in the Ruby Palace. Over the table, a discussion would leave Realm Marshal Manor's jaw hanging open. Maroon believed a war to be his next step as a ruler possessing the most potent weapon in all Gemotroplis.

"What? Do you think this is a wise idea, Maroon?" shouted Manor, slamming his fist into the table.

"Consider this, Realm Marshal! Our past was merely from our lack of magical strength. The other nations, especially Topaz, had the advantage when it came to spells compared to our Ruby magic. Maroon had no real knowledge of dark magic, thank the gods. However, I now possess all forms of magic. I can wield every spell there is to know! We no longer shall we be overpowered by those nations!" Maroon explained, his words laden with conviction.

Manor sank back in his chair, holding his head in his hands.

As the head of the Ruby Army, he had not been summoned to a meeting of such seriousness for decades. He was stuck. The emperor was not thinking straight.

Unlike anybody else, Manor held some power as the head of the Ruby Army. This was enough to disagree with the emperor partially. But when he went too far, just before the emperor burst with anger, he would concede, as he didn't want to end up in the dungeon.

Maroon rose from his seat and unfolded a massive parchment, which he spread across the table. Manor peered at the map of Gemotroplis laid out before him.

"Listen closely," Maroon said, smoothing out the creases.

"We will start here in Ravena. Then, we expand outwards from there. Like my father once did, we shall rally our forces and ascend the volcano, wiping out the Emerald, then Sapphire, then finally those reatrits, the yellow and filthy Topaz Nation." Maroon explained, his finger tracing a path across the map.

Realm Marshal Manor sighed, a sense of dread creeping over him. To convince Maroon to see the foolishness of his decision, Manor said, "Maroon, countless lives will be lost because of this," his voice trembling with concern.

Maroon didn't get it; in fact, it complemented his plans. His enthusiastic voice echoed through the boardroom. "Yes! Finally, you understand. Many Topaz, Emerald, and Sapphire lives shall be extinguished!"

For the next few minutes of the meeting, Manor fought desperately to convince the emperor he was making the wrong decision. Manor realised his words were falling on deaf ears, and he found himself searching for another excuse.

"Do you not remember what happened to your father?" advised the Realm Marshal.

"My father was a coward! Besides, I possess something he never had. This jewel." Maroon brandished it above his head. Maroon returned it to his pocket and pulled out another paper. After unravelling it, he slid it across the table.

"Now, all I need is your signature on this contract to approve this," Maroon declared, thrusting a quill and an ink pot towards Manor.

Manor's hand trembled as he stared at the contract before him.

"Okay. Sign it."

There was silence.

The emperor waited eagerly. The ink dripped from the quill's tip as the Realm Marshal lowered his hand toward the contract, hesitation brewing within him. Sweat began to form on his forehead. Manor's eyes skimmed line after line. He was not reading, merely trying to stall. Manor could see how outrageous this contract was.

"Come on now! I don't have all day," Maroon grunted impatiently, his fists clenched.

The quill touched the paper, and the red ink soaked into the parchment. Quite ironically, it looked like blood. Slowly, Manor began to spiral the quill and signed 'Realm Marshal M-'.

The weight of the decision bore down on the Realm Marshal, and he paused. He couldn't proceed with writing his name. It would validate the contract, making it irreversible. Maroon would gain complete control and unleash something devastating. This could not be allowed, and Manor knew it.

Maroon's frustration grew. "Sign it, you reatrit!" he ordered, his voice laced with desperation.

Those words pushed Manor over the edge, igniting a rush of adrenaline within him. Instantly, he sprang from his chair and lunged across the boardroom table, drawing a hidden dagger.

Without time to react, Maroon was pinned against the wall with a blade pressed against his throat.

"No! Please! Get off me!" Maroon pleaded.

He saw the fire in Manor's eyes and realised his fate was sealed, even before he felt the blood begin to trickle down his neck. The dagger was sharp enough to start slicing into his skin, even without much pressure.

"I won't let you do this, Maroon!" Manor yelled through clenched teeth. Maroon gurgled, feeling the flat blade of the dagger press harder against his neck, restricting his airflow. Manor didn't care if Maroon died from suffocation, blood loss, or even a heart attack. He had to take one life before Maroon killed thousands. For that moment, Manor believed he held the upper hand. Victory seemed within his grasp.

Yet, Maroon still had one last trick. With the dagger still pressed against his neck, he furtively reached into his pocket and grabbed the jewel.

Its radiance intensified, emanating brilliant rays of white light through Maroon's fingers. Suddenly, Manor was lifted off his feet and hurled toward the ceiling. Dust and debris rained down along with Manor, crashing into the table. In those precious seconds, Maroon gasped for air.

He ran towards the door. "Help! Guards!" he screamed, wrestling with the handle.

Realm Marshal Manor rolled off the table. Though stunned, he was a hardened soldier, determined now to kill Maroon. He charged toward him, the dagger raised above his head. Maroon spun around, his back against the door, watching Manor advance toward him. In one last effort, Manor thrust the dagger toward Maroon.

Maroon evaded it, leaving the dagger to bury itself in the door with a loud thud. Maroon scurried backwards, hiding near the table, while Manor struggled to free his weapon.

Desperate for a way to defend himself, Maroon retrieved one of the chairs that had snapped a leg from Manor's landing.

With limited options, Maroon hoisted the chair by its backrest, using it as a shield. "I trusted you!" Maroon screamed, a bit more confident now that he had the chair. Manor, finally managing to free his dagger, turned to face Maroon.

"I trusted you as well! But you cannot do this!" Manor shouted back. Manor began racing toward Maroon for one last time. Maroon knew that a chair alone would not be enough.

Fortunately, the bolt lock snapped back in perfect timing, and the door burst open. Guards flooded the room. Before Manor could reach the emperor, he was tackled to the ground.

"You won't win," Manor mumbled, his face pressed against the floor.

Maroon watched Manor as he was dragged away down the hall, his heart still racing. He sat down on the nearest intact chair, taking deep breaths to steady himself.

"Well, let's hope that was the biggest crisis of my time as emperor," Maroon uttered to himself, his scratchy voice serving as a reminder of the dagger wound on his neck. He explored the gash with his fingers before bringing his hand back up to his face, noticing the blood on his fingertips.

"Peroa. Guards, get me a doctor urgently," he called out, more concerned about the blood staining his brand-new robe than the injury itself.

He rose from his chair and stumbled over to the other side of the table, his gaze fixed on the contract.

"Hmmm, I think 'Realm Marshal M-' is enough. It's just like me writing 'Emperor M.' It makes sense. Good," Maroon smirked, finally satisfied with his ability to find a loophole.

Carefully, he stowed the contract away in his pocket.

The room still reeked of tension and shattered trust. Maroon glanced around, taking in the aftermath of the chaos, the broken chair, the dagger mark on the door, and the dotted trail of blood on the floor. Feeling a mix of relief and unease, Maroon knew he had to tread carefully. This encounter had stained Maroon with a new paranoia among his subjects, even amongst the people he trusted most. With a newfound determination, Maroon walked toward a grand window overlooking his sprawling kingdom. He gazed at the majestic skyline over a stunning blue ocean, contemplating to himself. "Perhaps…Perhaps it is time to act. I need not wait any longer," he proclaimed.

* * *

Back in the Crimson Forest depths, Lustre also felt his emotions conflicted. He was walking away, leaving Rusty's statue at the old well. He questioned his decision, feeling guilty for leaving behind someone so close to him, someone who had been his lifelong motivation. The mere thought of Rusty had driven him to walk an octave across the nation, and now he was moving in the opposite direction, uncertain if it was the right one.

Cranium broke the silence, urging Lustre to avoid returning and to travel toward the army camp.

"Lustre, remember, you must travel down south; that's where you will find the Territorial Ruby Army Preparatory."

Lustre nodded.

"Okay, but…Why is joining the army necessary for my revenge?" asked Lustre.

Cranium didn't explain; he only responded by pleading with Lustre to trust the plan and follow his commands.

Lustre replied with a resigned, "Okay."

After trekking out of the forest, Lustre saw the vast, grand palace in the distance. It was now just a golden silhouette against the high noon sun.

"It truly is beautiful." After taking it all in for one last time, Lustre turned his gaze away and set off on his new journey down south.

Alone in his trek, he found walking boring, so he found ways to distract himself. Watching his boots was a strange motivation, reminding him that progress was being made with every stride.

He tried not to think about his parents, Rusty, or the past. They were all behind him now; he had committed to this new journey.

Suddenly, the rustling grass interrupted the solitude, and Cranium's voice whispered again, revealing that something had occurred in the palace. "Listen, Lustre... Realm Marshal Manor has been turned to stone."

"What? What happened?" Lustre stopped, eager to know more.

"It doesn't matter. Just focus on getting to the army camp."

"Okay!"

Only seconds after, Lustre was interrupted by a friendly voice.

"Who's Cranium?"

Confused and startled, Lustre shouted, "Who said that?"

Lustre turned, only to see Jackie standing there with a nervous smile. The relief on Lustre's face was evident. "Jackie!" Lustre called out, fluttering with a mixture of relief and confusion. "I don't understand. Why are you here?"

Jackie stumbled over his words, trying to devise an excuse, "So... I thought I would bump into you here."

"What? I don't understand why you didn't come with me into the palace. I have been in the dungeon, you know! I couldn't have used some help!" Lustre showed his wounds, his wrists, and his cracked rib.

Jackie felt somewhat guilty; he mustered the courage to admit the truth.

"Look. I left for two reasons. First, as I told you, I had to go to the market and buy more hunting and brewing equipment and grab a book. But... truthfully. It's because there were too many guards in there." Jackie revealed.

"So what?" Lustre shouted.

"Well…It's because…" Jackie stammered.

Lustre's heart pounded in his chest; he refused to let this moment become a cliffhanger. He couldn't bear the suspense any longer and began blurting out random words in an attempt to complete Jackie's sentence.

"An Alcoholic?" Lustre called out.

Jackie's eyes widened. "Well, yes. But that's not why I-"

"An Abandoner?"

Jackie's voice quivered slightly as he tried to explain, "Look, Lustre, I am sorry for leaving you, but I had to. I am -"

"Mentally ill?"

Jackie snapped, "Okay! I get it!"

A heavy pause hung between them, filled with unsaid words and unspoken truths. Finally, Jackie mustered the courage to reveal the secret burden he had been carrying. "Listen, Lustre I am from… I am from Emer. I mean…" Jackie's voice trailed off, with hesitation weighing his voice down.

Lustre waited nervously, his eyes fixed on Jackie.

"I am an… outlaw," Jackie finally released the words.

Lustre was shocked at how difficult it was for Jackie to admit something so simple. To Lustre, being an outlaw was not a cause for alarm or shame. For a Ruby boy, it was a rebellion, a symbol of defiance against unjust rules, which the Ruby Nation had many of.

"What? Get over yourself, Jackie. We are all outlaws," Lustre snickered.

"But it's not like that." Jackie sighed.

Lustre strode towards Jackie. He placed a firm hand on Jackie's shoulder, his voice comforting.

"I am an outlaw, too. I have trespassed, punched guards, broken out of dungeons, and maybe even taken lives. We don't always have to follow the rules, especially when those rules are garbage," Lustre explained passionately, trying to reassure Jackie.

Despite Lustre saying it wasn't a big deal, Jackie still couldn't shake off his guilt. Perhaps Lustre wasn't fully understanding something, or maybe Jackie still had another untold secret on his shoulders. Nevertheless, Jackie was somewhat relieved.

A faint smile tugged at the corners of his lips.

The two outlaws exchanged smiles until something else caught Lustre's attention.

In seconds, an intense heat washed over Lustre, searing his skin. His eyes widened at the scene unfolding behind Jackie. Only yards away from the ground, a fire erupted. The grass surrounding it was fire-blackened instantaneously. The tongues of fire greedily licked at the sky, only to retreat into the ground seconds later.

Left in the fire's place, a disoriented figure emerged, stumbling towards Jackie. A drunken tone tainted his voice as he spoke.

"I've still got to get used to the feeling of Fazz Fire. I'd rather use Gone Gazz," the bearded man chuckled.

Jackie gasped, swiftly putting himself before the disoriented stranger, shielding him from Lustre's sight.

With trembling unease, Lustre asked, "Who is that?"

With a nervous tremor in his voice, Jackie uttered, "Uhh… Nobody."

Then, in a sudden realisation, Lustre burst into anger. "WINSTON!"

Lustre threw his hands at Winston, shouting, "Gamber Goth-Gorian!"

Only a tiny, dim fireball left his hands and exploded around Jackie.

Realising what was happening, Winston gasped and retreated, shielding himself behind Jackie.

"Wait! Lustre, stop this madness!" Jackie's voice pierced through the chaos as he dove for cover. Lustre stopped, keeping his trembling hands ready to cast yet another spell. As he hesitated, allowing the smoke to disperse, a pair of hands raised in surrender.

Winston stepped out into the clear, moving hesitantly toward Lustre.

Jackie was still sprawled on the ground, covering his head with his hands.

"Winston, you reatrit," Lustre uttered.

"I can't believe you've returned. You stole my precious jewel, partly destroyed the Crimson Village, and killed innocent villagers, and then you dare to show your face to me again? Unbelievable!" Lustre's words spat out like venomous daggers.

As the smoke finally settled, Jackie was relieved, "Phew, I'm not dead."

He mustered the strength to get up, quickly putting himself between Lustre and Winston.

"Lustre! Spare his life. At this moment, I hate him just as much as you, but he's still my brother! We don't need to kill anybody!" Jackie called out.

Reluctantly, Lustre lowered his hands, a storm of uncertainty churning within him.

With relief, Jackie stepped aside, Winston bearing a smug grin as if mocking him. His eyes glinted with amusement and malice, taunting him silently.

"Very well," Lustre said, his voice strained but with grudging acceptance.

"Explain yourselves."

Before Jackie or Winston could answer, Lustre was hit by a gust of wind. Carried by the wind was a lonely piece of brown paper, careening toward Lustre and slapping him across the face.

It stuck on his face for a few seconds, making Winston laugh. Lustre was slightly embarrassed; he hastily tore the paper off his face.

"Well, that's the answer," Jackie said.

"You better watch out! They're coming from all directions," Winston snickered with amusement, then added, "Indeed, this is one of thousands. The winds have swept them across the nation. They all say the same thing."

Lustre's gaze fell upon the paper clutched in his hand. It read, '*All male Ruby nationers must enlist in the Ruby Army or will be exiled*'. Jackie peered over Lustre's shoulder. Lustre clawed his fingers around the paper, his heart pounding—a puzzle of unanswered questions intertwining within his thoughts. He couldn't believe what he was reading.

Soldiers Wanted

All male Ruby nationers are to enlist for the Ruby Army immediately. If you fail to enlist within one octave, you will be imprisoned.

If you are foreign and not from the Ruby Nation, we recommend you leave now. The border will be briefly opened to let out the foreign population, but it will also be closed in one octave.

Emperor Maroon has taken full ownership of the Ruby Army, and Realm Marshal Manor has agreed to this proposed law and resigned.

All Ruby men shall travel down south to the Territorial Ruby Army Preparatory for enlistment and training into the army.

This letter will be delivered to every individual.

Your training will be completed in two octaves.

Signed, Emperor M.
Signed, Realm Marshal M-

"A few hours ago, when I left the Royal Ruby Town, I saw many flyers just like that one drifting through the air like a flock of colaies," Jackie explained.

"Yes, I still don't understand…" Lustre stuttered.

Jackie and Winston exchanged wary glances, sharing a sense of nervousness.

"Well…Lustre. We don't have a choice; we must obey the emperor no matter how outrageous. Winston and I came to ask if you wanted to travel down south…To the army camp with us? It would be better than going alone!"

"The letter didn't explain why we had to join the army," Lustre pointed out.

"Umm, well…"

Lustre didn't want to make another wrong decision, so he waited for Cranium to approve Jackie's offer. He felt like he had already made too many mistakes on his journey.

A strong gust of wind hurled past Jackie and Winston towards Lustre. This wind seemed out of place to them, but Lustre had gotten used to it by now. Cranium's chilling voice began to talk.

"Accept the offer, Lustre. Go with them down south," Cranium whispered. Lustre still had one question. He glanced upwards. "But you told me Manor was taken to the dungeon and turned to stone. How did he sign the flyers then?" Lustre asked, trying to mask his voice.

"Yes, I did. Something very sketchy is happening back at the palace," Cranium answered.

Lustre glanced back down.

"Okay, I will join," Lustre said.

"Fantastic! Now, let's get going." Jackie cheered.

"Wow, it sure is windy today." Winston was disturbed by voices in the wind and saw what had happened.

They began their journey south, the sun beaming above them. Soon, they were lonely figures trekking across a vast grassy field.

"If you are not there by the next octave, you will be exiled or arrested," Jackie said, re-reading the flyer.

Lustre's thoughts underwent a dramatic change over the past few hours. One moment, he was in tears, mourning the loss of his dear friend Rusty. The next moment, it was as if the memory of his friend had vanished. All sadness was gone, replaced with anger and a thirst for revenge.

He was no longer the kind, curious young boy. During the walk, the Fletcher brothers noticed an unsettling change in Lustre's attitude. One thing was sure: something was very wrong...

* * *

The three traversed a vast green field, with the sun beaming down. Lustre trekked behind. With his journey, he struggled with his mental state. Lustre now travelled with two individuals who had both tried to kill him in the past. Cranium was constantly reminding him. It was an understatement to say he was a little nervous. He followed behind so he wouldn't be stabbed in the back.

Lustre's senses were heightened; apart from the crunching of grass beneath his feet and the wind, he heard a whisper. Jackie and Winston were quietly talking to each other. Amidst the conversation, the wind carried his name. He hated people talking about him behind his back.

"What are you two whispering about?" Lustre snapped, abruptly calling to them.

"Nothing," Jackie swiftly responded, attempting to deflect the question.

Lustre knew that when someone answers a question with the words 'nobody' or 'nothing', it is an obvious sign that they are lying. Seriously, how boring would conversations be if they were always the truth?

"Nothing? Just nothing? I know you are talking about me," Lustre groaned.

"Indeed, you are a nobody," Winston retorted, bursting into laughter.

Jackie stifled his laughter so as not to stir Lustre further.

Nonetheless, Lustre's anger surged to unprecedented levels. It was perplexing, for an outburst of such magnitude usually stemmed from a culmination of preceding events concealed from prying eyes. However, Lustre's composure crumbled in a momentary lapse of reason on this occasion. Cranium then released a memory of the Paralapse spell from the book 'Dark Ruby Spells'. He and Rusty had found the book hidden under the bookshelf in Tether's Tavern. It had a list of very dark attack spells from era: 1st, such as the Bifurcation spell. They read through the book whilst drinking crimson cider. The spell was on a page labelled 'harm to disarm', featuring many others. At that moment, Lustre just snapped. He wasn't thinking straight and cast such a dark spell. He didn't even remember what it did, just that it would disarm.

"That's it, Paralapse!" Lustre yelled, crossing his hands above his head. In an instant, Winston's eyes turned an eerie white hue. He collapsed to the ground, spasming uncontrollably like he was having a seizure.

Jackie was the first to shout, "Peroa! What have you done?"

"What he deserved," Lustre responded.

The spell's success gave Lustre a twisted sense of gratification, momentarily overshadowing his remorse.

As Winston writhed on the ground, a disturbing change unfolded before their eyes. His skin contorted, growing pale and creased as if aging. The sinew and flesh receded, leaving behind a skeletal framework. An abnormal growth of snowy white hair sprouted from his chin and scalp while his fingers contorted into gnarled and bony claws. The rapid progression of aging rendered Winston almost unrecognisable. It took Jackie a moment to fully understand what was happening.

"Wait! Did you cast Paralapse? That's the spell that speeds up aging until death! It's a forbidden nightmare; it's irreversible! Please tell me you didn't do this!" Jackie's voice trembled with anguish as he rushed to Winston's side.

Lustre's countenance, once consumed by anger, now shifted to concern. He had never intended to inflict such harm upon Winston. His intent had been solely to disarm, to relieve his frustration. Lustre hurried towards Jackie and Winston with a storm of guilt, fear, and regret. "I... I don't know how to undo it!" Lustre cried out in panic.

With each critical second, they watched Winston grow older. Jackie, caught between despair and panic, remembered something.

"Wait! I have Muzzle Mud! Maybe it can help!" Jackie frantically rummaged through his belt, praying that he hadn't lost it. "Where is it? Please say I didn't forget to pack some." Jackie's voice trembled.

Abandoning his belt, Jackie delved into his pockets. When he felt something amidst the dread, a glimmer of relief flickered within Jackie's eyes.

"Found it!"

Swiftly, Jackie uncorked the flask and brought it to Winston's mouth. Almost instantly, the convulsions and rapid aging stopped. "Yes!" Jackie cheered.

Lustre was filled with relief; he thought for a second he'd just killed somebody.

However, as the seconds ticked by, Winston remained old, his wrinkled, frail appearance unchanged…

Winston's eyes fluttered open. "Jackie… I… I feel different," he muttered, his voice rough and raspy. Everybody was shocked.

After Winston spoke, he realised the difference in his voice, that it was much softer.

"WHY DO I SOUND OLD?" Winston cried in confusion. Jackie responded sombrely, "Lustre cast Paralapse on you. It made you age rapidly; you aged thirty rots in about thirty seconds. It's an irreversible spell."

Lustre, realising the seriousness of his actions, slowly backed away.

"What! Why would you do that?" Winston bellowed.

Lustre didn't know. He just lost his temper. Usually, he could control his anger pretty well, but for some reason, on this occasion, he just snapped. He was left with immense guilt and unable to explain. "I don't know…" Lustre's voice trailed off.

Winston's wrinkled face contorted with anger. He got up from the ground and began hobbling toward Lustre, struggling to keep his balance.

"Winston, stop!" Jackie urged. Lustre instinctively began recoiling backwards.

"You will pay for this!" Winston yelled.

Lustre's pace quickened into a full-fledged retreat. Panic coursed through his veins, his heart pounding in his chest. He knew he had crossed a line that should never have been crossed.

"Please, Winston, I didn't mean for this to happen," Lustre pleaded, his voice strained with remorse. "I let my anger get the best of me, and I'm truly sorry."

"Paralapse!" Winston screamed.

Lustre dived to the ground in an attempt to avoid the spell. Strangely, nothing happened.

"What? Why can't I cast any spells? Am I saying it wrong?" Winston grumbled.

"Uhh… Oh yeah!" Jackie remembered. "Once you grow old and frail, your magic wears off."

"WHAT!" Winston boomed in complete disbelief.

"Look! I'm sorry!" said Lustre, staggering to his feet.

Winston's anger refused to cease; his voice cracked with bitterness as he spat out his response. "Sorry, won't reverse what you've done. You've taken something from me, something I can never get back."

"Sorry, I know. I don't usually lose my temper over someone teasing me." Lustre tried to apologise sincerely.

"Jackie! Finish him off! He's why I lost my powers and beautiful chocolate hair!" Winston cried out.

Jackie hesitated, pausing for a moment to gather his thoughts. He leaned closer to Winston and whispered, "Winston, listen to me. You and Lustre need to get along. We are going to make this three-day journey to the army camp. Now, please, quiet down."

Winston's expression turned sour as he glanced at Lustre from the corner of his eye. "Fine, I'll go if my aged legs will get me there. But I still don't understand why the emperor is forcing us to do this," Winston groaned.

With that settled, the three of them embarked on their journey southward again, making their way toward the army camp. Lustre's trust in Jackie was still developing. While Winston and Jackie made him nervous, Lustre couldn't ignore that Jackie had numerous opportunities to stab him in the back, but he had chosen not to. Something was keeping them together, even amid their differences.

However, beyond ending Winston's magic and nearly his life, Lustre couldn't take his mind off Cranium's previous words.

The mention of Maroon's suspicious behaviour and why he sent thousands of flyers soaring through the air, demanding every man enlist in the army immediately, didn't add up.

"It just doesn't make sense!" Lustre exclaimed suddenly, causing both Jackie and Winston to stop. Lustre couldn't contain his thoughts any longer, unleashing a torrent of questions swirling inside his head.

"What is the emperor up to? What's so sketchy about it? It's highly unusual for him to act this way." Lustre ranted.

"Um, what are you talking about, Lustre?" muttered Jackie, clearly taken aback by the outburst.

"The emperor! Why would he suddenly demand that every man in Ruby Nation join the army out of nowhere? It's all so strange. Maroon has never acted like this before I gave...when... when I..." Lustre trailed off, his voice wavering. He finished with, "Gave him the jewel."

"You gave him the jewel! Please, tell me you're joking!" croaked Winston. "It all makes sense now! You gave Maroon the jewel; he's not just a mindless tyrant. He's now a fool with unimaginable power!"

An unsettling realisation struck Lustre like a bolt of lightning. Cranium joined all the puzzle pieces, forming a grim picture in Lustre's mind.

He stood frozen.

"Oh no," whispered Lustre, listening to the voice and seeing visions that filled him with dread.

"What is it?" asked Jackie, his voice tinged with concern.

"I know why the emperor is making us join the army!" Lustre declared, his voice now trembling.

"Me too. You do not need to be a genius," said Winston, straightening his hunched back.

Lustre words then barely escaped his lips.

"There's going to be another Ruby War."

End of Book One

Glossary

Acerbo-ironia: a brewed acid that can melt through almost anything. It must be stored in a glass jar or bottle, is not for drinking, and is dangerous to carry.

Archna-stela pelsitch-avia-bonwax-aroasiza: powerful, good magic, the bright light of Peroa, a spell from the mother of life.

Arachna-vire: a gemotro known as the 'Arac-vire' or locally named 'Wendy'. She is the mother wavire; cursed by Peroa, she retreated to her cave in the Banderian mountains.

aztel fern: a troublesome weed from the Emerald Forest; the only positive aspect is that they are edible and taste like muddy cabbage. A green fern with spikey leaves; see Bandeira nettle. In small amounts, it is used as a herb.

Bandeira nettle: the name for aztel fern in Bandeira; it's a vexing botanical pest across Gemotronia. In the verdant realms of Azareni, the Emerald folk have aptly dubbed it the 'azareni devil'. It has spread across the hunting grounds of Bandeira, the Crimson Forest and the Jackale. Other names include Bandeira bush weed.

bellowers: ghost-like figures wearing dark cloaks; first discovered in rot: 244 era: 2nd. Gemotros that transform to lure victims. Folk tales are told to scare children in the Irindorian village so as not to wander off alone.

Bifurcation spell: a forbidden Ruby spell to cut a man in half; dark magic.

blood orchid: a flower also known as crimson bloom, found in the Crimson Forest. Its pollen dust is flammable and glows bright blue when burnt. It runs some lanterns for a much brighter light. It's also a disinfectant when crushed.

Blood Orchid (the sword): a blade gifted by Emperor Maroon to the Realm Marshal of the Ruby Army, a curved version of Irisavire.

BlunderBee: blade of Emperor Cranium wielded in the first Ruby War, crafted long ago by the blacksmiths of Gorlith. The blade was passed to Emperor Maroon.

bracklia: a gemotro that inhabits Ravena, a most dangerous grombler thought to be extinct. Its body resembled a monstrous magical amalgamation of molten basalt and flesh, its thick, armoured hide undulating like flowing lava.

butter orchid: a flower, see golden devtark.

cobbler: a special grombler, much larger and more muscular than other gromblers; they use massive wooden clubs and can throw mountain boulders to start avalanches.

colaies: the birds of Gemotroplis, created with a song by Peroa.

Chapidodia: a giant female hexapus; a gemotro that inhabited the waters off the coast of Topaz Nation from rot: 330 era: 1st to rot: 2 era: 4th. After her death, she lay on the Beach of Neil. Some folks would say *'For the rest of her time and ours.'*

crimson berries: the fruit used to brew crimson cider, and are a secret ingredient for enhanced crimson oil.

crimson cider: a delectable elixir with origins in the early days of the realm, when rot: 34, era: 1st witnessed the discovery of

Crimson Berries within the heart of the Crimson Forest, by Sapphire traveller, Zeldil Haratchi, he covertly absconded with the cherished recipe.

Crimson Forest: the largest forest that dominates Ruby Nation, a forest of crimson trees.

crimson oil: precious oil derived from the sap of the crimson tree; when impurities are removed, it becomes highly flammable. When enhanced, it's the most destructive substance in Gemotroplis, better than magic.

Daradero: cold-hearted male god of death and war.

Dazzldern: a famous sword that the Topaz Emperor Irindor wielded during the Ferinthor cavalry charge during the first Ruby War, defeating Emperor Cranium. Also wielded by Richard Rallian against Emperor Maroon. The famous sword was forged by the IronShard family.

elder maroon: a fake ruby, like fool's gold. The word 'elder' means fake. Ironically, the name of the Ruby Emperor is also Maroon.

Emede Vinato: Emerald spell; Emedella green vines shooting from the ground, entangling and trapping your victim.

Emerald Mallet: named 'Gorungun Hengi', it unfolds as a remarkable testament to its power and enigmatic nature. This battle hammer bears an origin deeply intertwined with the annals of Gemotroplis.

egunis: also named a thornfish, is a Ruby gemotro, similar to a small plesiosaur with a barracudina head.

era: a timescale used in Gemotroplis; indicating each eruption of the volcano in Ravena; indicating a thousand rots - rotations; each rot similar to a year.

Fazz Fire: a teleportation potion only reserved for the Ruby Army. An alternative to the Gone Gazz.

ferinthor: large horses from the fields of Gondor in the Topaz Nation, gemotro with a mane of fire that scares off predators when threatened; used as cavalry.

fluro flutters: flowers of the Sapphire Nation used to preserve meats, better than salt, although with a minty taste; a Gemotroplis trading commodity.

Gamber Goth-Gorian: a knock-down Ruby spell, a small ball of magic fire that is more force than burn.

Gemotro: a unique creature, a non-human, given life by Peroa, the goddess of life.

Gemotronia: goddess of magic, the jealous sister of Peroa and Daradero. Her heart was shattered into eight shards, the basis of all nations' magic. She is also known as Queen Gemotronia.

golden devtark: Nicknamed butter orchid, it can be mistaken for a Topaz blossom. It's prized as it's used to brew the potion Gone Gazz and is an ingredient in a bandeiran bush weed poison. First discovered in rot: 51 era: 1st by King Jackale.

Gone Gazz: teleportation potion only reserved for the Ruby army. An alternative to the orange powder is known as Fazz Fire.

Grutoterian: the native language of Emerald Nation.

Hella-scaren-peta-shingo: Topaz spell; a summoned firestorm.

herpeta-mosa: nicknamed jabber, a large water-dwelling carnivore, species mosa-gac-lagas, similar to a crocodile. The first species of gemotro, emerged rot: 0 era: 1st.

Irisavire: sword of Emperor Maroon.

jabber: see herpeta-mosa.

King Richard's Wine: Richard's Wine, often dubbed the 'invisibility shot' is a truly extraordinary elixir with the remarkable ability to make anybody invisible.

Loomapa-lingera: powerful topaz magic used to turn your enemy to stone.

manes: see stephador.

Muzzle Mud: a potent dark blue potion, an elixir that heals wounds, knits fractured bones, wards off ailments, and even dispels intoxication and mental turmoil. Ineffective against infection.

muzzle-myers: or the root walkers, are herbivores that are critically endangered. Inhabit the Crimson Forest and Dalenia in the northern Areden Forest. First emerged rot: 1 era: 1st. Peroa spawned these tree-like humanoids. Myer blood is the main ingredient for the Muzzle Mud potion.

Obsidian Axe: during rot: 201 era: 1st, the Obsidian Axe was born, crafted from a colossal chunk of obsidian discovered deep within the mines. Its true power, however, was unveiled by Verneto Havata, empowering it to shatter the mythical demotrite, including the revered sword of Daradero.

octave: a timescale used in Gemotroplis; a 12-day week; five octaves per quintet.

Olde Hickory: A merchant from Crimson Village, a timber cutter who wanted to tame the Great Ruby River. He built a lock, dam and stone bridge during the late era: 2nd, all of which still stand.

Ornithialk: a giant eagle-like creature created in rot: 60 era: 1st by Peroa. Some say she remains nesting in the Bandeiran mountains.

Paxta-holla: Ruby spell; basic ruby fire-starting that replaces a flint & steel.

Paralapse: a forbidden Ruby spell to age your victim; dark magic.

pelata: or breed Pelor is a non-hostile herbivore whose diet consists of Banderian Bush weeds. It is an endangered species, basically a very large centipede. Pelatas were first discovered rot: 34 era: 1st in the early settlements in Galarie; early Bandeira.

Peroa: goddess of life, created all living things on Gemotroplis. A mother with the looks of a beautiful golden-haired lady.

quintet: timescale used in Gemotroplis; a month of 60 days; eight quintets per rot. Each nation refers to a quintet in its own customary way.

Ravena: area of basalt and fire, the very centre of Gemotroplis, a massive volcano.

Redemptias: a formidable Topaz gemotro akin to a gigantic gecko, indigenous to the treacherous waters of the Neilan Sea.

reatrits: giant rat-like gemotros that exist in all nations and can enter plague proportions. Also used as a derogatory term, being obscene to someone.

Re-tentro-mjana: Ruby spell; immobilising stun, can cause short-term paralysis, a guard's favourite.

rot: timescale used in Gemotroplis; a calendar year, a rot is 480-days.

sacro selester: Emerald gemotro, first emerged rot: 313 era 3rd, giant tame flying serpents similar to its ferocious cousins the sacro slither.

sacro slither: a flying serpent carnivore, an Emerald gemotro; the population is thriving, first emerged rot: 78 era 1st.

savanta: large, winged horses from the fields of Gorlith, a Sapphire gemotro. Savanta feathers were poached and harvested to produce the Muzzle Mud.

stephador: a very large gemotro akin to a tiger but the size of a hippopotamus. They hunt in packs and are aggressive. These beings originate from the forests of Areden and are locally referred to as manes.

sphyraena: locally named bloaters, omnivores (seagrass and plankton). Very large and similar to a blue whale, but not a mammal, it has four fins on its body.

saxumiaturpis: locally named boulder shark is a Topaz gemotro, a large hostile carnivore with razor teeth and a muscular tail. Imagine a tiger shark crossed with a humpback whale.

SluckStick: a machete-type blade of questionable quality.

starlight echoes: a flower thought extinct in rot: 20 era: 2nd. During the Battle of Emiella, soldiers would use the flowers for food to numb their wounds.

Sword of Daradero: the blade created by Daradero to assassinate Queen Gemotronia, the goddess.

Tipsy Tonic: a potion thrown on the ground that produces gas; when inhaled, it makes you drunker than a sailor.

turtur anguilla: Topaz gemotro, a large sea turtle about the size of a small whale.

terrortor: nicknamed Blue Blur, is a flying Sapphire gemotro like a medium-sized dragon; an omnivore.

Trio-Septeria: known as 'Fangs' is a mystical three-headed tiger guardian who dwells within the sacred precincts of the Temple of Gemotronia. Daradero guided Peroa herself to bestow life upon this enigmatic creature rot: 1 era: 1st.

stalker: nicknamed watcher, these hostile humanoids dwell in the Obsidian Forest. The population is estimated to be a few hundred. They bite with their teeth and claw with long fingernails; they only eat meat. First emerged rot 20: era 1st.

watcher: see a stalker.

wavire: a beastly gigantic Ruby gemotro spider. King Finch, a Ruby king thought these creatures symbolised the Ruby Nation, as they were fierce and terrifying and were growing rapidly in population.

Wav-va-wire stella lo-compo: part of a secret recipe for disinfectant, wavire juice; not the best drink.

Wezdorth Dazzagar: Ruby spell; lightning bolts used by Ruby guards.

Final Words

Please subscribe to my website.

www.gemotroplis.com

I first started my Gemotroplis pentalogy
when I was only twelve years old.

I aim to make the word 'autistic' a compliment.

People with autism are not so different.
We have talents, feelings
and want to be loved like everyone else.

So, if you enjoy this book, please share it
with your family and friends.

That way, you are part of the growing
community of Gemotroplis.

www.ingramcontent.com/pod-product-compliance
Lightning Source LLC
Chambersburg PA
CBHW070105120726
47909CB00002B/510